CONTEMPORARY FICTION
A NOVEL

NELLIE

Written by Andrea Bowman

Pen Press

First published in Great Britain

All paper used in the printing of this book has been made from wood
grown in managed, sustainable forests.

ISBN13: 978-1-78003-353-2

Printed and bound in the UK
Pen Press is an imprint of
Indepenpress Publishing Limited
25 Eastern Place
Brighton
BN2 1GJ

A catalogue record of this book is available from
the British Library

Cover design by Jacqueline Abromeit

For my Dad

Contents

CHAPTER ONE

Nellie

A cacophony of crows erupted above, rousing her reluctantly from desolate sleep to consciousness. She lay looking up at the sky through the great oak branches and she began to feel pain. Her head hurt. Her back ached. She sat up slowly and carefully. Gingerly placing her feet on the ground, she hoped that she would not find any injuries today. She gazed down at her misshapen broken boots and considered how much of a repair they would require for the day ahead. Reaching into one of her large plastic carrier bags, she dragged out the two lengths of rough green string she had found on the ground the previous day. Meticulously, she tied both pieces around the soles and uppers of her dilapidated footwear. Deep inside her being she felt the hollow ache of loss so acute, that she believed her soul to be crying. She cautiously eased up her body and rested it back against the bench, sighing deeply. She stared at the surrounding grass and borders, searching for signs of spring. She perceived the mere beginnings of buds on the shrubs adjacent to her seat. Invigorated by the hope they engendered, she tipped her head back to gaze at the giant limbs of the mighty tree and cried, "Good morning Quercus!"

Nellie stood, steadied herself and began her slow journey to the park toilets. From the position of the sun and the din of the dawn chorus she estimated it to be about seven thirty and would therefore be able to perform her morning ablutions uninterrupted. It was dank and gloomy inside, but she cheered as she washed and thought about her day ahead. She would look out for her friend, Maisie who could usually be found somewhere around the town centre. She did not have much to say but Nellie enjoyed having some company as they looked for leftovers and met up with the other homeless individuals that she had come to know in the last few years. Maisie spent her time collecting supermarket trolleys and returning them to their neat rows at the back of the shopping centre. Nellie did not believe that her friend was paid for this work or indeed that it was acknowledged, but Nellie knew that Maisie liked to feel purposeful and was disturbed when her environment was untidy.

Nellie caught sight of her reflection in the cracked, age-dappled mirror on the wall. Her face was puffy, lumpy and shapeless. She was shocked. As her eyes adjusted to the dim light she moved apprehensively, nearer to her image until she was able to focus on the detail of her face. Her skin was a bloated combination of deathly pallor and red-blue blotches. Anxiously, she moved even closer to study her eyes, which as a young woman had been green and had danced and sparkled with fun and optimism. Today, they were large, mournful and grey. She flashed herself a smile to brighten up the picture before her and thought better of it when she saw the gaping holes where her teeth used to be. As the smile was leaving her face she caught just a glimmer of the young woman she had once been and then it was gone.

She went back out into the sunny morning and as she bent to pick up her bags she saw the green shoots of bulbs bravely trying to break through the cold ground. Hot tears fell from her face as she knelt down to remove last year's decaying leaves from the earth around them.

She smiled, "There you go babies. Now you can see the sunshine. Don't worry; spring will be with us soon."

Creakily, she arose, gathering her belongings together and she shuffled out onto the sunlit path. It had been a long cold winter with very little sunshine so it lifted her spirits as she went on her way to the High Street. Most of the shop owners knew Nellie, but not as the young woman, who had lived there, brought up her children and had been a part of the community. Whenever Nellie thought about those days, she experienced pain in her belly which spread throughout her body until the only thing left for her to do, was to drink.

As she cut through the churchyard, she looked across the road and she saw George from the Wimpy Bar standing outside having a smoke. He looked like he was enjoying the morning air so she crossed over the road to say hello, hoping he might offer her a cup of tea.

"Hi Nellie," he said."It's a lovely bright day for a change. Do you fancy a cup of tea old girl?"

"Bloody cheek!" she thought, "He's older than me."

"Yes I'd love one. Thank you," she said.

She sat down at the window to watch the passersby and imagined, for a while, that she knew where they were going and what they were doing. She looked on with envy as people rushed off to work or to drop their children at school and felt keenly how little she really knew of anyone. George was approaching with the tea and a plate of hot toast. Nellie smiled in gratitude and tucked in. Maybe this was going to be a good day. She picked up the newspaper and to her great joy realised that it was Thursday and that it was benefit day. She felt a bubble of excitement well up at the prospect of having some cash for the next few days. She no longer pretended that it would last any longer than that. Whilst devouring her breakfast, she contemplated the inevitable soul destroying queue for her giro amongst the other itinerants, then the long haul back up the hill to the post office to queue again and cash the cheque. All of which, was worth it for the final, gleeful selection and purchase of alcoholic delights.

She thanked George as she left the Wimpy and started her slow journey down the hill. The pains in her joints eased as she created a walking rhythm and she felt moments of peace as she looked around. Passing the green, she saw snowdrops bravely waving their beautiful heads around in the sharp breeze and remembered how she had found it funny that grown men and women would take annual outings to visit spectacular displays of snowdrops. The same people going to the same place to see the same thing every year and now she understood how reassuring that must be and how she envied them.

She met Maisie outside the benefit office and they walked towards the glass door. Nellie admired Maisie. She always looked quite tidy, if not a little hirsute and seemed purposeful even though her purposes seemed a little pointless to Nellie. Maisie angered her when she lectured her on the perils of alcohol and criticized her inability to manage her finances. Nellie maintained that Maisie did not understand her plight. After all, Maisie lived in a hostel and therefore could not know what it was like not to have a roof over her head. On closer examination of course, this was not the whole truth, because Nellie had been given a bed in her hostel on a number of occasions but it never really worked out and she was eventually banned. Nowadays, if she was given the opportunity, she would expound on the benefits of the great outdoors where she was free to roam and her life was devoid of constraints. Her brave argument weakened significantly when, awakened by the cold, she would lay alone and afraid until dawn.

Nellie pushed open the heavy door and let the stuffy air of the office escape for a few moments as it swung shut. She turned to her friend and greeted her with enthusiastic bluster,

"Hello Maisie!"

"Hello Nellie!"

"How are you?"

"Cold"

"Yes it is isn't it? What are you going to do today?"

"The usual"

"Oh right."

Maisie was a woman who did not like to waste words. It was at moments like these that Nellie wondered if the falling out over her beard still rankled with her. Towards the end of last summer they had met up on a Thursday on the benches near the bandstand. It was early evening and there was a soft summer breeze blowing and life felt good. They had shared a couple of cans of brew and Nellie was unexpectedly experiencing a moment of euphoric contentment. She turned and looked at Maisie and the still bright evening light caught her face at such an angle that the full extent of her facial hair was visible. Her happiness developed into a sense of camaraderie with this strange little woman and she decided that it would be helpful to offer her some advice on facial hair removal. Maisie's response shocked her to the core. Nellie had never seen her so out of control. She shouted and cried and called her a nasty, rude old cow and said that no wonder she had no friends and that she was never likely to have any. The boys, a loosely used term applied to the disparate group of homeless men who tended to meet up at different and usually unplanned times of the day, had already arrived on the bench opposite and had been discussing the merits of space travel and its potential for the future. When Maisie started to rant, they looked over and Cyril, the natural leader of this diverse band, stood up to see if his diplomacy skills would be required, but sat down relieved when Nellie started to walk away feeling confused. Cyril, though concerned by the fracas, was thankful that his assistance had not been necessary and thus his immaculate appearance remained untarnished.

The benefit office door opened and Tom walked in. He was quite new to the area and had apparently previously been living on the Embankment. He was a Scot and had found himself in town after a drunken night during which he had fallen out with his best friend. To spite him, he had jumped on the night bus and remembered nothing more until he awoke the next morning in the local churchyard. He and Nellie had spent an early evening on the circle of benches by the market place, during which, he had shared his supply of Tenant's Extra and she had drunk it gratefully. Nellie had been surprised at his gentle manner which belied his burly, unkempt appearance and his harsh accent.

He saw Nellie as he limped in and loomed towards her with an idiot toothless grimace. She marvelled at the remarkable blends of yellow, blue and red which formed his face.

"Nellie! How are ye hen?"

"Cold"

"And what are ye gan te dee todee?"

"The usual"

Oh dear, she sounded just like Maisie.

"How about you?" she asked, trying to break the Maisie mould into which she seemed to have fallen.

"A bit o' scran and a wee drink. Would you care to join me hen?"

"Okay," she said and then immediately regretted it.

"Come round to mine about five and we'll paint the town red."

"Okay. See you then."

'Mine' was a boarded up terrace behind the library which Tom had been squatting in since he had decided to stay around and 'put down some roots'. Nellie was uncomfortable at the thought of company for a protracted period of time but the last few days out in the cold had really taken their toll on her. It might be good to spend an evening protected from the elements and she might even enjoy herself.

The queue stumbled along spasmodically until eventually, it was Nellie's turn. As she rustled up to the counter with her bags she remembered how she had loathed coming here when she was out of work as a young woman. She had never claimed benefits for very long and had found work as soon as she could. Now, she had no qualms about receiving 'handouts'; she just needed the money. So she smiled her ugly smile at the pretty girl behind the glass and gratefully shambled away.

Her feet were starting to really hurt as she made her way back up the hill to the post office. Her boots had begun to fall apart months ago. The uppers were detaching from the soles and she had been trying to rescue them daily with a variety of techniques. Her earlier intricate application of string was beginning to come undone on both shoes and she could feel the wind whistling through the gaping holes. To defend her toes from the cold, she wrapped her feet in newspaper and then covered them with two pairs of socks so that, where possible, the holes overlapped the good parts of the sock, offering reasonable insulation. However, this system did not work when it was wet and Nellie was aware that the need for a new pair was imminent.

By the time Nellie reached the Post Office, she was out of breath. Entering the large Edwardian building, she was enveloped by its warm, stale air and started to sweat profusely until she needed to lean against the wall for support. The temporary rest assuaged her breathing and she took the opportunity to survey the queue. Satisfied that it was not too long, Nellie joined it as inconspicuously as possible. The discomfiture that Nellie experienced each time she visited the Post Office was caused by people staring at her, then moving away but keeping her cumbersome profile within their sights. Since she carried all her belongings wherever she went, she took up a lot of space. Nellie often stood there wishing she could make herself smaller. Once she had established her position in the queue, she cheered considerably realising that she had a good overall view of the counters and was able to eavesdrop on a variety of transactions and observe how well the counter clerks performed their tasks. Nellie had worked on the counter in a building society for some years when the children were small and she had liked to pride herself in the quality of her customer care. Nellie used to brighten her day with a bit of conversation or on occasion, by helping someone who might be having trouble making ends meet. When she worked there she had accepted that she needed the job but had aspired to a more rewarding occupation when the children were older. Sadly, she recalled the level of conviction she had possessed in the planning of a career that was now unthinkable.

"Well that's over for another two weeks," thought Nellie as she pushed through the swing door and out into the February High Street.

She walked stoically against the northerly wind that was blowing discarded wrappers and cartons at her so fiercely that they seemed to create a dance all of their own.

"Now, let's get down to business." She said to herself as she entered the off licence and the door pinged its greeting.

"Hello Pat," she called to the man behind the counter.

"Hello Nellie. What's it going to be today?" He answered, smiling.

He was fond of old Nellie. She always came in, put down her bags carefully and then spent ten or fifteen minutes reading the labels of all the expensive wines and champagnes. She made polite remarks to him about the excellence of the establishment he was running and how the world would be a better place with more shops like his.

"I'm not too sure. You see I have a bit of a dilemma," she replied, enunciating each syllable as clearly as she could.

"Ah, and what would that be?"

"Well, you see I have received a dinner invitation from a friend of mine, don't you know? Unfortunately, I am unsure as to what we will be eating."

8

At this point, Nellie stopped and stood staring at the bottles neatly arranged in front of her. They were all different colours, shapes and sizes; each with its own individual promise of conviviality and hope. The spirits were blue, green, brown and their labels were beautifully crafted. This was Nellie's favourite section and as gleeful expectations rose from deep within and the bottles entranced her, she smiled at them and said,

"I do believe that one drinks white with chicken and fish and red with dark meat."

"I believe so," said Pat patiently.

"However, if I were to present my friend with a bottle of rose that would cover all eventualities."

"Yes..."

"Perhaps it would be wiser to purchase a beverage that lasts a little longer."

"Like a three litre bottle of Woodpecker's?

"Ooooh! Have you got those three litre bottles again? I'll have two and maybe just a half of vodka as an aperitif," said Nellie, looking up at Pat with twinkling eyes. "Throw in two of your best affordable cigars. After all you only live once. Caution to the wind and all that."

Nellie fumbled in her larger carrier bag to find her handbag and then the small purse inside it. Her hand was shaking with excitement, so much so, that the purse caught hold of an envelope, the only other thing that she kept in her handbag, and it flew out and across the shop onto a display of beer cans. Nellie leapt towards it and knocked the top two cans off the display as she lunged forward, grabbed it and shoved it back into the bag.

"Steady on Nellie," said Pat.

"I'm sorry," she said, looking down at the ground and feeling the colour rise up through her neck and on to her cheeks.

Suddenly, she felt the need for the outdoor air on her face and above all, to be alone. So she paid Pat, who gave her a discount for buying in bulk-or so he said-, then manoeuvred herself and her belongings through the door and on to the thrumming street outside.

The light was too bright and the noise was immense. Children shouting and little ones crying and that terrible noise of lorries, buses, vans and cars invaded her world and she had an overwhelming desire to throw back her head and scream and let them all know that she would not take that amount of intrusive noise without fighting back, without letting them know how painful it was.

And then she was afraid. She took a deep breath. "A drink," she thought, "That's what I need. A drink"

She turned into a side street and rushed down the nearest alley, put down her bags and started rummaging furiously in the bag that she knew contained the vodka. It was dark in the alley and she could not feel the smooth shape of the red-labelled bottle. Panic seized her for a moment and then it was there. She pulled it out, wrenched open the top with its familiar squeak and put the neck of the bottle to her mouth, upturned in readiness, and drank and swallowed, drank and swallowed until she needed to stop for air. Then she paused, breathing slowly and calmly measuring her heart beat and looking at the bottle to see how much there was left. She waited.

She leaned back against the wall of a house and started to feel the raw spirit permeate her body and her mind until she smiled and said, "That's better."

She put away the bottle, picked up her bags and made her way back on to the street. She had not wanted to linger in the alley since she had been forcibly removed one night by the police. They had been called by one of the residents of the flats nearby and although Nellie had tried to make herself inconspicuous whilst settling down for the night, the old lady had declared that she was a nuisance and that anything could happen and anyway didn't it lower the tone of the neighbourhood?

Her ordeal came to an end when a business man, on his way home from work, walked up to the marauding crowd and boomed, "What on earth do think you are doing? I have already called your headmaster and if you don't go home now I will also call the police and you won't look quite so funny and clever then will you? Now get off with you!"

The boys slunk silently away with their red faces bent towards the ground.

"Are you all right?" asked the man softly.

"Yes thank you," replied Nellie quietly.

"Have you got somewhere that you can go?" he continued.

"Yes," she said, "I'm just on my way to see a friend."

"Would you like me to walk some of the way with you?"

"No, I'll be all right now. They've gone. Thank you very much. You've been very kind."

"Goodbye then Nellie. Take care."

"Goodbye"

When he had walked around the corner, Nellie took out the vodka bottle and drank the rest of its contents before she embarked on her walk to Tom's. She placed the empty bottle in the bin next to the bench and started trudging wearily along the road. She felt very shaky as she thought about the boys but, more than fear she felt sadness and an uncomfortable moment of clarity.

"After all," she thought, "I am smelly. Smelly, smelly old Nellie."

The tears that she had held on to with fierce pride only minutes earlier, now fell from her eyes and on to her cheeks in such a torrent that she could barely see the way ahead and as she went to cross the road a car screeched on its brakes, forcing Nellie back on to the pavement with a jolt.

"Get a grip girl." She told herself sternly.

Nellie was cross at the time but she got a ride in a nice warm police car and a cup of tea from the young officer who dropped her back at the park entrance saying, "Now don't you go upsetting any more old ladies Nellie!"

Nellie continued up the side street and looking up, she saw that the sun was lowering in the sky and thought, "It must be about half past three. I'm a bit early for Tom's." She decided to go to her favourite bench in the town, collect her thoughts and, with an unexpected surge of enthusiasm, she thought, "Perhaps I'll sort out my bags. I haven't had a good clear out for some time." Her bags were feeling very heavy due to the six litres of cider she had now been carrying for the last half an hour and she mulled over the possibility of acquiring a shopping trolley. She had seen all sorts of different ones being used by ladies in the shopping centre and often caught herself assessing them for their size, strength and stability. The most suitable for her needs would be one of those large, and she thought somewhat unwieldy, affairs which looked like a cloth-covered box on wheels. The advantage to her of owning one of these would be its great capacity. However, she had often seen the more elderly owners using them either as a prop upon which to lean and steady themselves or as a warning to oncoming pedestrians to concede right of way. Nellie preferred to be less noticeable and she certainly did not like being in anyone's way.

The trolleys that she found particularly attractive yet seemingly useful, were the more modern ones which you could fold away inside another bag and only take out when necessary. She had watched enviously as the ladies in the supermarket took them out, constructed them deftly and expertly whist chatting to the person on the till. Nellie knew that she would have to have a fair amount of practice before she would be able to do this. The prospect of causing a queue pile-up while she battled with her trolley construction made her feel nauseous with fear. Yet,

11

the main reason for Nellie's yearning for one of these stylish shopping trolleys was that they were designed in bright colours with big loud flowery patterns and she would have been so proud to own one and wheel it behind her.

She rounded the corner and to her delight saw that the bench was empty. She sat down placing her bags on either side of her, immediately occupying the whole of the seat. This was the way she liked it because it prevented anyone even considering sitting next to her.

She remembered that she was going to tidy her bags and thought, "A little drink to get me in the mood methinks."

She felt in her bags and found the bottle. As she pulled it out she touched the envelope that she had rescued earlier in the off licence. She grasped it carefully and held it tightly in one hand as she took a drink with the other. As she paused, she looked across the road to the large, symmetrical Georgian building that stood proudly between two large oak trees. Nellie had always loved this house. It had been converted into modern flats some years ago but it had originally been a maternity hospital and both her children were born there. A warmth rose inside her as she remembered the time she had spent in its care when she was pregnant with Daisy.

She had been unwell and had enjoyed a month's enforced bed rest within its welcoming walls. The window by the bed she had occupied remained unchanged and she remembered fondly how she had watched for the visitors that came regularly to see her during that time. She had loved the attention she had received, but above all, was the joy of Daisy's birth and the pervasive, quiet elation that it brought her.

She put the lid back on the bottle of vodka and put it back in the bag. She was still holding the envelope and she tentatively opened it, deftly taking out the photograph that she kept inside it. Smiling, she looked down at the image of herself holding the

12

hands of her two children. It had been taken at the seaside and
three were tanned and dressed in shorts and plastic beach sh
ready for the day ahead. They were all smiling and both
children were looking up at their mother as if they were shar
a joke that only they were privileged to share. She sank in
reverie and felt that she was close to recapturing the feeling:
that long, lost day when suddenly, she was shaken from it by
harsh shouts of a group of school boys as they jostled each ot
on their way home from school.

"Hey look! There's Nellie."

They were nearly at her bench and she had just enough tim
put away the picture in the envelope before they reached her. Th
were five of them in school uniform, all about twelve or thirte
They surrounded her and then started to pick up her bags.

"What you got in here then Nellie?" said the tallest of
gang as he put his hand inside.

"Get out!" shouted Nellie grabbing at the air as he waved
big plastic carrier bag in front of her face.

"OOOooooh!" they taunted in unison.

"What is it then Nellie?" said the fat one. "Is it your se
soap supply?"

They all started to laugh and one of the smaller boys j
in saying, "We'd better not take it away then 'cos you ha
used it yet have you?"

"How d'you know that then?" said tall boy.

"'Cos she's still smelly!" said small boy gleefully.

"Of course!" said fat boy, "Its Smelly Nellie!"

"Smelly Nellie! Smelly Nellie!" they all chorused
becoming louder and louder with each chant.

Nellie sat on the bench clutching her bags as clc
body as possible, looking up at her tormentors with l
and resignation. Her big eyes glistened with tears of
she refused to shed in front of these beasts.

She put down her bags and started to rummage about in them until she found an old tissue. She dried her face and blew her nose.

"There we are," she said. She picked up her bags, crossed the road and turned into the street where Tom lived. She spotted his house. Nearing the front path, she thought genially how easy it was to recognise the building as it was the only one sporting boarded windows. She walked around to the back of the building. It was nearly dark now and Nellie knew that she needed to be careful because there was a lot rubbish and broken old furniture piled up against the fence. At the back door she hesitated, suddenly unable to knock on the door in case he had forgotten that she was coming or even worse, he had only been joking when he had invited her.

"Do I dare to eat a peach?" she quoted, chuckling to herself.

She was startled back to reality as Tom flung open the door, booming out in his broad Scottish accent, "What are ye stonning there fer? Come in hen its cauld."

CHAPTER TWO

Tom

Nellie walked into the kitchen immediately relaxing in its warmth and homely smell of cooking. She put down her bags.

"I brought us something to drink," she said, showing him one of the large bottles of cider she had bought earlier in the day. She did not want to show him both bottles. She was not keen on sharing her drink with anyone and always liked to keep something in reserve.

"Och! That's grand. Perhaps ye'd like to sample a wee dram o' whiskey to warm ye?"

"Ooh! That'd be lovely." She said enthusiastically.

He handed her half a tumbler full of whiskey and she started to drink. As she felt its warm glow move through her body, she inspected her surroundings. The kitchen was tatty and the walls were brown with grease. There were a few cupboards, some with doors and some without but the place was remarkably tidy. A single bulb in a rose hung from the ceiling, spreading its light upwards in a circle onto the peeling paintwork above and down on to the kitchen furniture and Nellie and Tom's smiling faces.

"Come through Nellie and bring your things with ye."

Nellie shuffled through the doorway into a living room and turning towards Tom said, "Its cosy in here. Mmm. Lovely and warm."

She walked towards an old three-bar electric heater and held her hands out to warm them. The smell of the dust burning reminded her of the large ungainly convector heater of her childhood home. On the opposite wall was a sofa. A mattress lay on the floor under the window. A piece of floral patterned cloth hung over the redundant curtain rail, separating Nellie and Tom from the dark, cold night outside. On the right, just inside the doorway, stood a small kitchen table set for two and decorated with two lighted candles and a small beer bottle containing snowdrops and yellow crocuses.

"They're just beautiful," said Nellie, reaching over to stroke their perfect petals.

"You do love your flowers don't ye?" said Tom gently.

"Yes, I do. They're all so different and special. I believe that they were put on this earth just to give us joy."

"Mebbee."

"I'll show you something," said Nellie, scrabbling noisily in one of her large plastic bags.

One by one she carefully pulled out a trowel, a hand fork and a pair of secateurs. Each tool was clean and polished and it was only the worn wood on the handles of the fork and trowel that showed any sign of their age. The secateurs were shiny and sharp and they caught the flickering candlelight as she proudly handed them to Tom for his approval. It tickled him to think of Nellie walking the streets with her gardening tools but he could see that they were very special to her and he turned the secateurs over and said admiringly,

"Ye've taken mighty good care of these Nellie. When d'ye get to use them?"

"You'd be surprised Tom. People can be very careless with plants. Sometimes I tidy and trim and prune the plants in the park. I know I'm not really supposed to but they can get quite overgrown and it troubles me. Usually, I wait until there's no-one about and I have a little go and then I feel better and so do they."

She stopped and looked up at Tom's face which was smiling down at her.

"Oh dear!" She said anxiously, "Now you think I'm quite barmy. Well maybe I am."

"Not at all, hen. Now come in and sit down."

He gestured toward the sofa which was large, low and covered in a stained red-coloured material. She misjudged the seat and found herself landing heavily, hitting her head on the wall behind and dropping all of her bags. As the bags hit the ground a glass object flew out with the impact and smashed on the floor.

"Oh no!" cried Nellie.

"Never mind, I'll clear it up. What was it?"

"It was one of those lovely snowstorm paperweights. It belonged to my little boy. He really loved it. Do you think I'd be able to fix it?"

"Och aye. Spot of glue it'll be as good as new."

As he left the room a tear rolled down Nellie's cheek. He returned with a dustpan and brush and she wiped her eyes and asked,

"Do you have any more of that whiskey Tom?"

"Aye that I do," going back to the kitchen to collect it.

Nellie heaved herself back up on to her feet. Taking the dustpan and brush, she tenderly swept up the pieces of her son's prized possession.

Squinting in the poor light she could see that a repair might be possible and thought, "I'll try and fix it tomorrow."

She took the pieces and wrapped them individually in tissue paper from one of her bags and placed them all into a small carrier bag which she kept 'just in case' and then returned it to her larger bag. She sat back on the sofa and Tom handed her, her refilled glass. Her head was starting to swim and she looked over at Tom, who was perched on one of the chairs at the table and asked,

"Why did you ask me over for dinner?"

"Well, I fancied a bit of company so I thought to myself,

"Now that Nellie seems a nice lady I wonder if she'd like to come over for a bite to eat." So I told myself, if I saw you this morning I would ask you. I thought you might like to come indoors for an evening. It's been such a long cold winter."

"Yes it has. My bones are really feeling it. They're just waiting for the spring. And my feet, my poor feet. They hurt and they ache and the cold eats into them. Sometimes I think that I won't be able to walk another step. So, I try to think about something else, or if that doesn't work I sing."

"What d'ye sing?"

"When I'm cross, I sing 'Nelly the Elephant'. I can stomp along to the rhythm and shout out the words, if no-one is listening. If I'm feeling a bit more poetic," she paused and looked over at her companion, "I sing 'Blowing in the Wind'."

"Och aye, now that's a good tune. Dye know the words?"

"Mmm, most of them," and she started to sing,

"How many roads must a Nellie walk down, before you can call her a man?" She chuckled.

Tom picked up the brush that was still lying on the floor with the pan, held the handle up to his mouth and started to sing with her. By the end of the verse they were sharing the 'microphone' and belting out the words,

"The answer my friend, is blowing in the wind,

THE ANSWER IS BLOWING IN THE WIND!"

Nellie fell back on to the sofa, laughing wheezily and tried to catch her breath, whilst Tom remained standing, also recovering himself.

"Away with ye! Let's eat," he said.

"Mmm, I'm hungry," said Nellie, "What's for dinner?"

"Mince and tatties."

19

Nellie followed him into the kitchen where the mince and potatoes were bubbling away. Tom took a bottle of red wine from one of the cupboards and took a corkscrew to its neck. The sound of the cork popping its way out of the glass aroused a wistful nostalgia in Nellie that she knew could only be quelled by drinking its contents.

"Would Modom care to taste the wine?" asked Tom his eyes sparkling with fun.

He poured a mouthful into the wine glass he had just polished with a bit of rag. Nellie took the glass slowly, held it up to the single naked bulb above her head, put it to her nose, sniffed it and then swallowed it.

"Not bad, my man, not bad. We'll have it seeing as it has already been opened. Shall we let it breathe?"

"I think not Modom. We wouldn't want it to evaporate now would we?"

"You're posh with all this wine and candles business Tom," said Nellie, as they sat down at the table and tucked into their dinners.

It was the first cooked meal that Nellie had eaten in a long time. Sometimes George at the Wimpy would give her bread and soup but Nellie was too proud to ask for it when she was hungry. Most of the time she lived on scraps from the bins or occasionally, she might steal a sandwich from the supermarket, but the prospect of getting caught and the ensuing humiliation would more often than not leave her hungry.

"It's a long time since I had any company at all and I wanted to make an effort for you."

"But I'm just a bag lady," said Nellie, looking puzzled.

"Let me correct you if I may. A singing bag lady, mind."

Nellie grinned and carried on eating, savouring every mouthful.

"You're a good cook Tom."

"Aye I am that. I learnt how to look after misself a long time ago."

Nellie heard melancholy in his words for the first time and she reached out and touched his gnarled, coarse hand. She raised her eyes to his and said softly,

"Tell me, Tom."

"I don't know where to begin"

"Where do you come from then?"

"Have ye heard of a place called Stornaway?"

"Yes, I have but I don't know anything about it."

"Well I was born and brought up there," his voice and accent softening with his memories. "It was a wonderful place to be. I had such a free and wild childhood. There were five of us boys. No girls. I think my Mammy would have liked to have had a wee girl to complete her life but she was a wonderful Ma and she loved to look after us and my Da. He was a fisherman and sometimes he would be away for weeks but he always came home bringing fish to eat and tales of the sea. They would rush into each other's arms like young courting lovers every time he came home and the house would be full of her smiles and their happiness.

We ran amok, my brothers and I. We lived on the edge of Stornaway in a fisherman's cottage and went to the only school in the town. I wasn't much good at school unless it was something that took my fancy and I was a terrible one for daydreaming. The countryside was pure heaven for the likes of us and we learnt about the plants and the animals and the weather-there was a lot of that- and the seasons. They would change one into another and then another year would have passed and Nellie, I never really thought about it then but I felt as if it would never end and that life would always be the same.

I used to help my Da on the fishing boat and sometimes I went out with him as I got older. I can still smell the sea and feel the raw wind on my cheeks as I stood at the helm looking out towards the horizon. I couldn't understand why it never got any nearer.

We used to go to the mainland a few times a year. The ferry journey was nearly three hours so it was a big deal and there were only two ferry trips a day-and that was in summer. The ferry took us to Ullapool, another fishing town not much bigger than Stornaway but it was surrounded by glorious, rugged mountains and that would be where we would head once we had eaten in the town. We'd return home exhausted and sleep the sleep of the just."

Tom looked dreamily into the candlelight and sighed. Nellie met his gaze for a moment and glimpsed the boy he had once been.

"Let's have another drink," he said, standing up to take the plates into the kitchen.

"How about a refreshing glass of cider to whet your whistle?" suggested Nellie.

"Aye that's a good idea"

When Tom returned from the kitchen Nellie had placed the two cigars she had bought earlier, on the table. Tom let out a rasping chuckle and said,

"Ooh! La di da!"

They sat for a while in silence as they attended to the business of lighting them and took long draughts of cider as though it were a hot summer's evening and there was a need to satisfy their furious thirsts.

"That's better," said Tom.

"Your Mammy sounds wonderful. Was she pretty?"

"She was beautiful and dark. She had deep brown eyes and long, black untamed hair and she sang like an angel. She used to sing and my Da would play along on his guitar. Celtic music was part of our life. Sometimes I think we were born with it in our bones and in the end, it changed my life forever."

22

"What happened?" asked Nellie.

"Well, every year we'd have a big festival on the Isle of Lewis; the Hebridean Celtic festival, to give it its proper name. It only lasted a few days but there was always a big build up to it and then a counting down of days until the start. It was mainly a music festival but there were loads of things for children to do.

The islanders loved it. They made quite a bit of money and they could show off their Celtic heritage to anyone that was interested. For us boys it was pure excitement. I can still feel the thrill of watching the ferries arrive and all the people spilling on to the harbour and out onto our streets. Their noise and colour marked the beginning of our summer. As I grew older I found work at the festival. I used to help set up the stage and the sound systems and one year I helped with the lighting. I have to tell you now that I thought that I was very important, in fact, they may have had to cancel the whole thing if I had been taken ill that year!

I had just turned sixteen and I met a girl called Jeannie and fell in love with her; there and then and for all time. She was slight and fragile-looking with a mass of curly, brown hair. Her looks belied her strength and we stayed up dancing 'til the wee hours and we spent the days out on the peaty moorland playing like children and when we were tired we would lie in the purple heather and look up at the sky and daydream about our lives. I took Jeannie to all the special places of my childhood. This place that I had always known now became clearer, more sharply defined and the colours were brighter and more beautiful.

Jeannie had come to Stornoway with her parents for a two week holiday over the festival period and on the day they were to return to their hometown of Aberdeen, I took Jeannie down to my favourite beach and asked her to marry me. I went down on one knee and wound a blade of grass around her finger and told her that my heart was now hers to keep. When I had waved her off I walked back to our house and told my mother that I was going to leave school and join the Navy. I knew that the fishing industry that my father had worked in all his days was not going to last long enough for me to earn a secure income to keep a wife and family and I had heard that men who had been in the forces were taught other trades."

Tom stopped, drank his cider and refilled both their glasses.

"So did you join the Navy then?"

"I did."

"What was it like?"

Tom grinned.

"Well I can't really say that it wasn't what I had expected because, to be honest, I gave it no real thought until I was there. I was suddenly so childishly driven by my love for Jeannie and my fantasy of living happily ever after that nothing would have deterred me from my path.

It was harsh at first, but as the years went by, it became my way of life. Jeannie and I married when we were eighteen and a year later she gave birth to our son Stuart. She couldn't settle on Stornoway. It was too quiet for her and I was away such a lot of the time, so we set up home in Aberdeen near her family. Nellie, I was a very happy young man and I felt blessed. Then came the war."

"What war?" said Nellie, looking puzzled.

Tom raised his eyebrows,

"The Falklands War."

"Oh yes," said Nellie, suddenly abashed, "I'm sorry. Of course the Falklands War. It seems like such a long time ago now."

"Well Nellie, since I'd been in the Navy I had really toughened up. I had been taught and shown how to cook and clean and look after myself and others. I had also chosen to learn an electrician's trade so that I would be able to work if I left the Navy. Along the way I had made some friends and when we were in port we would go out and have a riot of a time. I always stayed faithful to Jeannie, but I was starting to get a real taste for the drink. At that time, just before the war started I truly felt that I had discarded childlike ways and had grown into a man.

In March 1982 I said goodbye to Jeannie and Stuart and set off back from my leave. We had been training harder because there was talk of the trouble between Britain and the Falkland Isles but I still didn't believe that it would come to anything. I thought that it was just old Maggie Thatcher throwing her weight around again and puffing out a lot of hot air while she flexed her muscles. Who'd even heard of the Falkland Isles let alone cared about them. As the days went by I became more nervous. After all I hadn't joined the Navy to go to war and I began to feel afraid. I realised then that I hadn't ever really felt fear before and I could feel it gnawing at my bones. Before I could think about it anymore we were on our way out there and doing training exercises just off Gibraltar. Tension was rising alright but I still held on to my hope that it would turn out OK and life would return to normal. Six weeks later our ship was used as a decoy and the Argentineans bombed us twice and sank the ship."

"Oh my God!" exclaimed Nellie putting her hand to her mouth.

"That was it really Nellie. One minute I was up on deck. The next the sky fell in on me. I remember the crash and the pain in my ears from the explosion and the bright fierce light of the flames. Then the flames were on me and there was shouting and that was all I remember until I came to in the life boat. I could hear the men singing and someone said to me, "Hang in there. There'll be here soon." And I passed out again."

A shadow passed over Tom's face. Then he smiled and sang quietly,

"Always look on the bright side of life!"

He looked over at Nellie and said,

"That was it, Nellie. That's what they were singing in the boat."

"Then I was flown back to London and they tried to repair my body. It was burnt and mangled all down the left side and it took a very long time. Eventually, I was well enough to go home to Jeannie. All those weeks I had dreamt of my homecoming but when I got there it didn't feel real.

There was something dark looming between us and I didn't understand it. Jeannie was kind and patient, but we were uneasy with each other. I had been invalided out of the Navy and needed to find work. I had a few jobs as an electrician but they didn't last. My body was much stiffer and that made me slow. Worse than that, was my mind, I could only concentrate for short periods of time and then it was as if I was no longer there.

I was drinking most days by this time. I thought I deserved a reward for my pain and it stopped me thinking. The money ran out and we had to give up our little rented house and move in with Jeannie's parents. All the time, I kept thinking that things would pick up. I would get a decent job, keep my family and Jeannie and I would go back to Stornaway and we would grow old and happy together. But the darkness between us grew and became our very own albatross.

One day, I got up late and hung over and came downstairs to the disappointed faces of Jeannie's parents. The knowledge that they now despised me, made me squirm. I just couldn't seem to make things right again. Jeannie had taken Stuart to school and then gone shopping and I had another blank day ahead of me. I picked up the paper which was lying on the kitchen table and started to turn the pages. It was more to move my eyes from their gaze than for any real interest that I had in daily affairs.

As I was about to put it back down I caught sight of a small advertisement for labourers needed for a big building project in

London. I sat back in the chair and thought, "That's it. That's what I'll do." I waited until my in-laws had gone out, wrote a note to Jeannie and left for London, with a rucksack on my back and a few pounds in my pocket. Some days later, I realised that I hadn't even brought the advert with me and that perhaps it had only served to justify my flight."

He stopped suddenly, scratched his head and walked over to the fire. He stood looking in to the orange light of the electric fire.

"Tom," said Nellie hesitantly, not really wanting to disturb his reverie.

"Yes?" said Tom.

"I was wondering if I could use your facilities," feeling a little awkward now.

"Of course, let me show you," he replied seeming to brighten at the change of subject.

Nellie followed him into the dark hallway, past the staircase and to a door opposite the living room.

"What do you think of this then? Please help yourself to the deluxe amenities," said Tom, as he threw open the door.

Nellie walked into the bathroom and looked around in wonder. It was years since she had been in a proper bathroom. The room held a toilet, a sink and a deep enamel bath with a hose attachment on the mixer tap. The fittings were all old and had marks on their enamel but it was clean with fresh-looking towels hanging on the back of the door.

"You do keep the place nice," said Nellie.

Tom looked pleased and said, "That'll be my naval training. I was hopeless around the house before that. My Mammy used to do it all for us. Anyway make yourself at home." He gestured vaguely with his hand and left.

Nellie went into a daydream while she was there, imagining the possibilities of living in a place with a bathroom and kitchen again. She picked up the soap at the sink and slowly ran it under the hot tap, working up a lather. Holding the bubbles to her face she smelt the familiar fragrance and remembered how particular she had been about the brands of toiletries she used to buy with the weekly shopping. She sighed and wondered how soon it would be before she would take it all for granted again were she ever to be blessed with such luxury again.

"Not long I don't suppose," she thought ruefully.

As she returned to the living room, Tom was standing with his hands clasped together.

"Can I ask you something Nellie?"

"Yes Tom, what is it?"

"Well I couldn't help but notice that your boots have seen better days and you said when you got here that your feet were really hurting you..."

"Yes..." said Nellie expectantly.

"When I was in the Navy I learnt that it was really important to keep my feet in tip-top condition and I found quite a few handy tips for looking after them. So I was wondering if you would let me help you with yours. It's so grim when they hurt."

"Oh please do. I haven't been able to do anything about them this winter. I tie the uppers to the soles with string and then the string breaks and the cold and the damp get in. I need a new pair but I never seem to have the money, not even for some old pair from a charity shop. I get my supplies in when I get my money and then there's hardly anything left."

"I know exactly what you mean, old girl," said Tom, with a twinkle in his eyes. "Do you know what I do hen?"

"No, what's that then?"

"Well I take a little walk along the High Street, when everyone's gone to their bed and I pick up the bags that have been dumped outside the charity shops and bring them here. Then I have a good old rummage through and take out anything that might be useful-clothes I mean, and then I take the rest of the stuff back. If I've managed to wash any of my old stuff I put that in and then it doesn't feel so much like stealing and I have a new outfit."

"I've always been too scared that someone might see me rustling about in those bags, so I haven't dared to take anything."

"Anyway, what I was going to suggest to you was a footbath if you so desired."

Nellie suddenly blushed and looked down at the offending items and muttered almost inaudibly,

"I haven't washed them for some time. I think they might be a bit...you know..."

"Och nonsense! This is an old sea dog you're talking to. Now let me go and get a nice warm bowl of water."

Tom was starting to feel the effects of all the alcohol he had consumed and started to sway as he carried the bowl of warm soapy water back into the living room. He lurched forward and as he steadied the bowl it slopped back in a wave that splashed his face and wet most of the front of his shirt.

"Well that's me washed for the evening." He said laughing, "I think I could do with another drink to steady these old hands of mine. Then we'll sort out your tootsies. I think this is a whiskey sort of a job don't you?"

"I couldn't agree more!" replied Nellie, smiling.

Tom poured them both a large drink and took it over to the sofa where he gestured for Nellie to sit down and handed her the whiskey.

"What shall we drink to then, hen?" asked Tom, raising his glass to hers.

"This, all of this," said Nellie, making a slightly uncoordinated circular movement with her right arm and chinking her tumbler against his enthusiastically.

"Careful, old girl. We don't want to waste it."

They both took substantial gulps of their drinks and put them down on the floor next to the sofa.

"Now to business," said Tom, rubbing his hands together briskly.

He knelt down by Nellie's feet and took off each of her boots with care and deliberation.

"No wonder your feet hurt you so much. These boots are fit for the bin."

Then he gently removed the various and colourful layers of newspaper and filthy socks from Nellie's feet. As he removed the last layer on each foot Nellie winced and bit her lip to prevent her from crying out in pain.

Tom looked up at her and asked, "Are you OK up there?"

"Yeah, I think so."

Then he placed each foot carefully into the warm soapy water. Nellie could not believe how good it felt. She lifted them one at a time and studied them as closely as she could in the dim light of the room. They were both quite swollen and had various red blotches where her boots had been rubbing her. She inspected the cuts that had stung as her feet had first touched the water and wondered what on earth she could do about them. Tom remained bent over his task and was massaging the dirt away from the skin. The water soon turned a murky, brown colour.

"I think I'll just change the water and put some bubbles in it so you can sit there and soak them for a while."

"OK," said Nellie, suddenly aware that she no longer felt embarrassed about her feet. She held them up and wiggled her toes, while he took away the bowl.

He returned and replaced her feet in the bowl saying, "Let's leave them for ten minutes or so and I'll look out some socks for you."

Tom left the room and Nellie could hear him fumbling around in bags in the hallway. Nellie started to feel sleepy while she enjoyed the unusual sensation of relaxation.

"Ha! I have just the thing for your poor feet!"

"What's that?" asked Nellie, shaking herself awake.

Tom came bounding back into the living room with a look of achievement and satisfaction written into his lopsided grin.

"Look at these. I couldn't remember if I had taken them back. I thought they would do me as slippers around the house or something like that but they were miles too small. Anyway they're really ladies things."

He held up a pair of sheepskin boots that Nellie knew to be really fashionable. They had a special name which she could not remember. What she did know however, was that she had watched people walking around wearing them, thought how comfortable and smart they looked and had long coveted a pair of her own.

"Wow!" She cried out in delight. "They're absolutely amazing. Where did you get them?"

"I picked them up with my last haul from the charity shop. I was going to take them back tonight. I'm so glad I didn't. I think they're quite well worn though."

"No Tom, they're perfect."

And so Tom gently patted Nellie's feet dry and rubbed some cream onto the cuts. He put a clean sock on each of them and handed the new boots to Nellie. She was so excited that she nearly dropped one of them into the bowl of water. Tom swiftly moved it away from her and she pulled the boots on, one by one, her mouth dropping as she gasped in admiration at them.

"Look Tom! They fit me," she called out to him as he walked back into the room holding a small portable radio in his hand.

"I found this while I was looking through the bags. I wondered where it had got to. Shall we have a bit of music?"

"Oh yes. Let's celebrate my new feet," replied Nellie jumping up from the sofa and hopping from foot to foot with glee.

Tom turned on the radio to the sound of the DJ saying, "And now its party-time. Here are all those party sounds from the seventies you didn't know that you'd forgotten! Let's start with a bit of rock and roll from Sir Elton John. I give you Crocodile Rock!"

Nellie started to sway her hips in time to the music and looked over at Tom.

"Aren't you going to join me?" She asked, holding out her right hand.

He came over and took her hand as she started to jive to the rhythm from the radio.

"You're a very good dancer," he commented.

"You're not so bad yourself, for a bloke," Nellie replied, and then lost herself in the music.

They danced and sang along to the tunes until they were both breathless and pink from their exertion.

"I can't remember the last time I enjoyed myself so much!" exclaimed Nellie, panting.

"I'm right puffed from all that. I think I need a sit down," said Tom.

"And guess what," said Nellie.

"What's that old girl?"

"My feet aren't hurting," she replied.

"I'm thirsty," said Tom, looking around for the cider bottle. "Do you want a top up?"

"Oh yes please!" she said, holding out her glass for him.

He filled their glasses and as they were drinking another song came over the air.

"We must dance to this, Tom. It was one of my favourites."

And so they danced and sang to "Hi ho! The silver lining," with increasingly uncoordinated limb movements until they gave up and sat down heavily on the sofa laughing.

As their laughter subsided, they sat for a while not speaking, just enjoying each other's company. Nellie broke the silence asking,

"So do you ever go back up to Scotland?"

"I haven't been there for five years. I went up a few times after I left. I used to try and take some money home. I really wanted to watch Stuart grow up, but in the end Jeannie met up with a man who she had been to school with and they got married.

It broke my heart, Nellie, truly it did. Not that I really blame her. It must have been really hard trying to bring up the boy on her own, no man about the house to look after her and to take him fishing or teach him how to play football. I was very, very jealous and angry. I was angry with myself more than anything for letting them down; for not being there. I just couldn't do it however hard I tried. I'd thought I was a man when I was in the navy but now I'm not so sure...not so sure at all." He paused, and then turned his head towards Nellie and asked,

"You have a son, don't you? Where is he? Do you ever see him?" he asked.

"I have a daughter too, Daisy and my son's name is Freddie. I haven't seen them for a long, long time. I have a picture of them when they were little. Would you like to see it?" she asked, feeling strangely nervous and unsure of herself.

"Yes. Let's have a look at them," he replied.

Nellie pulled herself up to the edge of the sofa and leaned over reaching into the largest of her carrier bags. The envelope containing the precious picture was not in its usual place. Panic began to well up inside her and her breathing became more rapid, as she started to frantically pull out the contents of the bag. She remembered that she had put it away in its envelope when her tormentors had approached her earlier that day, but she had no recollection of putting the envelope back in a bag.

"Oh please let it be in here, please, please let it be here!" she chanted, as she emptied each item onto the floor.

Tucked away in a fold of the plastic, Nellie caught a glimpse of it and thrust her hand in, grasped it tightly, and then sat back on the seat, clutching it to her chest. As her breathing slowed, she said,

"I really thought I'd lost it. There were these boys who came up and started shouting at me when I was sitting on a bench looking at it and I had to hide it quickly so that they didn't take it or tear it or something..." she trailed off.

Then she took the photograph out of its envelope and showed Tom who had been watching her closely during the search.

"What boys were shouting at you?" asked Tom.

"Oh, just some school children. They've done it before, but they can be quite nasty and I'm a bit afraid of them. They call me..." Nellie paused.

"What do they call you?" asked Tom who now looked quite cross.

"Smelly Nellie," she replied quietly. Seeing the anger rise in his cheeks, Nellie found herself trying to appease him.

"Oh they're just silly little boys who think they're being funny. I expect it's only because it rhymes."

"Well they had better not shout at you if I'm anywhere near because I tell you they won't ever do it again. I'll make sure of that!" shouted Tom as he waved his fist in the air.

Nellie looked at him, and feeling a bit alarmed at his sudden burst of temper said, "Have a look at my children. Aren't they lovely?"

She passed the picture to Tom, who took it in his hands and peered at it with a puzzled look on his face.

"Is that you?" he asked, scrutinising the image of the young woman before him.

"Yes," she said simply. She knew that there was very little of the woman in the photo left in her.

"Och! Of course it is," he said, moving it closer to his eyes. "My sight isn't what it used to be and what with the light, but I can see it's you now. What handsome children too. You all look so healthy and happy. Where was it taken?"

"Bournemouth, it was a great holiday. I used to love going to the sea-side. I haven't seen the sea in years," mused Nellie.

"Well my girl, maybe you and I should plan a trip down to the coast sometime soon. What do you say?"

"That would be fantastic," replied Nellie, with a surge of enthusiasm. "Where would we go, do you think?"

"Well, I've always had a soft spot for Frinton. It's not the nearest but it's got lovely beaches. How do you feel about that?" asked Tom.

"Yes, Frinton would be great," said Nellie, not really believing that they would be able to go.

"So, Frinton it is then. I'll see what I can do. We could take a picnic and a few cans and sit on the promenade," he said.

"And listen to the sea and the gulls screaming overhead."

"And watch all the people walking up and down."

"And paddle in the sea with our trousers rolled up."

"And we could go to the town and eat fish and chips."

"And ice cream. Wouldn't it be great?"

"Aye it would hen. I'll drink to that," and he poured out another large whiskey for them both.

They sat sipping at their drinks for a while and then Nellie said, wistfully, "I really miss the children. When they were small it was the best time in my life. We had so much fun and we went to all sorts of different places. Not fancy, special places, but parks and woods and out for walks. We only went on holiday a few times but that was really exciting -for me- as well as them. Most of all I just miss them; their dear little voices, their arms around me at the end of a day, their sleepy smell. All gone now, I ruined it all. In one fell swoop, a moment of madness and they were gone forever."

"Do you want to tell me about it, Nellie?"

Nellie sighed heavily; she was suddenly overwhelmingly exhausted.

"I think I do, but I don't think I can tell you yet. I'm very, very tired. And Tom, my name's not really Nellie..."

"Oh," he said, bemused, "What is it then?"

"Lydia," she said.

"That's pretty."

"I've never told anyone before," looking anxiously up into Tom's eyes.

"Don't worry, I won't tell anyone. And now, you need to sleep."

"Yes I should go now," said Nellie.

"What out into that cold, dark night? I think not. You'll stay here in the warm. That's if you want to?" said Tom kindly.

"I do, but where will I sleep?"

"Over there on the mattress. I'll bed down here on the sofa. I'm tired now too. I think we may have overdone it. You go and lie down and make yourself comfortable and I'll go and turn off the lights and the fire."

Nellie pushed herself up from the sofa and wobbled the few steps to the mattress. She kneeled, then lay down on the soft bed and saw that she was still wearing her new boots. She smiled thinking that they would keep her feet warm during the night. She rolled onto her side. As she closed her eyes, she saw the image of herself with her children and fell asleep.

When Tom came back into the room he heard the sound of Nellie's gentle snores. He turned off the fire, walked over to where his guest lay peacefully slumbering, knelt down to kiss the top of her head and said,

"Sweet dreams, Lydia, sweet dreams."

CHAPTER THREE

Lydia

She walked out into the sunbathed March garden, looked around the early spring beds and settled on her knees by the border nearest to her kitchen window. The birds sang in the budding magnolia, darting from the ground to the hedges and back to the tree. She felt the light warmth of the sun on the back of her neck as she started to move the leaves left over from their autumnal fall. Delighted, she smiled as she saw the shoots of bulbs pushing through the earth that she had cleared. She picked up her hand fork and dug around the weeds that had already begun to grow. Happily absorbed in her labour, she was interrupted by the clear musical sound of her resident robin greeting her from the fence. " Good morning Robin!" she said.

Pleased with her efforts, Lydia took the kneeler and using it as a cushion; she sat for a while on the dew damp grass. She allowed herself to indulge in a daydream about her plans for the next few days.

"So far," she thought, "All eventualities have been covered."

Today was Thursday and tomorrow she would be on her way to Brighton to meet Michael. It was hard to believe, that after all this time and much heartache, she was to be with the man she had always loved. She winced at the disruption that it would cause Philip, but he too, would then be free to find someone with whom he could be truly content.

* * *

Lydia and Philip had met soon after she had finished her nurse training and had returned to her home town to work in the local hospital. They had met at a party and he asked her out for a meal. Lydia accepted and turned up at the restaurant with the intention of passing a pleasant evening with a well behaved man and returning home to nurse her wounded heart. She could not believe that she would no longer see Michael. After all, weren't they soul mates? And hadn't it always been each other's company that they had sought for solace and understanding? Lydia's stomach churned when she remembered the phone call she had received from his sister saying,

"Have you heard? Mickey's getting married."

"Who's this?" Lydia had asked, thinking it to be a random, wrong number.

"Oh I'm sorry, this is Chrissie, Michael's sister. I must have dialled the wrong number."

"OK," said Lydia, replacing the receiver.

She sat down by the window and fell into a trance as she watched everyone going about their business on the street below. She was perplexed. She had spent the weekend with Michael. There had been no mention of marriage. No mention of anyone else. Why had Chrissie phoned her? They knew each other but they certainly did not phone each other. Then an element of doubt crept into her thoughts. Perhaps the phone call was not an accident. Maybe she had made the call with the purpose of passing the information on to her and the intention of keeping Lydia away from her brother. She knew that she had to call him and find out the truth but she put it off until the evening, childishly clinging on to an ever diminishing hope that it was just a silly mistake. By the time she had plucked up courage to call him she had drunk the best part of a bottle of wine and was feeling angry.

When Michael picked up the phone with a cheery, "Hi!" Lydia snapped, "What's all this about you getting married?"

"Ah! How do you know about that?"

"Your sister phoned me, 'accidently' and blurted it out,"

"Well she had no right," replied Michael defensively.

"Never mind all that. That's really not the issue. Are you getting married, to whom and why didn't you say anything?"

"Um...to Jacqueline, I only just found out she was pregnant and then her Dad came round and threatened to kill me if I didn't do the right thing by his little girl."

"But, you said..." Lydia trailed off. "Well I hope you are all very happy together. Goodbye."

She stood still, looking at the telephone as if this inanimate object might have the power to rectify all the ills in her life. Then she walked across the room, picked up her coat and left the flat. She walked over to the pub across the road where she worked part- time to boost her student nurse salary and set about drinking away her woes.

* * *

Philip proved to be as courteous and reliable as Lydia had imagined him to be and soon they both settled into a routine of meeting two or three times a week and occasionally, going away for a weekend. He proposed to her in Kendal, one cold wet autumnal evening. He had been dithering about and acting strangely whilst Lydia had been trying to soak up the atmosphere of a local pub. She had just bought another round for the two of them and for the barman, when he beckoned her from the entrance, saying,

"Hey Lydia, come out here, there's something I want to show you."

Intrigued, she walked over to the door and as she walked outside, she felt the cold night air against her face and her head started to spin from the effects of the wine she had been drinking all evening.

"Oh dear, I do feel a bit wibbly," she said, laughing loudly.

"Come over here," urged Philip.

And so, with the sun disappearing behind the fells on the horizon, their orange bracken-clothed hills still aglow, Philip knelt down on one knee in the mud of the path and said,

"Lydia, will you marry me?"

Lydia was quite taken aback.

She had not been expecting this at all and as the rain ran into her eyes, she looked down at Philip, who was now completely sodden, and giggling, replied,

"Well yes, but you'd better come in and get dry otherwise you may soon die and there will be no wedding at all."

She took his hand and dragged him back inside.

"Let's celebrate," she said, raising her glass to his and then announcing their engagement to everyone else present. Philip was embarrassed by the immediate public declaration of their betrothal, but he was so relieved to have followed through with his plan that he sat quietly as Lydia accepted drinks and marital advice from the elderly locals.

* * *

Their married life took on a pace of its own. Philip worked as an engineer and became animated when discussing aspects of his work with friends and acquaintances. Lydia continued in her profession as a nurse until she became pregnant with their daughter, Daisy.

After her birth, Lydia felt that she was truly happy and gave herself to motherhood. She returned to nursing for a short period when Daisy went to nursery school, but she found that she had lost her confidence and no longer felt comfortable making decisions or, indeed having to deal with so many needy people. Her second pregnancy, therefore, came as a great relief. The rigours of a working life were no longer expected of her and she eagerly, settled back into the ease and comfort of her home.

Her experience had taught her emphatically, that she would never become a modern day superwoman. She had watched these women in their pinstriped suits swooping into the playground to pick up their progeny, bustle past waiting mothers to corner the teacher and demand reassurance that their offspring were continuing to take the world by storm. Then clipping past importantly in their too high shoes to their large, badly parked vehicles, they would speed off to the supermarket and buy delicacies for their husbands' corporate dinner parties. Although Lydia envied them their style, she knew that she could not emulate them even if she had the desire.

Lydia fell into a muzzy routine outlined primarily, by the needs of her children. Term-time required effort to ensure Daisy and Freddie's regular attendance at the local primary school and nursery school. Lydia felt amply rewarded for her efforts during the much relished afternoons she spent alone with Freddie. She would attempt a little housework while he constructed roads, railways and even town centres with the toys he had at his disposal, all the while, sustaining a tireless informative dialogue with his mother.

Occasionally, Lydia would join him in his imaginary world when she felt that the household was adequately attended to but they generally preferred to cuddle up on the sofa to discuss the relative merits of the Sesame Street cast. Bert and Ernie were their favourites, made all the more hilarious to Freddie, as the old man that lived across the road from them was called Ernie. Ernie, the neighbour, had a friend who looked nothing like Bert but he called him Bert anyway.

Their stroll back to the school was reliably gratified by Daisy's indomitably enthusiastic greeting and was often enhanced by her latest cardboard creation, usually presented to Lydia as a gift, thus absolving her of its responsibility. These were notoriously large unrecognisable expressions of her fervour for life which were, most notably, awkward to carry. All urgency now gone, they meandered back home; the children chattering cheerfully and Lydia laughing loudly at their jokes.

When she had made their tea and saved Philip's for when he arrived home from work, Lydia would sit in the kitchen at the table enjoying a few glasses of wine and looking out onto her beloved garden. She could hear the children playing upstairs and she would indulge in her daydreams. She mused over the job she would have when they were both in school. She imagined studying at the local college and pursuing her love of literature to a higher level or developing her already competent, gardening skills. As the clock on the wall turned its hands to the six o'clock position she would put the empty bottle in the bin, tie up the bag and take it out to the wheelie bin at the front of the house. Walking back indoors, she would call up to the children, "Bath-time!" and then slowly climb the stairs to bathe and read to them. As time passed, this return from fantasy to reality became increasingly arduous.

By the time that both the children were in full-time school, Lydia had become restless. She sought solace in second-hand book shops and soon found that, if she was not careful, the school bell would be already ringing as she hurtled into the playground. She would open the cover of the latest novel of her choice soon after she returned home from the school run. She then spent the rest of the day reading, interspersing this activity only with sporadic declarations avowing that she would just read a couple more pages. The detrimental effect that this had on the state of the house was apparent but it was Lydia's resultant inability to separate fact from fiction that began to torment her. Reluctantly, she admitted defeat and limited her devouring of other people's worlds to bed-time.

Her controlled reading regime left a void in her life which began to grow and to become darker. Lydia was constantly aware of the cloud that had begun to greet her when she woke and to hang around her most of the day. Lydia became so familiar with its presence, that she named it Clara. Clara faded increasingly and in direct proportion to the amount of wine that Lydia drank. Some days she thought she had all but disappeared. But sadly, she would be there at the bottom of her bed the next day.

She decided to take a practical course in gardening, partly, to enhance her keen interest in horticulture and also with a view to starting a small business; if she could pluck up enough courage. Mainly, she hoped that if she was outside with a group of fellow gardeners, surely her disquiet would ease. The course was one day per week for an academic year, leaving her ample time to meet her school and home commitments.

Lydia loved it and would come home on Mondays all fired up and ready to learn the Latin and Greek names of plants in her determination to excel. She took the children round their garden and showed them the perennials, annuals, shrubs and trees that she had learnt about in college. They dutifully listened and although neither of them was keen on putting their hands anywhere near worm-infested soil, they loved the passion that lit their mother's eyes during these guided tours.

She tried to share her blossoming interest with Philip. He had been working later in the evenings and at week-ends for most of that year and whilst Lydia was happy with the arrangement, she did occasionally have a niggling feeling that maybe she should make a little more effort with her marriage. Thus, on Monday evenings, when the children were in bed she would burble away to her husband about her day. She even asked him if he would like to join her at a gardening club one evening. He declined the offer, but on seeing the sparkle back in his wife's eyes he put his arm around her shoulder and gave her a brief hug of encouragement.

When Lydia's course finished, Philip started to work away from home during the week. He left the house early on Monday morning and returned late on Friday evening, utterly exhausted. He spent the whole of the weekend recovering, which left him little time to spend with her or the children. As time went by Lydia found that she had less and less to talk to him about. Most of the minutiae of the week was history by the time he was at his most receptive on a Sunday. It was hardly worth putting into words by then especially considering that most events made less than ground breaking news at their time of occurrence. Their weekends together became so uncomfortable that Lydia finally suggested that he leave on Sunday evenings. She suggested that he would be able to start the week feeling fresher, no longer having such an early start or an unpleasant journey to contend with before the working day. Philip agreed and the distance between them grew.

During the early years of her children's lives, Lydia was taken by surprise at the potential social pressures of motherhood. To begin with, when Daisy was in play school, Lydia would eagerly accept luncheon invitations from other mothers, pleased that someone liked her enough to want her company. She soon realised that receiving and accepting such requests was a minefield of etiquette, fashion, cooking abilities and the vainglorious vauntings of competitive mothers.

After attending a few such events, only to leave baffled and red-faced from the large amount of wine that she had drunk, she resolved, to excuse herself from any future offers. The deciding factor in this resolution was the horrifying prospect of returning their unnecessarily generous hospitality. In the haze of alcohol-induced bonhomie, Lydia watched these unflappable women glide around their guests with an ease and assurance that by the end of an encounter, she dared to believe that she could imitate.

However, in the cold light of day and in her own home, Lydia was stricken. How on earth would she compare to these confident, capable women? What would she cook? What would she wear? She knew in her heart, that her natural reaction to such fierce, but polite rivalry, was to wither. Finally, she stopped accepting invitations; then she stopped receiving them.

Lydia took a job working on the counter at the local building society when Freddie had been in full time school for a year. She had found that she had not been managing her housekeeping money as well as she used to and loathed having to account to Philip for every penny she spent. Unexpectedly, she reaped benefits other than financial from her new employment. She looked forward to her few hours spent with other adults and started taking a little more time on her appearance in the mornings. She even made a couple of new friends. She went out for a meal occasionally with two or three of the girls that she worked with and they very often ended up in the local pub exchanging amusing anecdotes about their children and husbands.

One night, Lydia had arranged for the children to stay at her neighbour, Alice's whilst she went out with her three friends from work. Tanya, Marian and Carol planned to go to their favourite curry house to celebrate Tanya's birthday. Lydia dropped the children off early so that they could play with Alice's two daughters. She came home intending to run a bath and relax while she prepared herself for the evening. She opened a bottle of beer and sat at the kitchen table. She felt apprehensive about the proposed outing. Money had been regularly short on the counters for the last two weeks and now the management were becoming agitated about the loss. Lydia was meticulous in her accounts, but knew that it was possible to make a mistake. The problem was that if money was being stolen, it would be by someone she knew and she liked all the people that she worked with.

"What if they think I'm stealing the money?" she thought, as she walked over to the fridge to take out another bottle of beer.

Then she wondered whether it was too late to cancel the meal.

"They might think it suspicious if I phone so late in the day," she reasoned.

Reluctantly, she took her beer upstairs with her and started to get ready. By now, she was feeling very nervous about going out and ran back downstairs to get another bottle.

"This is ridiculous! Calm down girl!" she told herself firmly.

She had taken her cigarettes, lighter and ashtray upstairs with her and was now sitting at the dressing table, drinking, smoking and putting on her make-up. She smiled as she thought how cross Philip would be if he could see her smoking in the bedroom. The beer was starting to have the desired effect and she felt more confident about the impending birthday celebration. Marian was driving and she would be there soon. Lydia made her way downstairs and missing the last two steps, slipped and landed on the floor with the contents of the ashtray on her jeans.

"OOpsa daisy!" she said as she stood up and brushed the ash from her clothing.

She looked at her watch and thought, "Just time for a small one for the road!" and went into the kitchen to open the bottle of vodka she kept for emergencies only.

She poured out half a tumbler and added a little orange juice. The door bell rang just as she drained the glass.

She answered the door, "I'll just get my handbag," she called to Marian and to her dismay she found that she was slurring her words.

"Oh dear! she giggled, "It's a bit early for that, I'd better watch my step tonight."

Then she launched herself unsteadily down the garden path and toward the waiting car.

"Hello girls!" she called out too loudly as she sat down heavily on the back seat of the car.

They all greeted her and she thought she caught a glimmer of disapproval from Carol, as she turned to look out of the window.

"You all look nice," said Lydia, suddenly aware of the strong smell of conflicting perfumes that pervaded the limited air in the car. Gradually, she became conscious of the fact that she must smell strongly of cigarettes and alcohol. She wished that she had brushed her teeth again before she came out.

"Who's looking after the children tonight?" enquired Carol.

"Th'lady next door," slurred Lydia.

Lydia was horrified. She'd only had a couple of drinks and she was feeling drunk already. She resolved to limit her drinking during the night out and avoided talking anymore while she was in the car. Fortunately, it was only a short drive to the restaurant and she moved very carefully as she stood up and walked to its door. They were greeted by the owner, Ravi, who knew them well and he led them to the bar where they usually sat before a waiter would come along and seat them at their regular table.

"What would you ladies like to drink?" he asked.

"These are on me as I'm the birthday girl," said Tanya.

Lydia realised, to her consternation, that she was the only one wearing jeans. Her friends were all wearing dresses and had a freshly made-up look about them. Obviously, they had all thought the occasion warranted a slightly more formal dress code than was usually assumed. She wondered why it had not occurred to her, but abandoned her train of thought when she became aware that the drinks order had reached her.

"Come on Dolly Daydream, what are you having?" asked Tanya, tapping Lydia on the shoulder gently.

"A sparkling gin and tonic with a refreshing slice of lemon," she said with a wry smile, "Large of course, if you don't mind."

As they raised their glasses to Tanya, Lydia was shocked to recall her previous pledge to drink less than usual. How could she have forgotten?

"Oh well, it's done now. Better not let it go to waste," she mused and drank greedily from her glass.

* * *

The next morning Lydia was woken by the loud insistent ring of the telephone next to her bed. She rolled over slowly and picked up the receiver.

"Hello," she said croakily.

"Hi Lydia, its Alice, would you like me to take the children to school for you this morning?"

At first, Lydia was completely mystified by this simple question. Why would Alice want to do that? Then she remembered that Freddie and Daisy were at Alice's house and not upstairs in their bedrooms as she had automatically supposed. She looked at the clock. It was a quarter past eight.

Realising that she was possibly taking a long time to reply, she cleared her throat and said, "Yes, thank you that would be great."

"Are you OK?" said Alice, sounding concerned.

"Yes," replied Lydia hastily, "I'd just got out of the shower and I rushed to the phone. Are the children alright?"

"Yes they're fine. I thought you might like a bit of extra time before you go to work. Anyway, I'd better get going, we wouldn't want all four of them to be late. See you later."

Lydia rested her thumping head back on the pillow. She'd forgotten that she was expected at work.

As she lay there she could feel her stomach churning and had to suddenly run to the toilet.

As she came out she thought, "It must have been the curry, I wonder if the others have got upset tummies."

She went downstairs holding onto the rail as she went. She was feeling quite clammy and faint as she made her way into the kitchen and embarked on the hunt for headache tablets. At the sink, she ran the water for a few seconds and then sat down to her breakfast of paracetomol and fresh tap water. She put on the kettle, which seemed to be much noisier than normal and gazed out onto the back garden while she waited for it to boil. She was perplexed. She could not recollect the events of the previous evening after their arrival. Was this the onset of pre-senile dementia? She could remember drinking at the bar but however hard she tried she could not recall what she had eaten or anything that was said. She sat drinking her coffee and gradually, a few recollections emerged in the form of images. She cringed as she saw herself dancing maniacally to the sedate, sitar music of the reputable restaurant.

"Oh no!" she thought, "I don't think I'll be able to go to work feeling like this."

She looked up at the clock on the kitchen wall. It was eight forty-five. If she phoned the building society now, the answer-phone system would still be on and she would not have to suffer the awkwardness of speaking to any of her colleagues. She left her message and went back upstairs to prepare herself for the day. As she turned on the shower, she felt a sharp pain in her right shoulder. She glanced at it and was astonished to see a large, dark, bruise covering her shoulder and beginning to make its way down her upper arm.

Then she remembered, "Oh my God! I fell over in the restaurant, in front of all those people. How am I ever going to show my face again?"

When she had washed and dressed she went back downstairs and contemplated the day ahead. She decided to stay at home because she did not want to run the risk of being seen by anyone from work, or Alice who had taken the children to school on the strength of her need to get there on time.

"A day to myself then," she said, "What'll it be? Gardening and a spot of lunch, methinks. How nice. I don't think I'll go out for meals anymore. It's much safer to stay at home."

Lydia stuck to her resolve. She made polite excuses each time a night out was suggested and she hoped that the memory of her antics in the curry house would be replaced by the horror of someone else's misdemeanours.

* * *

It was around this time that Lydia renewed her contact with Michael. She had taken to nightly musings over a few drinks after the children had gone to bed. One night, during her reverie she started to think about him and how life may have been had they married and settled down together.

"Why don't I try and get in touch with him. We could have a chat and catch up with each other. After all, it couldn't really do any harm. We were such good friends apart from anything else," she thought.

Michael had phoned Lydia's mother twice one Christmas in an attempt to contact her. However, she had not received this information until sometime after the event. She decided not to respond to the calls. She had only recently given birth to Daisy and she was still enjoying the marvel of her creation. At this juncture, the prospect of speaking to Michael felt somehow wrong and her mind could not cope with thinking about him. Now, some years on her cheery outlook on life had been tainted by disappointment. Her marriage to Philip was becoming increasingly remote and Lydia was growing more isolated and detached from life. Her idea of romantic love had remained the same since childhood. It was an abstract concept unrelated to worldly things and overwhelmingly apparent when it arrived. An ethereal meeting of the mind and spirit between two lovers was her personal definition of this elusive state. The nearest she had ever come to experiencing this was during her relationship with Michael and she now became eager to restore their bond.

She took out her address book and found his parents' telephone number. Pouring herself a large vodka, she dialled the number and waited for her call to be answered.

"Hello," said the man's voice through the receiver.

"Hello," said Lydia, "This is Lydia, I don't know if you remember me. I used to go out with Michael."

"Oh yes, I remember you. How are you?" answered Michael's father amicably.

"I'm very well, thank you," she replied, amazed at how easy it had been, "I was wondering if you had Michael's telephone number, I seem to have lost it and he called me the other day."

"Yes, have you got a pen?"

"Yes," she replied, "Fire away." She wrote down the number as he called it out.

"Thanks very much," said Lydia cheerily, "I hope I didn't disturb you."

"Not at all. Take care now," he said and rang off.

She heard a sound from upstairs and went to investigate. It was Freddie making his way noisily back from the toilet to his bedroom. He was sobbing quietly taking involuntary deep breaths between sobs. The children rarely woke in the night and Lydia felt a pang of guilt as she took the small, distressed boy in her arms.

"Did you have a dream?" she asked him as she lay him down in his bed. She kissed the shampoo fresh fragrance of his head.

"No Mummy, it was a night-mare," he replied, carefully pronouncing the last two words for emphasis.

"Of course, silly me, it was a night-mare. Was it very nasty?" she enquired, softly, stroking his head.

"Very nasty indeed. There were lobbers. Lobbers everywhere. Under my bed, on the walls, on the stairs, in the toilet," he paused and looked up at his mother.

Freddie had a disproportionate fear of lobsters, considering that he had had very limited contact with them in his short life. Since he now had his mother's undivided attention he proceeded to elaborate on his night horrors.

"And there were enormous spiders driving a red Ferrari Testarossa 385 bhp, which they'd stolen off me just because I was asleep," he finished indignantly.

"Do you want me to read you a bit of Winnie the Pooh to take your mind off all your troubles?"

"Yes I think that will be a very good idea. Then all the lobbers will be gone. Can I have the bear of very little brain, please Mummy?" he asked, chuckling, "He really does have a very little brain. Poor bear." He shook his head and then lay down while Lydia read their favourite part of Winnie the Pooh. He was dozing, as she left the room and went downstairs.

She did not ring Michael that night but she wrote the number in her phone book resolving to follow up her plan in the near future.

* * *

Later that week, she called the number. She had been uneasy since she had phoned Michael's Dad and became aware that she was avoiding phoning. She was afraid that he would not want to speak to her. After all, a long time had elapsed since they had last spoken. Thus it was that with some trepidation, she found herself dialling the number of, as she believed, the only man that she had ever truly loved.

"Hello," said the voice that she felt that she had always known.

"Hello, it's me," she said hesitantly.

"Lydia, blimey! How on earth are you?" She exhaled in relief at the pleasure she could hear in his voice.

They talked for an hour, during which time, they arranged to meet the following Friday. They agreed upon a pub that had been a favourite haunt of theirs all those years ago.

"Do you look the same?" Michael asked her.

She paused and considered whether she had borne the years well.

"I think I do, more or less, maybe a bit older looking."

"My hair's gone grey," offered Michael, "Still you can let me know whether or not it suits me next week."

"OK then I'll see you there," said Lydia.

"Yes, bye then, it's been great talking to you," replied Michael, and she waited until she heard the click of the receiver going down.

Lydia had kept in touch with a friend, called Jane with whom she had been to school. She now lived about thirty miles away. On the occasions that she went to see her, Lydia would stay overnight to avoid a long, late journey home. It also meant that she did not have to worry about drinking and driving. After arranging to meet Michael she had started plotting her escape for the evening and she decided to use her friend as an alibi. Although she was undeniably uncomfortable with her duplicity, she had, by now, begun to think of herself as a thwarted romantic heroine and therefore vindicated in her actions.

On the night of their assignation, Lydia found herself driving down the North Circular Road singing along loudly to her Bob Dylan tape.

"How many roads must a girl walk down, before you can call her a man!" she bellowed out laughing loudly.

She was surprised and relieved that she could still remember the route without the use of a map. Everything was going according to plan. She sensed that their tryst was predestined. Any resultant consequences would be dealt with as they arose.

As she swung the car into the pub car park, she was unexpectedly struck by a surge of nostalgia. It was not so much the pub, although she did have very fond memories of the misspent hours she had whiled away there with Michael. It was not even a yearning for the girl she used to be, but much more a longing for her youthful, blithe spirit. As she walked towards its entrance, she breathed in the air and just for a moment, felt a minute part of that once familiar sensation; then it was gone.

She paused at the door, then pushing it open confidently strode across the floor past tables, chairs and animated conversations to march purposefully up to the long bar. Michael was already seated on a stool and finishing a pint of lager. He looked up as she arrived and they both smiled and hugged each other warmly.

"What were the roads like?" asked Michael.

"They were good," replied Lydia, studying the face of the man she had ached to see for so long.

It was true, his hair was grey, nearly white in places, but his face was the same. She had the same sensation that she always had when she met up with him. For a man of such singular importance to her, he really was quite ordinary to look at. Pleasing, but ordinary.

"So what do you think then?" he asked, pointing to his head.

"Well, yes its grey. What can I say? Your face hasn't changed though," she answered.

"Neither has yours. In fact, you don't look any different at all to me," said Michael, grinning, "Pint of lager?"

"Sounds good, thanks," And they settled down, at the bar immediately at ease with each other.

Lydia told Michael about her marriage to Philip and their children. She fondly recounted adventures she had shared with Daisy and Freddie. Michael watched on with affection as she became more and more animated. Her eyes shone with pride as she said to him,

"Oh it would be so wonderful if you could meet them. I know you would all get on so well."

He took her hand and said, "Maybe I will."

They laughed at times they had spent together and remembered fondly the bedsitting room that he had rented during the early days of their relationship. There, they had exchanged experiences of childhood and related the traumas of their teenage years. The lack of understanding shown by their parents was a common theme and they both felt that they were making a stand and showing the world that they were now grown up and therefore would do exactly as they pleased. They recalled how they would sit up late in the evening and into the early hours of the next day, drinking, talking and listening to Pink Floyd and Led Zeppelin. They giggled at their inability to get up in the mornings and how they had been constantly dashing in to the hospital where they were both employed, either just in time for a shift or reprehensively late.

Lydia and Michael were encapsulated in the glow of their own exclusive world. Towards the end of the evening the conversation turned to the possibility of, not just reliving these memories, but creating new ones. It was Michael who had suggested that this dream could become a reality. He had told Lydia in some detail about the trials of his sudden marriage to Jacqueline, who since the birth of their daughter twelve years ago, had suffered intermittently from depression. He adored his daughter Emma but felt constrained and unhappy in his union with Jacqueline. He said that there was no comparison to the freedom of spirit that he felt when he was with Lydia.

Lydia had not felt so happy in years. She had come home. There they were unchanged in their mutual understanding of each other. The logical conclusion was for them to be together as she had always known they should. Swiftly, Lydia and Michael went over the details that needed to be considered for their plan and decided that they would meet again in a couple of weeks to make preparations for their prospective reunion. As they were parting Michael said,

"We never did go for that meal we planned,"

"No, maybe we can do that next time," said Lydia. She kissed him on the lips and turned to walk to her parked car.

"Bye then!" she called out as she opened the car door, "See you in two weeks. Same time same place."

"Yes, drive carefully," he replied and walked away with his hands in his pockets.

* * *

As she offered up her face to the warmth of the sunlight, she thought about the last few weeks. She had met Michael on two further occasions and they were now in the final stages of their preparations. Michael and Lydia would meet in a hotel in Brighton. They had chosen this as a rendezvous in memory of a happy holiday they had shared there. They planned to spend the weekend together and return to Lydia's house to discuss future living arrangements with Philip.

Philip was pragmatic and would see that, not only did he not require the family home for his housing needs, but also he would appreciate the necessity for the children to remain there. The only detail left undone was the letter to Philip, telling him of her plans, so that when she returned on Sunday he would be prepared to discuss practicalities. Lydia leapt from her trance, as the sound of the telephone ringing from deep within the house directed her mind firmly back into the present.

She ran into the house and picked up the receiver, "Hello," she said cheerfully.

"Hi, it's me," said Philip on the other end.

"Is everything alright?" asked Lydia, guiltily aware that his whole world would be changed by Sunday evening.

"Yes, fine, I was phoning to let you know that I will be late home tomorrow night. The project is taking longer than anyone thought it was going to and I just wanted to try and gain some ground."

"You haven't forgotten that I'm going to Jane's for the weekend, have you?" said Lydia.

"Oh yes, well I had actually. Can't you go later or take the children next door or something?"

Lydia sighed impatiently. "Yes I suppose so. I'll sort something out. I'll leave you a note letting you know where they are," she said briskly, "I'll see you on Sunday."

"Don't drink too much," said Philip and put the receiver down.

Lydia felt strangely relieved by the annoyance that she now felt towards her husband. He had neatly replaced the discomfort of her deceit with a justified irritation at his lack of concern for her needs and the assumption that she would rearrange everything at a moment's notice.

"And," she thought vindictively, "I'll drink just about as much as I bloody well like!"

She went into the living room to search for a letter writing pad and a decent pen. Pens were such coveted items in their house that she usually hid a couple away from the children otherwise they all disappeared in the name of some urgent creative venture. She picked up a photo album lying open on the floor. She was about to return it to the shelf where it belonged, when she caught sight of a photograph of herself walking along the promenade at Bournemouth holding hands with Daisy and Freddie. She smiled wistfully as she recalled the eagerness with which the three of them had bounded down to the beach that day. Daisy had been so excited she had fallen out of the door of the chalet and cut her knee. They had all had to go back in while she had the wound cleaned and Lydia staved the bleeding. Lydia squinted at the picture and could just about see the plaster stuck at an angle over the cut. She walked back into the kitchen putting the pen, paper and picture on the table.

"I think I'll have a spot of lunch, before I attempt to write The Letter," she said to herself wryly.

She opened the fridge door and was greeted by the jelly she had made for their pudding and a pound of mince which she had bought on the way back from school that morning. She wanted to make Daisy and Freddie's favourite dinner because she would not be seeing them for most of the weekend. The thought of the Sunday afternoon homecoming made her feel panicky. How would it go? Would the children be OK?

"Well it's now or never old girl," she said, as she reached for the opened bottle of wine sitting in the fridge door.

She poured herself a large glass and sat thinking about the weekend ahead. Her overriding emotion was one of joy. At last she was to be happy. She knew that it would probably be a bit difficult at first for everyone to come to terms with the changes, but she also knew that she had not felt fulfilled in her relationship with Philip. She was not naturally malicious, but she believed now with an unwavering certainty, that she had been given one chance at life and that if she did not follow her heart now that she would never have another opportunity to flourish. She called Alice to make the necessary arrangements for Daisy and Freddie, made a sandwich and when she could procrastinate no longer she opened the writing pad and began:

Dear Philip,

I hope that you got in at a reasonable hour and that you are not too tired. As you may have gathered the children are at Alice's. She was very kind and said that you needn't rush over for them if you wanted to catch your breath when you got in.

This is a very difficult letter for me to write, so I had better get straight to the point. As I'm sure that you are aware, we have not been getting along well for quite some time. I really don't know how you feel because you haven't told me and we see so very little of each other these days.

Anyway, recently I renewed contact with Michael, the chap that I had been seeing before I moved back into the area. I am not proud of this but we have met up three times in the last couple of months and we have both realised that we were destined to be with each other. His marriage is on the rocks and it seems that we get on even better than we did before. Maybe that is something to do with the fact that we have both had to grow up quite a lot.

You may, by now, have gathered that I am not staying at Jane's this weekend. I have gone down to Brighton to meet Michael and we have decided to come back here and start a life together. We need a couple of days to sort a few things out and then we will come up together on Sunday afternoon. One of the reasons for me writing this letter before I go is that I wanted you to have some time to think about where you would like to live. The obvious choice would be for me, Michael and the children to live here in our house because there is enough room. You may however, want to sell it straight away, in which case we can come to some agreement over what we can do about accommodation in the meantime.

I do hope that this has not come as too much of a shock to you but I believe that it would have happened at some stage and although it may be difficult now, there does not seem to be any point in putting off the inevitable. I hope too, that like me, when the dust has settled you find someone that you can truly love and cherish.

I would also like to take this opportunity to ask that you forgive me for not turning out to be the wife that you needed. I say this now in case I don't have the chance to say it to your face when I see you on Sunday,

Tell Daisy and Freddie that I love them very much and look forward to seeing them Sunday at 3pm.

Love Lydia

She read through the letter slowly. Although she had found it hard to write, she was satisfied everything necessary had been said. She folded the piece of paper in half and set about looking for a matching envelope. She found one in the living room on top of the cupboard where she had found the paper. She was pleased. She had always been particular about using good stationery and felt that it would have been disrespectful not to do so on this occasion. She wrote his name on the envelope and placed it between the salt and pepper pot, facing towards the door to the hall so that it would catch his eye when he walked into the kitchen.

She sat down at the table and breathed a sigh of relief. Thank goodness that was over. Of all her preparations, this was the one that she had dreaded most. She poured herself another glass of wine and considered, in detail, what she was going to pack in her hold all for the weekend. She started to feel confused. All of a sudden, a seemingly small task had taken on ominous proportions. She became panicky at the prospect of forgetting something important so she decided to make a list. As she noted each item on the piece of paper, her fear diminished. By the time the list was complete she was looking forward to packing her belongings.

She looked up at the clock. It was already two thirty and she had to leave at three to collect the children from school. She rushed upstairs and embarked on the awkward task of extricating her faithful red hold all from the loft. She took the step-ladder out of the airing cupboard set it up under the loft hatch and proceeded to climb its steps pushing open the soot smudged wooden flap inwards and onto the loft joists. Her eyes had to acclimatise to the darkness and then she saw it- just out of arm's reach to her left. The next part of the exercise was more than a little dangerous as she needed to hoist herself up from the top of the ladder and wedge her thighs over the threshold. She began to laugh at her ungainly posture and had to quickly grab at the bag before she came out of the loft crashing on to the landing bringing down the ladder with her. She lay there for a moment stunned. She let go of the bag. Then she felt her head where the ladder had hit it on her way down. She felt the wet stickiness of blood dripping down her cheek.

"Oh bugger!" she cursed and pulled her body out from underneath the ladder.

She went to the mirror in the bathroom. She cleaned up the wound and held a towel to it until it stopped bleeding.

"That looks alluring," she said sarcastically to her reflection.

She tidied away the ladder and took the bag into the bedroom. She had left her list downstairs so she threw a few likely items inside it and then rushed to the front door picking up her keys and coat as she went.

The playground was nearly empty by the time she arrived. For an instant, she felt a surge of alarm. Where were they? She breathed a sigh of relief as she looked over into the far corner and saw Daisy and Freddie walking along with Mrs Lane. Even from a distance, Lydia could see that Freddie was engrossed in a meaningful conversation with his teacher. He was no doubt asking her some very involved questions about how leaves grow and why. Lydia was watching the three of them intently as she rushed to meet them and she could see a lot of gesticulating and pointing at the trees. Daisy was skipping energetically with the rope that Lydia had bought her last weekend and on seeing her mother skipped adeptly towards her, puffing out the words,

"Where have you been, Mummy? We thought you'd fallen asleep again."

"Oh I'm sorry, darling, I had some jobs to do and I lost track of the time," she answered, taking Daisy's hand and marching as quickly as she could up to Mrs Lane and Freddie.

Daisy got her foot caught in the rope and hopped next to Lydia until it freed itself. She looked up at her mother and said in a worried tone,

"Mummy what have you done to your poor head? It's all bleeding and lumpy."

Lydia put her hand automatically up to the wound on her forehead and said, "I had to go up into the loft and the ladder slipped and I fell and it landed on top of me. It's alright though, Daisy it doesn't hurt."

She realised, as she spoke, that this was not entirely true and became increasingly aware of the throbbing as she reached Mrs Lane.

"I am so sorry, Mrs Lane, I had a bit of an accident and I didn't realise how late it had got. Thank you so much for looking after the children."

"Are you sure that you are alright?" asked Mrs Lane peering at the oozing gash on Lydia's head and her slightly wild but glassy-eyed gaze.

"Oh yes I'm fine. I fell out of the loft. No real damage done. Now come on Daisy, stop bouncing up and down and Freddie come back we're going now."

The three of them trundled off. The journey had seemed longer than usual and Lydia opened the front door with a sigh. She took their school bags from them and hung them carelessly over the banister.

"Careful Mummy," said Daisy, "There's a secret surprise in there and it's very delicate."

"I've got a secret surprise in mine too," said Freddie, not to be outdone by his older sister.

"Yes, but mine's probably a bit better than yours because I'm older," retorted Daisy folding her arms and looking superior.

"Well I'm sure they're both just as lovely. Anyway, why are they secret surprises?" asked Lydia.

"Silly! If I told you it wouldn't be a surprise would it?" said Freddie triumphantly.

"OK, if you say so," said Lydia, suddenly tired of the whole secret surprise business, "I'm going to put the dinner on. Guess what we're having tonight?"

"Is it spaghetti?" asked Daisy, watching her mother while she waited excitedly for the answer.

"Well done! And we're having jelly and ice cream for pudding," finished Lydia.

"Wow! Jelly and ice cream! Yummy!" shouted Freddie while he jumped on and off the bottom stair.

"Stop jumping," said Lydia. She sat down on the stair as the children sat themselves either side of he. She put her arms around them gently and said,

"Do you remember that I told you that I was going away this weekend?"

"Ye-es," they said in unison.

"Well I thought that we'd have a special tea and then, if you want we can go to the park and feed the ducks."

"That would be nice," said Daisy, "But when are you coming back?"

"Sunday afternoon," answered her mother.

"What time?"

"Three o'clock, why?"

"I just needed to know," said Daisy.

"Because it's a secret surprise day! Oops!" said Freddie, holding his hand up to his mouth.

In an attempt to deflect his mother's attention from his obvious mistake he asked casually,

"Can I take my pedometer to the park with me? I really need to know how many steps it takes to get there."

"Of course you do," replied Lydia, catching her daughter's twinkling eyes, as she raised her eyebrows knowingly at her brother's demand.

She pushed herself up into a standing position and made her way to the kitchen. As she walked into the room her eyes were immediately drawn to the letter addressed to her husband, which stood on the table where she had placed it hours earlier. She picked it up with the seaside photograph and slid them both in to the kitchen drawer and commenced cooking.

Lydia opened a fresh bottle of wine to celebrate this special dinner they were having and by the time that she had served it up she was experiencing a pleasant, light headed sensation. She sat looking at her two children, while they ate heartily and recounted events of the day, both fancied and real. She loved the sound of their happy chatter and she drifted off in to her own dream about her prospective adventures over the next few days.

"Mummy, you're not listening to me," said Daisy emphatically, "I said shall we bring some bread to feed the ducks?"

"Yes, that's a good idea," she answered, returning her mind to the present.

She got up unsteadily from the table and walked into the hall to check the injury to her head. The bleeding had stopped but she could see the beginnings of a dark bruise appearing around the cut. She pulled her fringe down over the area and picked up their jackets.

It was the first week of later spring evenings and Lydia knew that they did not have to rush. It was mild and sunny with a gentle breeze blowing through her long hair. They ambled up the road towards the park contentedly. As they rounded the bend and entered the park gates Daisy and Freddie raced off to the well-planted pond to seek out the ducks.

Lydia caught up with them and put her hands on their shoulders saying, "Are they all present and correct?"

"I think one of the daddies is missing," said Daisy, "He'll be cross when they tell him that he's missed all the bread."

"He's probably looking for a laydee duck," offered Freddie.

"But he's got lots of lady ducks here," argued Daisy.

"I s'pect they're not beautiful enough for him. I bet he's found a gorgeous lady duck. I bet he lurves her and wants to bring her back here but the other lady ducks will be angry and bite his beak off and then he'll die. Ducks can be very psychopathic, you know," he finished with a definite air of satisfaction.

"Now you're just being stupid," said Daisy impatiently.

She walked away and started skipping and chanting a rhyme in time with her jumps. She stopped skipping abruptly as she neared the bench under the big oak tree. An old man was sitting there and was waving at Daisy. Daisy ran back up to where her mother and brother had started to walk away from the pond. She took her mother's hand and pulled on her arm.

"Mummy, there's a scary man over there," she trembled, "Look, there he is!"

Lydia followed the direction of her daughter's finger with her eyes.

"That's not a scary man, Daisy, that's just Old Joe. He's a nice man and Daisy, don't point at him it's not polite," she said, taking both her children's hands. "Come on let's go and say hello to him."

She could feel the weight of her children's reticence on her arms but continued over to the seat.

"Hello Joe," said Lydia, "How are you?"

"Hello, I'm OK. And who have we got here?" replied Joe, directing his gaze at Freddie and then at Daisy.

Freddie gave a little cough and said in a clear voice,

"My name is Freddie and this is my sister Daisy."

"Yes and we've been feeding the ducks," volunteered Daisy, not wanting to be outdone by her younger brother.

"That's grand, and how were they?" asked Joe, flashing a crooked grin at them.

"They were very well, thank you, but I think they will be putting their pyjamas on soon."

Joe laughed heartily and said, "Well I suppose it is that sort of time."

"Talking of which," started Lydia, "It's time we were making tracks. Bye Joe."

"Bye bye Joe!" chorused the children.

As they strolled away Daisy whispered loudly,

"You're right Mummy, he is nice but he's a bit smelly and dirty."

"Why is he smelly and dirty Mummy?" piped in Freddie.

"Sssh! Well he doesn't have a comfy house to live in like we do. So it must be difficult for him to wash and to keep his clothes clean."

"Oh I see," said Freddie thoughtfully, and then, "Oh no! I forgot to bring my pedometer."

"Count your footsteps then," suggested Daisy impatiently.

As they entered the house, Lydia called to them both as they rushed past her and up the stairs,

"Start running the bath and I'll be up in a minute!"

"OK!" they replied.

She sat down for a moment at the kitchen table and suddenly felt overwhelmingly tired.

"I'll get them ready for bed and then I can organise myself for tomorrow. I might even have an early night," she thought, yawning loudly.

She lumbered up the stairs wearily and went in to the bathroom to turn off the water.

"You first Daisy, I want to wash your hair," she called out.

While Lydia washed and rinsed her hair, Daisy asked, "Can you do me a fat plait like yours, Mummy? Then it will be all curly wurly when I take it out in the morning."

"Yes of course. I'll leave you to wash. Don't forget to leave the plug in."

She walked into Freddie's bedroom and chuckled. He had taken off all his clothes and was rehearsing his latest dance moves to the rhythm of "I wanna be like you," from the Jungle Book tape which was blaring out from his cassette player.

"You see it's true oo, that an ape like me-e, can learn to be hu-u-uman too!" He sang out joyfully, whilst perfecting his ape impersonation. He looked up and saw his mother laughing.

Lydia clicked off the tape and clapped her hands together, saying, "Come on! Chop! Chop! Time for a bath," and he scurried off giggling, to the bathroom.

"You know that Alice is going to pick you up from school tomorrow, don't you?" she asked.

"Yes!" they said at the same time.

"Daddy will pick you up when he gets in from work," she continued.

"That's alright," said Daisy. She enjoyed spending an evening next door because she could play with Alice's daughters and it generally meant that they stayed up past her bedtime.

Daisy and her mother sat on the edge of Lydia's bed in front of the dressing table mirror. Lydia was brushing her daughter's damp hair and preparing three sections for the requested plait. Daisy was looking at her mother's reflection in the mirror.

"I look like you don't I Mummy?"

"You certainly do."

"You're pretty. Some Mummies aren't pretty like you. I'm very lucky."

"My bruise isn't very pretty, is it?"

"Why don't you try some make-up?"

She reached over and picked up a tube of Lydia's foundation and handed it to her. Lydia did not really like wearing foundation but was impressed by Daisy's pragmatism and applied a small amount over the affected area. She winced as she felt the cut sting at the contact with the liquid. She leaned towards the mirror and said,

"Aren't you clever? It looks much better already."

"I'm going to get into bed now. Will you come and tuck me in?"

"Yes let me just get Freddie into bed."

She read Freddie the moving tale of Eeyore's birthday and then tucked him in and kissed his forehead,

"Night, night, see you in the morning,"

"Mummy?"

"Mmmm?"

"Isn't it strange how life just goes on?"

"What do you mean?" asked Lydia, frowning at what she thought was either a very advanced or a very disturbed statement for a six year old boy to make.

"Well, there's Christmas and then there's birthdays and then the next year it's the same all over again."

"Yes..." said Lydia, walking away in bafflement.

"Night, night, Daisy," she said as she walked into her daughter's room.

Daisy was propped up in bed, reading her latest book.

"Do you want me to read to you too?" she asked.

"No thank you Mummy. I like reading to myself." Lydia felt a pang of redundancy, but decided to say nothing.

"See you in the morning then."

"Night, night Mummy."

Lydia tidied the bathroom and picked up a few toiletries to pack into her hold all. She made her way downstairs to the kitchen, glanced around at all the displaced items they had used that evening and decided to have a glass of wine before she started tidying up. She sat down at the table and went over the plans for tomorrow.

She had arranged to meet Michael at seven thirty in the bar of the hotel she had booked for the weekend. Now that she had permitted herself the luxury of drifting into the anticipation of their approaching reunion she experienced a rush of elation. Although, she remained physically in the same position, mentally she was transported to the train journey, the walk from the big station at the top of the hill and eventually to the hotel. She wondered how it would feel when they actually met. She revelled at the prospect of having him all to herself for a whole weekend. She had always delighted in their exclusivity. She wished that she had someone with whom she could talk and share her happiness but she did not want to mar her exceptional fortune with the opinions of anyone who might merely misunderstand her.

She felt a sense of loss when she realised that she had no-one to whom she could confide anymore. Her friend Jane, who she had grown up with, had become increasingly disapproving of her over recent times. She no longer had the sensation of ease and acceptance that had been the prevailing force between them until the last couple of years. Lydia had seen less and less of her during this time. When they did arrange to meet she found that she was dreading the barrage of disparaging remarks that would surely be rained upon her when they did finally get together. She picked up the wine bottle and refilled her glass. Taking a long draught from it she thought,

"Why am I wasting my energy on all these negative thoughts? This time tomorrow, I will be the happiest woman alive."

She glanced up at the clock. It was ten-thirty. She thought about going to put her feet up on the sofa in the living room, but remembered that she had fallen asleep there a few times recently. Woken by the pain of a full bladder and with the vile buzz of the television in her head, was not the way to achieve the well rested effect that she desired for her important morning. She decided that an early night was in order. She checked that the front and back doors were locked and bolted and went upstairs to bed. She picked up her book from the bedside cabinet and tried to read a few pages.

It was her favourite book, Wuthering Heights. She had read it a number of times but could always lose herself on the bleak, wild moors with Cathy and Heathcliff. Philip mocked her love of romance and said it just showed how devoid of reality her world actually was. Lydia did not take too much notice of his scathing comments. She pitied him his inability to escape in such an effortless manner. She fell asleep with the book on her chest.

CHAPTER FOUR

Brighton

Lydia was woken by Daisy running into the bedroom. She called out to her still sleeping mother,

"Mummy! We're all late again," as she drew back the curtains letting in the early morning sunlight.

Lydia opened her eyes, befuddled by the din. She lay still for a moment to orientate herself. Then she remembered; this was the day. She was going to Brighton to meet the love of her life and then they were all going to live happily ever after. She leapt up out of bed and then feeling dizzy sat back down and eyed the clock. Half past eight! Oh no! They were very late. She pulled on her clothes that were lying on the floor where she had left them the night before and ran down the stairs.

"Have you two had your breakfasts?" she asked them, pulling on her jacket and slipping into her shoes at the same time.

"Yes, we're ready. I made Freddie's breakfast and I've washed the dishes," said Daisy, glancing up at her mother in anticipation of the praise that she promptly received.

"You're such a good girl, Daisy. I don't know what I'd do without you. Really I don't."

Daisy smiled content with the outcome of her efforts and taking her brother's hand they left the house and scurried down the road towards the school.

They walked through the gates at ten to nine and Freddie turned to Lydia and said, "Phew! That was a Close Shave Gromit!" and ran off to join a group of fellow six year old boys blocking the school door with their constant wiggling, jumping and shouting. On reaching his friends, Freddie became immediately absorbed into their world.

"Well Daisy you have a lovely weekend and I'll see you on Sunday." Daisy flung her arms around Lydia's waist and nestled her head into her body.

"I'm going to miss you, Mummy," she said plaintively.

"I'll miss you too," returned Lydia, "But it'll be Sunday before you know it, you wait and see."

She kissed her daughter's head and caught the sweet, clean scent of her hair. She watched her walk over to the entrance and disappear inside.

Lydia went home and made coffee and toast. While she was in the shower, she decided to make an early start on her trip as Alice would be collecting the children from school. By ten thirty, she was washed and ready to go. She was about to leave the house when she remembered the letter she had written to Philip, in preparation for this moment. She took it out of the kitchen drawer and placed it again between the salt and pepper pot. On impulse, she picked up the photograph that had lain with it and put it in her handbag.

As she closed the front door, she thought, "I'll be a different person, next time I walk through this door."

She walked down the garden path noting that there was still some spring tidying to be done. Nevertheless, the daffodils were starting to bloom and she knew that their distraction alone could temporarily mask any amount of minor neglect.

Lydia marched eagerly in the direction of the tube station, bought her ticket, and settled in the carriage near the end of the train. Checking that her ticket was secure and accessible in her jeans pocket, she resumed her adventures on the Yorkshire moors with Cathy and Heathcliff. She looked up briefly when she heard the train launch itself rattling into the tunnel. She inhaled as she always did at this point of the journey and hoped fervently that the train would not crash or if it did, that she would survive. That done, she returned to her doomed lovers. Cathy had just died but her spirit was living on and Lydia let herself be swept away by the tragedy of their plight.

Suddenly, she was there. She put away her book. She leapt up and oozed out of the carriage and onto the platform with the other passengers, joining the steady flow of travellers on the escalator and eventually emerging, in their midst, at Victoria Station. Taking a second or two to find her bearings, she assembled her bags more comfortably. Standing with her red holdall in her hand and her pink rucksack on her back, Lydia perused the timetable board expectantly. Her train was due to depart in seven minutes from platform one. She felt a rush of youthful anticipation at the prospect of her imminent train ride.

"I'd better hurry up," she thought, searching for a ticket office.

With seconds to spare, she ran to the platform and boarded the train to the sound of the whistle. Bursting into the nearest carriage, she spotted a forward facing seat by the window and lunged towards it, bag first. Pleased with her achievement she glanced around her and to her delight saw that the carriage was only about a third full. She waited for the sound of the train starting and again for the initial slow rhythm of its exit from the big, grey Victorian station. She gazed out onto the dirty, drabness of London, wondering what it was like to live in those tall inhospitable buildings whose only view was of the railway sidings carrying droves of people in and out of the city.

Her ruminations were disturbed by the arrival of a rather large, red faced gentleman of indeterminate age who proceeded to place his bulk on the seat diagonally opposite hers. She tried to avoid eye contact, but was unsuccessful and found herself returning his jolly greeting with a rather insipid, "Hello." He puffed with the exertion it cost him to arrange his ungainly body into the space provided.

"So where are you off to?" he inquired in an unnecessarily loud voice.

"Oh dear," thought Lydia, "Where would I be going on the non-stop London to Brighton train."

But she reminded herself that she was off to have a glorious time in Brighton with the man she loved and this interloper may just be lonely.

"Brighton?" she said, raising her eyebrows and smiling at him.

As the mighty, image of the now defunct Battersea Power Station crept into view, Lydia sighed as if all was well with the world. Smoke no longer poured from its chimneys as it had when she was a child, but she felt that it continued to earn its place as one of London's more gratifying landmarks. Preparing to settle back into the angst that was Cathy and Heathcliff, she was once more called to attention by the disembodied tone of a distinct, but slightly mocking voice, announcing that the bar was now open.

"Would you care to join me in a drink?" asked her rotund neighbour enthusiastically.

Lydia put away her book in defeat. The better man had won. She accepted his kind offer and then checked the window for a sign and the arms of the seat for ashtrays. Exhaling with relief, she took a packet from her rucksack and lit a cigarette.

Mr Wobble re-entered the carriage amidst much fumbling and swaying to the motion of the train, presenting Lydia with four cans of lager, two glasses and two packets of crisps. They made a brief and hurried introduction to each other and Mr Wobble became Harry.

Lydia visibly relaxed as she cautiously poured her lager into a glass, took several large gulps and sat back to stare out of the window once more. The buildings were rapidly thinning out and soon she would be passing the reassuring countryside of England.

She looked over at Harry, raised her glass to his and said, "Cheers!"

"Cheers!" he replied heartily, "Are you down for the weekend then?"

"Yes I am," said Lydia, aware that she did not want to taint her plan by talking about it to a stranger. She decided to use her deflection technique, which involved turning the question back to the questioner. This practice was dependant on the fairly reliable theory that most people really enjoyed talking about themselves.

"Here goes," she thought.

"How about you?" she enquired.

"Ah well," he replied, showing visible signs of relief, "I'm on my way to Hove to attend my mother's funeral."

"Oh I'm sorry," said Lydia genuinely.

She had not been expecting a sombre response but on hearing it his black suit and tie became instantly apparent to her.

"Thanks," he said graciously. "It's a funny old situation though. You see I only got to know her in the last six months, and now, well it's all over."

"Oh," said Lydia, intrigued, as she looked at her travelling companion moving a stray tear from his eye in an attempt to recompose himself.

She could have sworn that he had shrunk, as if he had literally had the stuffing knocked out of him. Her curiosity was aroused but she did not want to seem callous or prying, so she waited for Harry to continue his story. Her patience was rewarded and he began his tale.

"I was adopted when I was a baby and I was brought up in a very loving family. I was told about my adoption when

I was a teenager. Although part of me was angry because I thought I had been tricked into believing in a world that was suddenly no longer as it had always seemed, I didn't really want to think about it. I just wanted to maintain the status quo and felt that this was the best way of doing just that, at least, for the time being. Part of me also thought that if I didn't mention it, then my family would not focus on it and I would not be treated any differently. Many years went by, and obviously I did think about if from time to time, but even if I had wanted to find out more, I was too afraid to ask. I thought that I might find out something truly gruesome about my natural parents.

I married and had children of my own and although a mother's love for her children is supposed to be stronger than a father's, I could not have imagined any circumstances that would be so bad that I would have voluntarily given up my children."

Lydia was listening intently to Harry's story, and nodding in agreement with his sentiment.

"Do you have children Lydia?" he enquired.

"I do. I have a little boy of six and a girl, Daisy, who is ten. I cannot imagine ever agreeing to have them taken from me for any reason," she concurred.

"Well then you'll probably understand that, as a parent myself, I began to judge my mother. I had been told all those years ago that she was a teenager when she had me and I knew that it was a possibility that there would be no trace of my father so I directed my judgements at her. In hindsight, it seems so bizarre to criticise someone I had never met before but I was so far up in the sky on my moral high ground that I had lost all sight of reason."

"So how did you get in touch with her then?" asked Lydia, now confident that he would not mind her asking questions. He certainly seemed to be inviting her interest.

"Judge not lest ye be judged," he started, "About five years ago, my wife became ill. She'd always been so healthy, so it really shook me." His voice was starting to falter. He paused and took a gulp of his drink and continued,

"Anyway, she died two years ago of cancer. It was a truly terrible time for the children and I. We really struggled to come to terms with it. In fact, we struggled with everything. David was fifteen and Miriam was thirteen, so although it possibly made matters worse emotionally for them with all that hormonal stuff going on, they were physically independent. I found it really difficult to look after them. I was so disturbed by my own loss that I couldn't even think about theirs' and I suppose that I neglected them. I understood then, and for the first time that sometimes parents are not able to look after their children however much they love them.

The three of us have got through the worst of it and life is a lot better than it was but what happened to me during that time, was that I started to feel some genuine compassion for my own mother and I started to want to know more about the reasons why she had given me away.

I asked my parents to tell me everything they knew about her and then I set about trying to find her. It wasn't particularly easy but now that I had begun the whole idea had got a grip on me and I wasn't going to give in without a struggle. The day came as I had hoped it would when I got news that she was alive and living near Brighton."

"Did you go and see her straight away?" asked Lydia.

"No, I was stricken with fear again, but I plucked up courage to phone her about a week after I got the news. She knew by this time that I had been looking for her and really, she was waiting for the call. It was the strangest and the hardest thing I have ever done. I listened to the frail voice of an old lady over the phone line, knowing that she had given birth to me and that I knew nothing about her least of all, what she looked like.

We made arrangements and the next week I found myself on the train to Brighton with a scrap of paper with her address scrawled on it. The children were worried about how it would affect me but since my wife's death I had become more or less obsessed with my quest and I knew then that I had to see it through to the end."

"It must have taken a lot of courage to make that journey," said Lydia looking at Harry's animated face.

She was fascinated by the change that had taken place in Harry in such a short space of time. This oversized middle-aged man who she had thought would be little more than an irritation on her much awaited train journey, with whom she had hoped to have as little interaction as possible, was now telling her the most moving story she had heard in years. As she waited for him to continue, she willed the meeting between Harry and his estranged mother to be agreeable.

"I haven't ever told anyone the details of my visit. I just tell people, if they ask, that it was OK. She was little and old with white hair that looked like it had just been done for the occasion, but maybe I'm flattering myself. When she opened her door I was struck by how tiny and then how ordinary she seemed. We stood staring at each other on the doorstep for a few moments and then we went through the awkwardness of me entering her house and taking off my coat. I felt terribly self-conscious.

She made some tea and brought it through on a tray which had already been prepared. I kept watching her closely and then trying to avert my gaze. It was all very strange but it got easier when we started to talk. She told me about how she had become pregnant as a teenager and that my father was a married man who had left the area with his family on hearing the news. Apparently, they came up to London and stayed there and my mother heard that he had died about ten years ago. At the moment she told me that, I realised I had lost all desire to know anymore about him.

Then she turned my world upside down. She said that my adoption was arranged by her family and she assumed that it was the only solution to the shame of her being pregnant.

When she had given birth to me she held me in her arms and talked to me calling me Harry from the very start and she said, "Harry, you are a very beautiful boy and I want you to be happy always. For this reason I am going to give you to a good family who will give you all that you will ever need. I know that I am not able to do that for you because if I were, I would not let you go. They won't love you as much as I do now but I know they will love you because you are wonderful and special. Maybe one day when you are grown up you will look for me and find me. I will wait for that day."

She told me that she waited every year to hear from me, especially around my birthday. She was convinced that one day she would see me again. She said that she had waited such a long time but when she did finally hear from me on the day of our first phone call she said her heart nearly burst with the happiness that welled up inside it. She also told me that she would be able to let go of life absolved of the guilt and the worry she had felt since she gave me away.

I remember that I joked on that first visit and said not to be too hasty as we had a lot of catching up to do. But she was already old and although I saw her on two more occasions, I was not surprised when I received the news that she had died."

Lydia was sitting quietly as he finished his tale.

Harry sat back in his seat and sighed. His transformation was complete. He was quiet. The nervous bluster had evaporated and he seemed more compact. Lydia finished her drink and tidied up the rubbish. The train was slowing as it approached Brighton station. They both stood and shook hands.

79

Harry said, "Thank you, have a good weekend."

"Goodbye," replied Lydia, as she turned the handle of the door.

She walked down the platform thinking about Harry and his personal tragedy. She hoped that the knowledge that his mother's abandonment had not been complete and that he had remained in her heart all those years would console him today and continue to comfort him in the years to come.

"Enough!" she thought as she stepped out into the Brighton sunshine and started her walk down the hill. Lydia had not visited Brighton for some years but was struck by the sense of security it evoked in her. She walked past the still familiar buildings. The dingy philately shop had been there since her childhood and the over ornate gilt clock tower at the cross roads never failed to lift her spirits as it coincided with her first sighting of the sea. At this juncture, her hair was swept back by a gust of sea breeze escaping through the streets. She gasped and smelt the salt air in her nostrils. She stood on the corner and glanced up at the clock.

It was midday. What she needed was a plan. Spotting a coffee shop with seats outside she decided to sit there while she thought about her day ahead. She bought a large, strong cup of Italian coffee and cheerfully mused over possibilities while she watched the colourful parade of people passing her table. She speculated over their destinations and their lives. Did they live there? Were they visiting? Or did they work in Brighton having to contend with a gruelling journey twice a day? If so, was it worth it?

Aware that she was drifting from her purpose, she said to herself,

"Come on girl deal with the matter in hand."

Her bag was quite heavy so she decided to check in at the hotel and deposit her belongings. Then she could spend the afternoon exploring her old haunts. Michael would not be there until seven thirty that evening and she was determined to make the most of the few hours before they met. After all, that was why she had made arrangements for the children to be picked up by Alice. She wondered what Alice would make of all this and then stopped herself as she started to feel uncomfortable at the thought. She would know soon enough and it made no difference now what anyone thought because the letter had been left and the deed was done. Lydia paid for her coffee and ambled slowly down toward the street where their room was booked. Making her way down this familiar road she perceived a griminess that she had not been aware of before. The greyness was alleviated by a brightly coloured pub arrayed with hanging baskets opposite the hotel.

"That'll be handy," thought Lydia, smiling as she pushed open the door of the hotel.

There was no-one at the reception desk. As she let her eyes become accustomed to the dim lighting of the establishment she noticed that it smelt fusty and damp. She stood for a while contemplating the invitation to ring the bell for service, when a small stout woman with a burning cigarette hanging from her mouth, entered the room and looked at Lydia suspiciously.

"Yes?" she asked, unceremoniously.

"I have booked a room for the weekend," said Lydia apologetically.

The unfriendly woman made a grimace which Lydia identified as a smile and gave her name.

"Oh yes, here it is," said the woman, rustling through a diary and spilling the untapped ash on to the pages.

She turned and reached behind her for the keys which were hung numerically on a dark wooden board.

"Number eleven. Up the stairs, turn right and at the end of the corridor. Breakfast is from seven thirty to nine. Out by eleven on Sunday." She uttered the words with a mechanical monotony, handed Lydia the key and turned away, lighting another cigarette as she walked back through the door through which she had appeared.

Lydia picked up her bags thinking how much she and Michael would have laughed at their greeting had they arrived together. Undeterred, she followed her instructions and opened the door of the room which would be their haven for the weekend. The same fusty smell caught her as she opened the door. It was dark as the curtains had not been fully opened but she could see that the room was furnished with twin beds and she had a surge of irritation recalling that she had specifically requested a double room. Walking over to the window she pulled back the drapes to let in the light and to admire the sea view she had also been promised. Her vista included the back of a building and the two backyards between them, containing a variety of wheelie bins. However, on closer inspection, she caught a glimpse of the sea at the end of the next street. She could see the sun twinkling on its surface as it met the horizon.

"It's a good thing I'm long sighted," she thought drily.

She put down her bags and tidied a few items into the eclectic pieces of furniture and took her toiletries into the barely adequate bathroom. Checking her face in the mirror she saw that the bruise around her eye was starting to change colour and become more noticeable.

She applied some foundation and then some lipstick, smiled at her image and said, "You'll do. Let's go and have some fun."

Back on the street she turned seaward and skipped with glee. She joined her fellow promenaders and walked on in the direction of Hove. She thought for a moment of Harry and hoped that he was surviving the day. She suddenly felt very lucky and decided to celebrate her good fortune with a sumptuous lunch. But where would she go? There were so many different places to eat. What she really fancied was sitting in the plush restaurant of the Grand Hotel and taking coffee on the verandah with all the wealthy ladies of Brighton.

"Why not treat yourself?" she said, considering the cost and remembering that she had the cash card to her and Philip's joint account.

"Blow the cost!" she said, smiling as she walked up the steps and in to the hotel restaurant.

Lydia gasped as she walked into the richly decorated hallway which led to a winding wrought iron staircase.

A young man carrying an empty silver tray walked towards her and asked, "May I help you Madam?"

"Yes I would like to eat lunch here. Is that possible?" she asked, feeling naive and desperately underdressed.

She was only relieved that she had bothered to touch up her make-up and hoped that she did not appear to have just lost a fight.

The young man, apparently unperturbed, asked, "Will you be dining alone?"

"Yes, could I sit in the window?"

"Certainly Madam, please follow me," and he led her to a table set for two in front of the most glorious, panoramic view of the sea and the esplanade.

The restaurant was fairly busy but not full and she felt cushioned by the muted muffle of conversation punctuated by the clink and clank of crockery and cutlery.

The waiter handed Lydia a large leather bound menu and asked,

"Would you like a drink while you decide?" he asked.

"Mmm, yes please," replied Lydia enthusiastically, "I'll have a large gin and tonic with ice and a slice, thank you."

"And will Madam be wanting wine with her meal?" he asked, offering her the wine list which seemed to have appeared from nowhere.

"Perhaps he's a magician in his spare time," she quipped to herself, and to him replied,

"Thank you I believe I will,"

She ordered a fancy red wine and a starter. Then she settled comfortably in her seat to wait and to observe the bustling outside world.

"This is the life," she congratulated herself.

She was thirsty and drank her gin and tonic with gusto. Its effect enhanced her now immense feeling of well-being and she started to eye the other diners with interest. There was a well-dressed couple sitting in earshot of her table and this pleased Lydia greatly. She always found that a smattering of dialogue improved the quality of the imagined lives of those she chose to watch.

He was tall and lean with white carefully cut hair and a matching moustache. She was of medium height and slightly plump. Her outfit was a perfectly co-ordinated navy blue and white piped trouser suit contrasting with her crisp white blouse and row of fat genuine pearls. Lydia thought how delightful she looked and smiled broadly in her direction when she caught her eye. The lady nodded with one eyebrow and turned back to her husband who was showing concern at Jessica's apparent difficulties settling in at Cambridge.

Drifting back out of their lives Lydia was pleased to see her waiter heading towards her table laden with her starter and an uncorked bottle of wine. He stopped at her table and presented her with an interesting array of salad, goat's cheese and toasted croutons. Placing this before her he proceeded to display the label of the wine she had selected and prompted by her smile proceeded to open it for her, pouring a small amount into her glass.

"Would Madam care to taste the wine?" he asked.

Lydia did as was suggested and swallowing the contents of the glass said,

"That's very good, thank you."

He refilled the glass and left her to enjoy her food.

As she started to eat, she became aware that she may be the only person sitting alone in the restaurant. She drank from her wine glass and scanned the restaurant for other lone diners. There was one gentleman in the corner near the entrance who was reading a newspaper and she relaxed thinking,

"Well I could always get my book out if they think I'm a bit odd, but my nice waiter doesn't seem to think it matters. And that's the main thing."

She continued eating, drinking and gazing out at the magnificent, sun drenched beach of Brighton. She drifted into a reverie about her future with Michael and the children. He would want to spend time with his daughter Emma. Lydia was confident that Michael and her children would all get on with each other. She did not know Emma but Michael had often spoken about her to Lydia and she was optimistic that when everyone had reconciled themselves to their new circumstances that Emma would be eager to come and stay with her Dad. Emma was fourteen and soon would be able to decide where she wanted to live. Lydia had an unexpected pang of guilt when she thought of Michael's wife, Jacqueline possibly ending up alone.

She looked at her watch. It was two thirty and according to the plan, Michael would have already told her that he was leaving her and would soon be starting out on his journey to Brighton. She genuinely hoped that Jacqueline was able to cope with the upheaval, but also felt sure that it would not be long before she met someone else. After all she was a very attractive girl. She sighed and looked down at her plate. Her main course was nearly finished, as was the bottle of wine; she suddenly had a desire to leave and to look for a diversion while she waited for Michael to arrive. She asked for her oversized bill, paid it and left.

Lydia turned on to the congested coastal road and made her way back towards town and the Lanes. The Lanes had always held a fascination for Lydia partly because of the non-essential nature of the goods sold in the quaint little shops and partly because of the vibrant crowds that frequented them. She wound her way into the square and was immediately enchanted by an old man wearing a straw boater busking outside one of the pubs.

The sun was shining down on the hanging baskets behind him as he gave a reasonable rendition of, "Baby please don't go."

Lydia stopped to listen to him and smiling at him, she dropped some coins into the guitar case that lay on the ground before him. He winked as she walked past and she turned into an alley lined with antique shops and restaurants.

She was becoming disorientated as she weaved in and out of the alleyways and was finding it increasingly difficult to avoid colliding with other pedestrians. In the midst of her mounting confusion, Lydia recalled a very exclusive boutique that she had visited some years earlier and thought that it would be amusing to try on some of its weird and wonderful fashions. By chance, she happened upon it as she turned the next corner and composing herself, she opened the door. Greeting her effusively was an overly made up woman in her late forties. She was much taller than Lydia and to her disappointment, was wearing neat clothes which failed to represent any of the merchandise on display either in the window or on the rails.

"May I help you?" said the woman, peering down at Lydia.

Unaware of her own dishevelled appearance and the strong smell of alcohol she was emitting, Lydia proceeded to enter into the spirit of the game.

"I am going to a party tomorrow night and I would like a new dress for the occasion," she replied, knowing that it would be far more fun to have help in selecting possible choices.

Lydia's experience of clothes shopping was limited to buying fairly durable items with the occasional pretty top. She had found that if she was let loose with an indefinite amount of money and a special event to shop for, she invariably ended up with something uncomfortable, inappropriate or both.

"You are a size ten Madam?" she enquired.

"Usually, sometimes a twelve," replied Lydia, momentarily distracted by the colourful display of garments in the far corner of the shop.

"Ooh, this is lovely," she said, reaching over to pick a floating, pink blue and white chiffon affair from one of the rails.

She surreptitiously glimpsed the price tag as she swept it up under her chin and admired it against her figure in the mirror.

"One hundred and fifty quid!" she thought.

Looking more closely at her reflection, she noticed that the bruising around her eye had worsened and the foundation that she had applied earlier had worn off. She pulled her fringe down over her eye as the shopkeeper asked,

"Would you like to try it on?"

"Yes please," responded Lydia, glad of an excuse to hide behind the curtain of the changing area.

She pulled the floral screens together and studied her battered face closely.

"Oh dear," she thought, "What will Michael think of this?"

Then she consoled herself by thinking that he would find the story of how she fell out of the loft highly entertaining.

"All the same," she thought, "I had better touch up this make-up."

As she set about fumbling in her rucksack, she heard the clacking of the woman's shoes approaching the cubicle.

"Is everything alright in here Madam?" she asked, pulling the curtains apart a little and peering at her customer quizzically.

"Yes thank you," said Lydia cheerfully.

"I had better get on with this fashion parade before she thinks I'm going to steal the dress," she thought.

After much wriggling and struggling, Lydia crept quietly out of the cubicle to exhibit the uncomfortable creation. She gawped at the image in the large shop mirror and had to control a very strong desire to giggle. She could see that, without a shadow of a doubt, she looked utterly ridiculous. Even the proprietor had no words to express the awfulness of the sight before her. Lydia was slim but the dress was cut in such a way that it showed none of her attributes and all of her unflattering traits. The offending item was cut away in swathes perhaps with the intention of producing a nymph-like effect which was lost on Lydia. She let out an involuntary snort of laughter.

"I look like an elephant in a tutu!" she shrieked.

"Well maybe not an elephant," said the lady who glanced at her watch and walked to the door to turn the 'Open' sign to 'Closed'.

"Goodness is it that time already?" said Lydia, walking back to the cubicle.

She spent some time disentangling herself from the delicate, almost friable material of the dress. In her desperation not to damage it she nearly fell over and found herself crashing in to the mirror on the wall. Trying to suppress her sniggers, she dressed hurriedly and burst out from behind the curtains. Handing the dress back she said,

"Thank you very much for your help, goodbye."

Walking back out on to the Lanes she sensed a change in the atmosphere. People were moving faster and with a greater sense of urgency than before. Some were rushing home from work and others were excitedly hastening towards an early evening assignation. Lydia enjoyed the frisson of anticipation that she was experiencing and remembered that soon she would be joining them. She had a momentary sense of belonging to the determined droves that swept her along with them, as she set off to the hotel to prepare for her romantic evening ahead. The seagulls called mournfully, as they swooped and rose above the endless tide of the sea. She turned on to the promenade for one last look at the beach before darkness fell. Deeply inhaling the salt-scented air, she walked back to her room.

By seven fifteen, Lydia had showered and changed in the inhospitable bathroom provided and was waiting excitedly for Michael's arrival in the reception area of the hotel. The door of the entrance swished open and Lydia's heart lurched as a slight, bespectacled man walked in past her and up the stairs giving her a perfunctory nod as he did. There was a small mirror in the dingy lobby and Lydia approached it while she was alone. She had done a good job of covering her bruise and was pleased that she gave the appearance of a well-groomed woman. However, something was different and she could not work out what it was. She moved her gaze away from the glass and then swiftly back again. It was a hint of darkness crossing her face and resting fleetingly in her eyes.

Justifying her nervousness she thought, "After all, anyone would be feeling anxious in my situation."

She became aware of a new sound in the apparent silence of her surroundings. Puzzled, she tried to identify it by inspecting the room more closely. She twisted around and saw on the wall behind her an old large-faced Victorian clock bearing Roman numerals and a swishing pendulum. It was nearly eight o'clock. Although erratic in many ways, Michael had been consistently punctual during the years that Lydia had known him and she was beginning to feel apprehensive. What if he had had an accident in his car? What if something had happened to Emma? It was at this point that Lydia began to wish that she had one of those mobile phones that everyone had started talking about. She had never understood the need for them but this was one of those situations where the benefit was obvious. Mind you, Michael did not have one so what good would that be to her now?

As the clock above her chimed the hour she decided that she would telephone his house if he had not arrived by eight thirty. Fortunately, she knew his number by heart. She was glad that she had taken the time to learn it. She was not overly keen on speaking to Jacqueline but she would be aware of the situation by now and after all, she just wanted to know that he was safe. In the few minutes leading up to the half hour, Lydia recalled slowly and meticulously, the events of their last rendezvous. She could find no room for error or misunderstanding. In fact, she recollected their parting words exactly.

"I'll see you in Brighton at our hotel," said Michael.

And Lydia had replied happily, "Yes I'll see you there. I can't wait."

"Neither can I, goodbye 'til then."

The clock struck once.

"This is it then. I'll have to phone his house. I can't sit here all night worrying."

She left the hotel and walked across the road to the pub. It was busy and she felt self-conscious as she pushed open the heavy door. She glanced around and saw that there was a public phone right next to her. She was relieved because this meant that she could still keep a look out for him while she dialled his number. She listened to the ringing tone.

"I'll listen to ten and then I'll ring off," she thought, losing her nerve. But the phone was answered on the third ring and a clear, female voice enquired,

"Who is this?"

"It's Lydia," she replied, feeling suddenly sheepish.

"Ah yes, I was expecting you to call. This is Jacqueline just to clarify any possible confusion that you may be experiencing. Michael has told me all about your hare-brained scheme and so I assume that I am honoured with a call from distant Brighton?"

"Yes," said Lydia, cut by her icy tone.

She continued in a flustered manner, "I am so sorry to bother you at this time but Michael is very late and I was getting really worried that he might have had an accident. What time did he leave?"

"Michael is very late because he is here with me. He does not want to speak to you. I am aware that he can be unpredictable and selfish at times but please know that he loves me and Emma. Not you, you are just a whim there to reinforce the fantasy that he can still live in a dream world where he does as he pleases. Michael would no more lose us than stop breathing."

Lydia's hand was sweating on to the receiver as she clutched it tightly to her ear.

"B-but...," she stuttered, having no formulated sentence prepared but aware that this may be her last opportunity to save her relationship with Michael.

Obviously, Jacqueline was very angry and Lydia quite understood, but why was Michael still there?

"I was going to wait a few more weeks to tell Michael but on hearing of your ridiculous plans I thought it important that he knows that I am pregnant with our long awaited second child. He, as I'm sure that you will understand, is absolutely delighted as we have been trying for a brother or sister for Emma for many years."

Lydia was experiencing sharp, stabbing pains in her guts and her breathing had become rapid.

"So to be crystal clear, do not telephone this house again. Do not contact Michael. I am his wife, not you. Now stop bothering us. Goodbye!"

Lydia heard the ring tone change and knowing that it was over put the receiver back on the rest. She had started to see stars in front of her eyes and her mouth was so dry it felt as though her tongue was stuck to its roof. The noise from inside the pub seemed to be getting louder and louder as she held on to the door jamb.

"Are you alright lady?" said a voice from somewhere nearby. She held on to the post for fear of losing control and collapsing on the floor. The owner of the kindly tones took her by the arm and guided her gently to a seat near the door asking,

"Would you like a drop of brandy to steady your nerves?"

Lydia nodded and realised that her whole body was shaking. When the man returned to the table he handed her the large glass of strong smelling liquid. Lydia took it, trying to show gratitude in her stricken green eyes. Her tremors were causing such turbulence that she was unable to guide the shaking tumbler to her lips.

The man sat down next to her and held it for her. She took large gulps and swallowed waiting for the spirit to do its work. As she felt it make its way to her stomach, she visibly calmed. Finishing the drink, she leant back in the seat and tried to get her bearings.

For a moment, she wondered how she had got there and who the benevolent gentleman was that sat with her. In a flash of darkness, she recalled Jacqueline's chill words and the venom through which they had been transmitted. Lydia felt helpless and afraid. How had this happened? Why hadn't Michael spoken to her? And in that instant, the excruciating truth of the situation became apparent. Michael was a weak-willed dishonest man and always had been. He may have believed what he had said to her at the time that the words were uttered but to follow through on what Lydia believed to be the realisation of a much yearned for dream, had been, for him, an impossibility.

The agony of her loss and the humiliation that she felt began to overwhelm her. She could feel the tremors returning to her limbs and looked over at her companion in a plea for help. She was afraid of attracting any more attention from those around her and was relieved when he offered her another drink.

While he was up at the bar, she thought about the enormity of the actions she had taken in her pursuit of happiness. She thought of the letter that had sat on the kitchen table awaiting Philip's return. She had no idea how he would have reacted to it but felt certain that there would be an element of relief in the knowledge that they would no longer have to keep up what she had grown to believe was a sham of a marriage.

She yearned to see her children's faces and to put her arms around them but she knew it would be better if she arrived at the time she had stated. Philip would have had time to assimilate his feelings and then they would be able to discuss their future. She wondered if he would be pleased by her humiliation and whether he would consider continuing to live with her despite everything. The promise of a fulfilled life had spoilt her in that regard and she could no longer envisage their now tainted life together. Her head was throbbing with all these unanswered questions and she felt as if it would explode if she did not stop torturing herself.

The man arrived back at the table and sat down.

"There you go, get that down you," he instructed her firmly.

She picked up the glass and drank.

She took a deep breath and said, "Thank you very much for looking after me. I think I'll be alright now."

"I won't hear of it. It seems to me that you've had a big shock and you may well not wish to dwell on it but perhaps you would like to join me and my friends at the bar?"

Lydia raised her eyes to the group of men at the bar. They were quite loud but did not seem to be threatening in any way, so she decided to take him up on his offer and walked unsteadily towards them.

"Who's this then?" asked a large, dark haired man in his late thirties.

"My name's Lydia," she replied, suddenly immensely grateful that she did not have to go back to the dingy hotel room yet.

She also reflected that if she had some company she would not have to listen to the cruel thoughts which were hurtling around her head. She breathed a deep sigh of relief and threw herself into the conviviality of the crowd.

Astonishingly, she found that the pain of rejection, from which she had felt sure she would die from only an hour earlier, was already easing and soon she was laughing at their jokes and even telling some of her own. All too soon the bell for last orders sounded and with it, Lydia felt her heart sink.

The man who had rescued her earlier whispered in her ear, "If we're lucky we may get a lock-in. I'll give you the nod."

And so it was that Lydia sat with her new acquaintances while she chased oblivion.

Much later she stood falteringly and slurred, "I musht go now."

She saw that she was the only remaining guest and that the barman was leering ominously over the bar in her direction.

"No, no," he said insistently, "Stay for another."

Lydia, despite her intoxicated state, was disquieted by her vulnerability and his persistent manner. She pitched her body at the door and discovered that it was locked. She jumped at the raucous laugh erupting behind her.

"I said stay for another," he repeated, more forcefully than the last time.

In an attempt to placate her captor she acquiesced, hoping to talk him into unlocking the door. Unfortunately, her plan was misunderstood and he brought her over a drink and proceeded to launch his body at her in what she presumed to be an embrace. She pushed him away and took her chance and ran behind the bar searching desperately for the back door. She found it despite the dark and frantically trying to control her shaking hands, she managed to turn the key and run out onto the street.

94

The street was quiet: it was very late. She ran across the road to the hotel and pushing the door open, ducked in and spotting a bolt on the inside pulled it over and ran all the way up the stairs to her room. Once there she threw herself on to the bed and lay there trembling and sobbing until the alcohol and exhaustion overpowered her and she slept.

Lydia awoke from a deep but unsatisfactory sleep with a crashing headache and an almighty thirst. She rolled on to her side and put her feet on to the dirty carpet beside the bed. She went into the bathroom and took long draughts of unsavoury water and sat down on the edge of the bath.

She recalled the latter events of the previous evening and shuddered at the potential danger she had inadvertently encouraged. These recollections were swiftly replaced by the memory of her conversation with Jacqueline and all its implications. What on earth was she going to do now? Her plans had been crushed in one fell swoop. Should she go home today? Would she call Philip to see how the land lies? Somehow, this seemed a cowardly approach and she settled on keeping it simple. She would return home tomorrow at the time arranged and would face Philip and allow him to tell her what he wanted to do in regard to their future. After all, he may well take the children somewhere in the morning and she did not want to be the one to spoil an outing.

Lydia speculated on the ways in which she could spend the rest of her time in Brighton while she washed and dressed. Entering the reception area on her way to breakfast, Lydia saw that it was eleven o'clock. Sighing at her tardiness, she abandoned all hope of eating; she felt in no fit state to enter into a discussion with the chain smoking woman of the lobby on the very slim chance of acquiring food. She walked out on to the street, careful not to look in the direction of the pub she had been in the night before and headed towards the sea. She had a strong desire to see the sea and to hear the familiar sound of the waves rushing over the Brighton pebbles. It was a lot colder than the previous day and the wind blew viciously up the road forming a funnel between the houses. Lydia pulled her duffel coat around her and continued on her way.

There were very few people walking along the front and Lydia felt inordinately disappointed when she realised that a thick mist hung over the beach and was making the sea indistinguishable from the sky through its cloying dampness. She stood for a few moments at the railings trying to breathe in the air, but soon began to shiver and turned back disconsolately towards the town. Her hangover seemed to be abating and she started to feel hungry. She set out with the intention of finding a cafe that served bacon, eggs and toast, but finding this difficult, she began to be seduced by the luscious menus of the more salubrious restaurants. The lack of food was making her feel lightheaded and she knew that she would have to make a decision soon. A delicious aroma of frying garlic emanated from the kitchen of an Italian restaurant on the corner of one of the lanes and Lydia walked inside.

She was immediately greeted by a shiny young man in a white shirt and black trousers who showed her to a seat in the corner. It was still early and the bistro was quiet. Lydia sat down and ordered some food. She tried not to order wine when it was offered because she had felt so ill that morning, but when it came to it she could not resist the temptation.

She justified her action by saying, "Well I am away for the weekend. I might as well make the most of it," and promptly thought no more of her previous resolution.

As the large, newly decorated room filled with the lively chatter of cheerful diners eagerly awaiting their lunches, Lydia began to sense her isolation. Her self-consciousness grew and she surveyed the scene searching for a likely soul with whom she could pass the time. There was a group of young men and women all listening attentively to each other and a few couples of varying ages intent on their quest for food. She envied them their freedom of spirit. As the wine took effect she became bolder and smiled at the group on the next table but they simply continued their conversation without interruption. The only acknowledgement of her approach was a slightly bewildered frown from one of the diners as he resumed his dialogue.

"Oh well," thought Lydia, not yet disheartened, "I'll have a little read."

She took out the book from her bag and tried to immerse herself in the agonies and ecstasies of Wuthering Heights. She waited to be gripped by the passion of the novel but however hard she concentrated, she sensed that its power was dwindling. She became aware of a slight irritability towards Cathy and disconcerted by this sentiment, decided to put the novel away before she had any more negative emotions towards it, possibly ruining any future flights of fancy on the Yorkshire moors.

The restaurant was now full and the waiters had been hovering around her for some time. She became aware that they were waiting for her to leave. After all, she was occupying a table for four which could be filled by the next influx of hungry customers. She asked for her bill, secretly hoping to be congratulated on her selflessness and feeling unexpectedly deflated when this did not happen. Telling herself that they were unlikely to be able to read her mind, she ambled gloomily back down to the beach.

The mist was even heavier than it had been in the morning, and she could not see the sea at all.

She was at a loss as to what she should do and thought grumpily, "What's the point of coming to the sea side if you can't even see the sea?"

She walked down the slope and on to the stony beach. She trudged laboriously towards the rushing waves and breathed in the air. She was very tired. She looked around her and there was no-one about so she lay down on the cold pebbles, pulled her ungainly duffel coat around her shivering body and fell asleep. The mist swirled and clung to her dormant form.

She awoke a couple of hours later, stiff and cold to the desolate screeching of the seagulls. She felt miserable, alone and dejected. She toyed with the idea of phoning home but reminded herself that Philip needed some time to think but felt unsettled by an increasingly insistent yearning for her children.

She remembered that there was a tea hut in the gardens of the Royal Pavilion and she cheered at the prospect, thinking that she could also use the toilets while she was there. She stood up and dusted off her coat as she made her way to the promenade. The sleep must have done her some good because as she re-entered the thrum of the town, she found that her spirits had lifted. She once again breathed the air of possibility that Brighton had always promised her.

She turned into the road that led to the pavilion and noticed the theatre on her left.

"Maybe I'll treat myself to a night out," she thought.

She walked up to the boards and saw that they were showing an Alan Aykbourn comedy. The play commenced at seven thirty and she could purchase her ticket at the door.

"Lots of people go to see shows on their own, so I shouldn't appear out of place," she convinced herself.

Proud that she had made a decision about the evening, thereby giving her day structure, she sauntered serenely into the pavilion park. The tea hut had recently been given a fresh coat of green paint and it boasted all manner of cakes and sandwiches.

"Oh good," thought Lydia.

She made her way to the public conveniences and smiled at the young attendant who was whistling as she mopped the floor. While she was in the cubicle, she heard an older lady saying,

"Ooh! You shouldn't whistle you know."

"Why's that?" asked the young girl.

"Well, when I was young I was told that it was very unladylike to whistle and that young men did not like it," was the reply.

"Oh well, I'm gay," she responded lightly, "So I suppose it doesn't count."

There followed the mere hint of a pause and then the lady said, "No, maybe not."

Lydia came out of the cubicle and the lady smiled over at her. Her friend was standing at the door chuckling.

She said, "You must be very happy to be whistling away all the time."

"I am," she stated, "I'm nineteen, I have a job that pays the rent and a lovely friend to go home to in the evening."

"Is she a good cook, your friend?"

"I haven't asked her yet," she answered, glancing down at her mop.

Lydia walked over to the happy youngster and handed her some coins saying, "Keep whistling."

The girl smiled up at Lydia and said, "Thank you," and continued her cheery cleaning.

At the tea hut Lydia bought a sandwich, a packet of crisps and a large mug of coffee. Carrying her tray, she assessed the seating arrangements. There was a choice of smart green outdoor furniture from which the optimum vantage point was one of the tables situated by the railings. From here, all the activities in the park could be seen and there was also a very clear view of the patrons of the tea hut. All these were occupied. As she chose a vacant seat in the middle of the ground she happened to notice a rather peevish looking older man staring down at the ground from one of the coveted railing seats.

"What a waste of the best seat in town," she thought, "I'd be up there and taking notes!"

She then proceeded to muse over the possible reasons for his disconsolate demeanour. Perhaps he was a lonely old widower who felt he had to sit out in the park for amusement but whose bones were aching with the cold. However, Lydia doubted from his appearance that he would easily give up his chair for anyone. While she was tucking into her snack, three old men walked over to his table. One of the men particularly caught her eye because he had a lined, leathery face topped by a shock of white hair cut in a strangely modern fashion and gleaming out from the dark skin of his ear lobes were several earrings. He strode up to Mr Grumpy flanked by his two companions and as Mr G stood to greet him they kissed full on the lips and embraced. Lydia's jaw dropped. And as they all moved back towards the seat chatting she could see quite clearly that her "lonely widower" was very much gay.

Lydia was not shocked by their homosexuality but by how frequently and how dramatically wrong she could be about her fellow human beings. She thought about the transformation Harry had made in front of her very eyes. An oversized, potential nuisance of a man with a grating bumptious manner converted into a humble, unassuming chap in the space of an hour. A gentleman who was simply pleased to have come to terms with his true parentage. He wanted only to honour and respect his mother, who had unbeknown to him, sacrificed her own joy and peace of mind for all those years so that he may thrive.

Watching the group of men chatting so easily amongst themselves, she wondered at the trials and tribulations they may have experienced in their early years when their way of life was considered socially unacceptable. It warmed her heart to think that their friendship had overcome the prejudice of years.

She thought of Michael now at home with his newly pregnant wife settled in the bosom of his family. She was angry with him for his dishonesty and her resultant mortification. She did not understand why he had led her to believe that they were to live happily ever after together when he had probably never intended to leave Jacqueline. Despite herself, she considered that she was in a better position than her. At least she would not spend the rest of her days fretting over his likely infidelities and fearing that one day he may finally leave.

Lydia had always held to the theory that having an affair with a married man was insanity. Based on the fact that if he were to deceive his wife at that point, then there was no guarantee that at some time in the future he would not do the same to her. For some strange reason Lydia had believed that her relationship with Michael was exempt; that their bond rested on a higher plane and therefore could not be affected by the problems of mere mortals.

"What arrant nonsense! What was I thinking?" exclaimed Lydia aloud.

People turned to stare at her. She scattered the remains of her sandwich in the direction of the persistently pestering pigeons and headed towards the glorious architecture of the Royal Pavilion.

Lydia cast her mind to Freddie who could always be relied upon to appreciate the wonder of a magnificent building. He would have adored the overly ornate 'days of the Raj' design, especially the domed roofs and turrets.

As she neared the palace, she heard the sound of a guitar and some doleful singing. Glancing in the direction of the music, she saw an unexpectedly happy, young man serenading an enthusiastic Chinese girl with a camera. She suddenly handed her bag to her friend and started an incongruous dance in front of him, consisting of both balletic and frenetic movements. She took a picture of him and waving goodbye, headed towards the pavilion's main entrance.

Lydia made her way to the pillared doorway. Debating whether or not she would enter and perhaps join a guided tour, she decided against it when she realised that it was nearly due to close.

"Maybe another day," she thought, turning in the direction of her hotel.

She thought about what she should wear that evening and was relieved when she remembered that she had hurriedly thrown in one smart outfit just before she left the house. She would spend the remainder of the afternoon preparing herself for the theatre and having a meal.

* * *

Lydia was ready and queuing for her ticket for that evening's performance by seven fifteen. She was pleased that she had followed through with her plan but was beginning to feel conscious of her aloneness now that she was thronged on all sides by eager fellow theatre-goers. Fortunately, she did not have to wait too long before she was at the kiosk and was seated in the stalls just before the first bell.

Lydia luxuriated in the lavishness of her surroundings, loving the decor and the velvet curtains. As they went up and the lights went down, she was launched into an absurd world of misunderstanding, ambiguity and innuendo. The play did not interest her as much as the people around her. She studied their outfits and listened to their muffled comments wondering when the interval would take place.

Traditionally, this was when Lydia would rush to the toilet leaving just enough time to grab a drink at the bar before hurrying back for the rest of the performance. On this occasion, her awkwardness kept her rigidly in her seat uncomfortably awaiting the second half. She contemplated the possibility of leaving before the end, but this would also have drawn attention to her solitude. Not wishing to be defeated by her own frailties, she stuck it out until the end, trying to concentrate and to appreciate the choreographed humour.

By ten thirty she was back out on the street, relieved to be able to breathe the air rather than the combination of noxious perfumes which had increasingly assaulted her nostrils throughout the performance. A little disappointed in her evening of culture she felt, nevertheless, quite proud of herself for seeing it through. She felt thirsty and wanted to celebrate her success but was reticent to render herself as vulnerable as she had the previous night. She glanced in at the pub adjacent to the theatre and reassuring herself that it had a civilised ambience she entered and strolled nonchalantly up to the bar to order a drink. As she stood waiting for someone to serve her, she observed a group of men in the corner who certainly did not look as if they had been to the theatre. Their conversation was loud and frequently interspersed with raucous laughter. The noisiest amongst them glanced over at Lydia and with a lurch of the stomach, she realised that it was he that had accosted her in the small hours of the morning. She panicked and ran out of the door and all the way back to the hotel. When she reached her room and had locked the door, she sat on her bed panting, wishing that she was safe at home with her children asleep in the next room.

"What a mess I've made of this weekend," she thought, "At least I'll be home tomorrow."

* * *

The next morning she awoke early and happily in time for breakfast. She paid her bill and set off up the hill to the station. The climb was tedious and its shops had lost their charm. She was thankful to be sat on the train heading for home. Her journey was uneventful and the excitement of seeing Daisy and Freddie began to bubble up from within. By the time she had alighted from the tube at the end of her journey, she had regained the spring in her step and she trotted gladly down her road almost skipping as she approached her house.

She looked up at her home with affection noticing that all the windows were uncharacteristically closed. She looked at her watch and saw that she was a half an hour earlier than she had expected and assumed that Philip had taken the children out for the morning and was late returning. She walked up to the front door and put her key into the lock. It did not turn. She tried again and it still did not move.

"I knew I should have had another one cut," she thought.

The lock had been sticking for some time and she had kept forgetting to have another key cut because it was an intermittent problem. She tried one last time and then decided to go next door and see if Alice was in. She had a set of their keys due to the frequency with which Lydia had taken to locking herself out or simply mislaying her own. She recalled how much it had irritated Philip.

Alice opened the door and Lydia called out cheerily, "Hi Alice, how are you?"

"I'm OK," she said with a slightly puzzled and less than welcoming expression on her face.

"Do you have our spare door key? Mine seems to have finally given up the ghost," asked Lydia, undeterred by her neighbour's greeting.

"Lydia, haven't you spoken to Philip?" she asked, now sounding quite disturbed.

"No why? I assumed that they had gone out and would be back soon," she answered.

"I think he's gone," Alice started, but was quickly interrupted by Lydia.

"What do you mean, gone?" she asked, a feeling of dread rising up through her body.

"He's gone somewhere and taken the children with him," she replied.

"Where? Where has he gone?" ventured Lydia, needing to hold on to the doorpost for some stability.

"Lydia, I have no idea what has been going on but he was very angry. He said that you weren't with your friend but that you had gone off to Brighton with some bloke. He said that it was the last straw and that he was going to make sure that the children would be cared for by a responsible adult from now on."

"Oh my God!" exclaimed Lydia as she reeled from the words.

Concerned that Lydia may collapse on the doorstep; she beckoned her in and took her into her kitchen.

Lydia sat down at the table while Alice brought her a glass of water.

As Lydia took a few sips, Alice asked, "What on earth were you thinking of Lydia?"

"I didn't meet up with Michael in the end," she said, weakly, "It just didn't work out the way that I had planned."

"So you did plan to go off with another man. You are the absolute limit, Lydia. You have a lovely house, two wonderful children and a decent husband and you decide in your infinite wisdom to blow it all on a whim!"

"B-but I thought it was the real thing. That I had found my soul mate..." she trailed off as she heard the hollowness of her own words.

She jumped at Alice's snort of derision.

"This is it Lydia. You have really done it this time. He said that he never wants to see you again and that you are not to try and find him or to contact him or the children," continued Alice, in an exasperated tone.

"Do you know where he has gone?" asked Lydia plaintively, "Please tell me if you know."

"He didn't tell me," she said sharply.

Finally registering her neighbour's disapproval, Lydia stood up and with gravity asked,

"May I please have our door keys then?"

"You may but I don't think they'll be any good. There was a man there yesterday morning changing the locks," she handed Lydia the keys and continued, "I really must say goodbye now. My children are in the front room waiting to give me my Mother's Day surprise. Oh and Freddie left this behind on Friday evening when Philip rushed off with them both. By the way they were fine since you haven't asked."

"That's not fair Alice you know how much I adore Daisy and Freddie," retorted Lydia indignantly.

"I don't know anything anymore," she replied.

Lydia opened her mouth to respond but Alice was already hurrying her out of the house, handing over the snowstorm paperweight that was Freddie's pride and joy, as she went. As Lydia stood in the porch feeling bewildered, she shook it and the snow fell prettily on the winter scene inside the glass. Lydia opened her holdall and wrapped the precious object in a sock before placing it in the middle of the bag and then she walked up the path to her own house.

Alice had been right. The locks had been changed. She opened the back gate and wandered dejectedly around the side of the building and into the back garden. She admired the bed that she had been working on at the end of the previous week and craved the normality of weeding and digging. Lying at the side of the bed, were her hand fork, trowel and secateurs.

"How careless of me," she thought and knelt down with the intention of picking up her tools and putting them away.

Instinctively, she started weeding where she had left off and became completely absorbed in her activity. As one area became clear and tidied, she shifted along to the next.

She moved her fork in and out of the soft, damp, earth rhythmically and as she did she muttered, "Careless Lydia that's what you are, careless."

The movement soothed her troubled soul but after a while, she had to stop and shake her aching arm.

Resting back on her heels she thought, "Oh my God, what am I going to do now?"

She stood up wiping the soil from the tools and automatically put them into her holdall. She walked over to the French windows leading into the living room and pressed her nose against the glass. As she leaned there, she tried the handle of the door which was resting under her hand. She knew that it was pointless. The whole house was thoroughly locked up and she was excluded. She let her eyes adjust to the different light of the room and searched for clues and evidence of her children's rapid departure.

She could see some glue and felt tip pens next to some red coloured card on the low table in front of the sofa. She could feel tears pricking her eyes at the thought of little Daisy making something elaborate for her homecoming. She could see the scene more clearly now and made out the words on the front of the card 'Happy Mummy's Day' in big ungainly print. In smaller letters underneath it said, 'To the best Mummy in the World'. She had drawn a picture of Lydia flanked by Daisy and Freddie. She recalled the children's muffled whisperings interspersed with the word surprise. She had not even remembered that it was Mother's Day.

Overwhelmed by shame Lydia began to cry. Silently at first and as the pain increased, she sobbed in tidal waves of grief and regret. Holding her stomach she staggered to the garden bench on the patio and howled until the aching in her belly subsided.

There she sat, looking out at the garden, numb with sorrow.

The hours went by and Lydia sat reflecting on the horror of her situation. Over and over again she wished that she had not acted so impulsively. She knew now that she had been deluded in her quest for happiness. She had never considered that her actions would result in the loss of her children. Those two dear beings for whom she would have gladly died in order that they should live, were gone. A wave of discomfort coursed through her and manifested itself as rage.

How dare he take them from her? Where were they? And how was she to find them? Darkness was falling on the garden and she picked up her belongings. She would find a telephone booth and find his mother's number and call her. She would know where he was. Perhaps he had gone there.

After much trouble, Lydia had managed to obtain her mother-in-law's number and she nervously dialled the number.

"Hello?"

"Hello, its Lydia," she said apprehensively.

"Ah Lydia, he's gone I'm afraid. He stopped here briefly late on Friday night before they left for the airport."

"Airport!" shrieked Lydia.

"Yes, he's gone abroad. He said that he had been offered a job overseas a while back and that now that things had changed between the two of you he had decided to take it."

"But where? Surely he can't just take my children abroad like that and not tell me where they are," said Lydia.

"I'm sorry Lydia he didn't tell me which country he was going to because he knew that you would phone me eventually. He didn't want me to be involved. But what he did say is that he has put the house up for sale and that it is in the hands of his solicitors. When you have found somewhere to live you can give me your address for the solicitors to contact you."

Lydia could already hear that the conversation was coming to a close and knowing that she was to be given no more information; she put the phone back down on the receiver and left the booth. As she trudged aimlessly around the town she remembered that Philip had never put her name on the mortgage. There had been a specific reason why, at the time, it was preferable and Lydia had thought little of it. Philip was an honest man but she knew she would not do very well out of the sale of the house now. She thought about it and realised that she did not really care whether or not she was treated fairly financially. She could not see a way of finding her children.

She did not know whether or not Philip's actions were legal. She was woefully unprepared. She had never had cause to believe that Philip would leave her and therefore had no contingency plans. Philip had managed all the finances, insurance and expenses. For the second time that day she cursed her carelessness. Lydia had thought in the past that her vagueness about the minutiae of life was something that she could not help. At worst, an irritation for her husband, and at best, an expression of who she was; the slightly bohemian woman who believed that ethereal matters were more important and thus more rewarding than reality.

Meandering through the High Street, she stopped at a cash point machine to draw out some money. While she was there, she decided she had better check the balance of the account before considering what she was to do next. She looked with disbelief at the piece of paper in her hand. One hundred pounds was all that was left. Horrified, she realised that Philip had removed all the funds. How long did he think that one hundred pounds would last her? She started to panic. She had always treated her wages from the building society as pocket money. She certainly did not earn enough to live on. For the first time in years she had to think about how to fend for herself.

Lydia walked into the off licence and bought four cans of

lager and sat on a bench nearby to reflect on her predicament. Thinking about her job, she suddenly realised the humiliation it would cause her to work there in the light of her new situation. She deliberated on the possibility and concluded that it would be too painful to admit to her foolishness let alone confess that her actions had caused her to lose her children.

"I lost my children," she said, "I've misplaced my children," she tried, "Perhaps that sounds better."

She drank her beer and tried to formulate a plan. Firstly, she needed a place to stay and then she would have to earn some money.

Recalling her mother-in-law's words, "When you have found somewhere to live you can give me your address..." she felt a glimmer of hope.

Philip's Mum had not been unkind. Perhaps she would help her if she contacted her in a few weeks with her new details. Her instinct was to return home. If Philip had changed his mind and thought it too cruel to deprive her of her children he may go back to the house. She had finished her cans and found the thought of having nothing to ease the pain unbearable, so she went back into the off licence and bought a bottle of vodka.

Traipsing back, she remembered that Philip had made sure that there was an electricity supply to the shed in their garden. Relieved, she quickened her step in the knowledge that she had a roof over her head for the night. She walked with hunched shoulders gazing at the ground beneath her feet, only raising her eyes to furtively glance at the owners of the footsteps that passed her by. The thought of a crushingly awkward encounter with a cheerful but inquisitive acquaintance, was more than she could bear.

She opened the side gate noiselessly, let herself into the garden and walked up the path to the shed. Once inside, she felt for the light switch and silently thanked Philip for his attention to detail as its contents were illuminated. In front of the digging tools stood 'Mummy's sunbathing chair' which she took out and unfolded. Opening her vodka bottle, she sat in her shelter, took a large swig and considered her options for the future. She was keenly aware of the strong sense of shame which was overriding her turbulent emotional state. She had no desire to face the people she knew and undergo the humiliation of informing them about her personal crisis. Although she suffered from tidal waves of wrath towards Philip, she could not overlook her responsibility for the consequences of her ill-advised weekend.

As she made her way steadily through the vodka which had not left her hand since she had sat down, she was struck by an inspiration, "I'll take an early tube up to London and find a room to rent," she thought, and galvanised by the prospect, "Then I will set about looking for a job."

No-one would know her there and she could start afresh. When she was established she could contact Philip's mother with her address and perhaps Philip would have calmed down enough for Lydia to attempt some sort of mediation or conciliation. As her idea began to take hold she felt a resurgence of hope. Eventually, due to the vodka and the events of the day, Lydia fell into an uncomfortable slumber.

Her nightmares woke her several times and just before dawn, she conceded to them and decided to face the day. It was cold as she tidied her hair and put the vodka into her hold all. She opened the door of the shed to the early birdsong and stepped out into the garden. She bid farewell to her plants and slunk quietly down the side passage and onto the deserted street.

Lydia approached the tube station with trepidation but as she bought her one way ticket, it evaporated and was replaced with a diffident anticipation at the possibilities of the Metropolis. Sitting on the tube, she rummaged in her holdall for her hair brush and pulled out the picture of Daisy and Freddie holding hands with her by the sea-side.

"Don't worry little ones, I'll find you. This is just the beginning," she said, swallowing hard to prevent the tears from leaving her eyes.

"I must find an envelope to keep the picture nice," she thought as she replaced it carefully into her holdall and then pondered the possibilities of the day ahead.

CHAPTER FIVE

London

She resolved to leave the tube at King's Cross, deeming it as good a place as any to make a start. She recalled that it had a high concentration of offices and hospitals in the vicinity thus increasing her potential employment opportunities. As she left the station, the sun dazzled her and the noise of the traffic caused her to put her hands to her ears in an attempt to muffle it. The early morning commuters were racing each other and the rest of the world for the best seats in the tube and nothing was going to stop them. Amid the apparent chaos, Lydia relaxed into its anonymity, aware that it was this that she had sought.

She stopped at a cafe for a coffee. There was a card in the window advertising for an assistant with accommodation provided and an invitation to come inside for further details. Lydia wary of its serendipity, decided to order a coffee and spend a little time trying to get a feel for the place. She was greeted at the counter by a large olive skinned man wearing an unclean white T-shirt stretched over his protruding belly.

"Good morning," replied Lydia, "Could I have a cup of coffee please?"

"One coffee coming up," he said gruffly.

Lydia paid for it and sat down at a table by the window. The table and chairs were old and rickety and everything appeared to be coated with a greasy, yellow film.

"I'd have to give this place a thorough clean if I were to work here," she mused.

Driven by necessity and buoyed by the half hearted smile that the proprietor threw her way, she went back up the counter and asked,

"Are you still looking for an assistant?"

"Why you interested?"

"Yes I may be, I have an interview later on this morning but I thought that I would enquire anyway," she said, colouring at her lie.

"What your name?" he asked brusquely.

Lydia panicked not wishing to relinquish the obscurity that London had offered her.

"Eleanora," she lied.

"Very nice," he said, peering at her suspiciously, "Have you had experience in cafe before?"

"Yes, some, I can cook, clean and tidy and I am very organised," she replied, wincing at the lack of truth in the second part of her statement.

"Can you start tomorrow?" he asked abruptly.

"Yes," she answered, thinking, "Oh no, what have I let myself in for this time?"

"See, I need someone to be here at seven in the morning. So you have to be able to get up in time. There's a small flat upstairs if you need somewhere to live."

"Yes that would suit me well," said Lydia, "May I see it?"

"Yes, here is the key. The last tenant isn't very tidy and I have no time to clean."

Lydia took the key and following the direction of his index finger, she found the foot of the stairs which led up to the accommodation. The stairs were rickety and she was accompanied by a strong, unidentifiable smell which increased ominously as she neared the top. The light switch was a timed button and she had just enough time to line up the key in the lock before darkness fell again. She pushed open the door and walked in to a small hallway carpeted by old newspapers. Trampling over the debris, she stepped gingerly into the living area containing a battered settee and more piles of rubbish.

Uninspired by her prospective home, she quickly glanced in at the bedroom, kitchen and finally the bathroom. Horrified, she saw that the sink and surrounding area were bloodstained and there were needles and syringes around its base. Recoiling at the thought of even contemplating living in such a place, she left hurriedly and ran downstairs and back into the cafe. She found herself in close proximity to her potential boss and intuitively moved away. He was grinning at her now,

"So flat OK? You start in the morning?" he asked.

"Well as I said earlier, I do have this other interview so perhaps I could let you know later?" she replied.

"OK, but midday latest," he said grumpily.

"I'll see you then," said Lydia, having no intention of returning.

She strode out on to the busy street and continued along until she reached its end. Lydia felt raw from the episode in the flat and her spirits were plummeting. What was she to do? She was unprepared for any possibility of being considered at the many nearby offices. As she deliberated on the impression she might give if she entered one of them, she became aware of her shabby state. She had not washed in over twenty four hours. Her hair was unkempt and her clothes were dirty. She needed a place to sleep and very soon she would run out of money.

Reluctantly, she turned back and trudging slowly, she eventually re-entered the grimy snack bar. Inhaling deeply, she glanced at her new employer and trying to show some enthusiasm said,

"I've decided I would like to take up your kind offer of employment."

"Very good," he said, handing her the key to the upstairs rooms, "Get settled in and I show you ropes."

Lydia took the key from him and went back out to search for a shop that sold cleaning fluids and bin bags. Her enthusiasm for the project was enhanced by the careful selection of a vase with artificial flowers and some promisingly fragranced air fresheners.

"Mmm, lily of the valley or freesia, which shall it be?" she asked herself, "It's a bit stinky. I think I'll take both."

She stood in the queue waiting to pay and noticed that there was a comforting row of bottles behind the till. She added some cans of beer and a bottle of wine to her shopping.

"I'd better make sure that I get up in the morning," she thought, vaguely aware that her latter purchases were not entirely wise, "I must celebrate my new found home," she concluded as she sauntered back to her digs.

"Hello," she said as she walked back into the shop, "Do you know I don't even know your name!"

"Stav," he said, holding out a sweaty palm. She shook his hand and continued on her way.

Back upstairs, she flung open the windows and started cleaning. The worst part of her ordeal was the removal of the drug abuse equipment. She picked up each item warily with her rubber gloves and placed them in a rubbish sack. She was surprised to feel a certain melancholy for the person who had been so desperate before her. However, the need to rid the place of all traces of its previous misery became imperative.

She stoically stuck at her task, finally placing the vase containing the unauthentic plastic and linen flowers on the stained coffee table in front of the shabby sofa, with a flourish. Pouring out a beer into one of the two unmatched glasses she had retrieved from the kitchen chaos, she sat and sipped with a mild sense of satisfaction.

As she gazed ahead, she listed the other jobs that needed to be done for her to be ready for work in the morning. Most importantly, she must buy an alarm clock and then there was the small matter of not having any clean laundry to wear. Perhaps she would spend some of the last money in the bank account on a new wardrobe. After all she would have a wage packet by the end of the week.

She set off to the shops, after promising Stav that she would be back within the hour. She decided to take out all the money from the joint account just in case Philip removed anymore and put it all in her purse. She turned off the main road and found a dilapidated row of shops in a side street. The traffic blackened facades and peeling paintwork were uninviting. Just as she was contemplating turning back, Lydia caught sight of a charity shop at the end of the small parade and headed towards it.

The door stuck as she pushed it open then suddenly thrust her forwards into the middle of the chaotic shop. She stood reeling from the fusty smell peculiar to second-hand shops. She recovered herself and started to rummage through the assortment of garments arrayed eclectically on round display rails. She gathered a number of items and glanced around to see if there were any facilities for changing. An extremely old lady was sitting behind a glass showcase which boasted all manner of jewellery and watches. Drawn by the twinkling of the rings and necklaces, she remembered that she had planned to buy an alarm clock. She scanned the shelves and saw a colourful clock with a nodding Winnie the Pooh head.

"Please may I have that clock?" she asked the elderly woman, who appeared to have dozed off. For a moment, Lydia thought that she may have stopped breathing. To her relief, the woman made a strange snortling noise, opened her eyes and tried to focus on her customer. She shook her head and then stared blankly inside the cabinet. Finally, after many attempts, she managed to lay her hand on the item. She spent several minutes searching for tissue paper and meticulously wrapping it up, despite Lydia's pleas to just put it in a bag. Lydia had lost any desire to try on her clothing and estimated that most of it would fit. The prospect of requesting the location of a changing room seemed suddenly too arduous. Whilst waiting for her jumble to be gift wrapped, she turned her attention to the selection of books on a nearby shelf. Picking out 'Crime and Punishment' and 'Metamorphosis', she lay them on the counter next to the other items adding a pair of large dangly earrings that had caught her eye during the protracted packaging process. Philip had an aversion to showy jewellery but she realised with chagrin that she was now free to wear whatever she pleased without fear of his inevitable disapproval. She left the shop with her strange smelling goods and went back to the cafe to be given her instructions.

Stav instructed her on the idiosyncrasies of the coffee machine and the water urn for the tea. He then told her where to find the bread and sandwich fillers, interspersing this information with an intermittent resumé on what to expect during a day's work in the cafe. It was open from seven in the morning until five at night. The early morning clientele were usually in a hurry and it was therefore imperative that the hot drinks were served as quickly as possible. Apparently it could be very busy with a post lunch lull during which time, she would be expected to stock up where necessary.

Lydia's head had begun to spin but she managed to ask her boss the all important question, "How much will I get paid?"

She was disenchanted by the meagre amount she could now expect to receive on Friday evening from which her rent would be deducted, but was comforted by the thought that she would be able to leave when she found a better job.

"At least I'll have a roof over my head for the time being," she thought.

The clock on the wall informed them both that it was time to close for the night and Lydia turned around the sign in the window. Picking up an unclean rag from the draining board behind the counter, she started to systematically clear and wipe the tables. As she finished her task, she stopped, glanced around at her efforts and sighed with satisfaction. Perhaps she could make something of this opportunity after all.

"OK Nellie," said Stav, "I'll see you in the morning. I usually here about ten, but I try and get here bit early tomorrow as it's first day."

"My name's Eleanora," she said, enunciating her new identity with care.

Stav stood waving a tea towel around in a dismissive manner,

"Too long, too difficult to say, Nellie's much better, very nice name don't you think?"

Lydia had an almighty rush of irritability and in attempt to control her temper she muttered, "Mmm..." and walked past him and up to the rooms above the shop.

She stamped her feet on the first three steps to assuage her anger. She had chosen the name Eleanora because she thought it was romantic and quite beautiful and had she had a second daughter that is how she would have named her.

"Nellie is an ugly old lady's name," she thought, but by the top of the stairs she just shrugged her shoulders and opened the door to her new abode.

She was exhausted by the exertions of the day and planned a hot bath, something to eat and a good read. Lying in the bath, she remembered that she had no food in the flat. She would have to go out again and she could see through the frosted glass that night had begun to fall. Racing against the darkness, she jumped out of the water and quickly dressed in some of her newly acquired clothes.

She ran out onto the street, reflecting that her haste had been unnecessary as there were still people milling about and some of the shops were open. Slowing her pace she counted the money she had left in her purse. She crossed the road and entered the telephone kiosk situated directly opposite the cafe. She took out the piece of paper with her mother-in-law's number scrawled on it. She dialled the number anxiously, but consoled herself with the thought that she had been invited to phone with her new address. She did not dare to think that there may be any news of her children.

She was surprised when there was no ringing tone and it just jumped to a sharp female voice saying, "The number you have dialled has not been recognised. Please try again."

Thinking that she had misdialled, she followed the instructions carefully reading the number out loud as she did so. The result was the same. She tried several more times and then gave up.

Defeated, she stood outside the telephone box thinking, "She must have changed her number so that I could not call again."

Crushed by the knowledge that her last tenuous link to her children had been severed and sensing betrayal at its deepest level she added the change to her severely dwindled funds.

"I might make it through to Friday if I'm careful," she thought. Her hunger was being taunted by the distinct aroma of a kebab house.

"Maybe I'll treat myself just this once," she said and strode into the restaurant. Standing in the take-away queue, she felt lonely and vulnerable. Everyone else appeared to be chatting and in high spirits. She tried to talk to the man behind her, but he grunted at her and looked down at his boots. Gathering her large, greasy package under her arm, she set off back to the cafe, recalling that she had been instructed to use the back entrance outside business hours.

She turned down a small, deserted side street and then a short way down an alleyway which ran parallel to the main street until she came to a wrought iron fire escape. Lydia was becoming increasingly nervous and panicked because she was unsure which of the back entrances was hers. It was dark and uninviting. She tried to tread silently so that if anyone was hiding in the shadows she could not be heard. She jumped and screamed when she saw a teenager swaggering towards her.

"What the matter lady?" the youngster said, "You think I steal your kebab?"

He laughed menacingly, baring a shiny set of gold capped teeth and sauntered past her with a sneeringly slow strut. Lydia ran the last few steps to the base of the fire escape and following a perfunctory search for potential attackers ran up all the steps and to the back entrance of her lodgings. She fumbled with her keys and eventually unlocked the door. Once in, she immediately pulled over the bolt, for which she was immensely grateful and sat on the grubby sofa shaking.

She knew that she needed to prevent the flood of tears from falling. Afraid that on acquiescing to this urge she would never stop, Lydia hunted out the wine and beer left over from her earlier home making efforts. She drank a couple of cans very quickly in the certain knowledge that she would then be able to sip her wine. She picked up the bottle to admire its contents and made the disconcerting discovery that it had a cork and she had no opener. The next half an hour was spent searching frantically for a likely implement with which to solve her problem and she settled on a knife and a shoe to hammer it in.

She sat huddled on the corner of the seat waiting for the alcohol to numb her soul, occasionally picking at the congealed kebab meat still in its wrapper. As her thoughts turned to her children, she rummaged in her holdall for the holiday snap she had so casually packed on that fateful Friday morning. Lying uncomfortably on the sofa, she kissed their dear trusting faces and held it to her breast. Eventually Lydia dozed off and slept fitfully for fear of oversleeping.

The brutal tones of her new alarm clock seared through her reverie awakening her into a bleak, new world. She made her way lethargically to the bathroom. As she was dressing, she put together a colourful outfit consisting of a brightly coloured, gypsy style skirt with a red top. Lydia finished the effect with the gold hoop earrings she had bought the day before and a daub of scarlet lipstick. Slightly cheered by the ensemble she went downstairs to open up the cafe and start work.

With difficulty, she was able to operate the various machines and after a halting start she fell into a routine whereby she could serve, take money and ensure that she had not run out of anything. By ten o'clock she was exhausted and convinced that she would not survive the day, but Stav arrived soon afterwards to alleviate her of some of the work load.

During the quiet time, the establishment was frequented sporadically by vagrants and other marginalised individuals. Lydia enjoyed the company of some of them and when Stav was not watching she would refill their cups. If anyone asked her name, which did not happen often, she resigned herself to being Nellie. It was not quite the new persona she had imagined, but it was important that she did not reveal her original identity. Separation from her previous life meant that she would not have to divulge the true reason for her arrival at the cafe.

Although her exertions were great and her fatigue sometimes unbearable, Lydia found constant activity preferable to the evening spent alone in the rooms upstairs. After her first evening there she was loathe to leave the premises if it involved coming back after dark, so she spent the evening reading and then fell asleep on the settee after saying "Night night!" to the picture of Daisy and Freddie.

For two weeks Lydia settled into a reasonably comfortable routine. She made sure that she ate during the day and in the evening, was so weary from her labour that she sat reading until she fell asleep.

She had intended to buy some bed linen when she first moved in but as time went by she became used to the sofa as her bed. She only had a very small amount of money left and there seemed something quite distasteful about sleeping in the same bed as the previous troubled inhabitant. She rarely tidied up and had no enthusiasm for cleaning. She was concerned however, with the state of her clothes and resolved to visit the local launderette as soon as possible.

Her first opportunity came when she arose on Sunday shuddering at the prospect of the unfilled hours before her. She packed up her washing in her holdall and rucksack and set off. Lydia had not been outside the building for nearly a week and treated the expedition as an outing. She took the remains of her paltry wage packet from which the rent had been deducted and packed her now battered copy of Crime and Punishment.

Stopping at the twenty four hour shop a few doors along, she stocked up with some beer and tasty snacks for her jaunt. Lydia had not had an alcoholic drink since the night of the kebab and in her excitement, threw all her clothes in the same machine, organised the change and soap powder and burst back out onto the street to find a bench. Once settled, she took out one of the cold beers and a cigarette from the packet she had succumbed to as the ultimate indulgence, lit it and surveyed the scene.

The menace of Monday night had evaporated into the miasma of the spring sunshine. She was sure that she could even hear the sound of birds above the urban landscape. Content that all was well, she pulled out her book and resumed the account of Raskolnikov's anguish. Pausing to open another can, Lydia reflected upon the reasons why she identified so closely with his predicament. After all, she had not murdered anyone, nor had she had any desire to do so. The explanation lay in the fear that his guilt and shame evoked in her. He had justified his actions with a slightly dubious rationale and yet he could not rest. At this point, Lydia felt another pang of recognition. Had she not validated her deeds of the previous weekend with all sorts of tenuous reasons? Although she believed that she had not intended to cause harm by her conduct, was she not wracked with guilt, shame and remorse at the resultant damage? She wondered whether the pain would ever subside. The guilt would remain with her for ever but she did not have to relive it by revealing her crime. At that moment she vowed that she would never tell another living soul the story of how she had so carelessly abandoned her children. And so Lydia became Nellie. No longer caring that it was not the name she had chosen, only relieved that by changing it, she might be able to leave behind her, if only in part, the woman who had so recklessly lost her children.

Her burden thus temporarily eased, she sat back on the seat and drank her beer. She placed the unfinished book by her side happy that it had helped her with her own dilemma. As she picked up another can, a man stood in front of her and tipped his pork pie hat at her.

"Good morning Madam. I see you are enjoying the air," he said.

"I am indeed," she replied, recognising him as one of the disparate afternoon visitors to the cafe.

"Do you mind if I join you?" he asked.

"Not at all."

He took off his hat and placed it on his lap as he sat next to her.

"It's Nellie, isn't it?" he enquired politely.

"That's right," said Nellie, "What's your name if you don't mind me asking?"

"William," he responded, delighted that she had asked, "Not Bill or Willy or any other ridiculous curtailed version of a perfectly good name, but William. W-I-L-L-I-A-M," he spelt out painstakingly.

"And a very nice name it is too," said Nellie, trying not to smile.

She glanced over at her companion who had picked up her book and was thumbing through it.

"Cheerful buggers those Russians," he said sardonically, "Not the sort of stuff you need on a fine spring morning such as today."

"You might be right about that," she replied ruefully, "But I've nearly finished it. Have you read it?"

"Oh yes," he answered, "A long time ago."

He was eyeing her supply of beer now.

"Would you like one?" she offered, not wishing to appear churlish.

"If you can spare it," he said.

Not waiting for a reply, he seized a can, opened it and started to gulp it down. When he had nearly finished it he came up for air, wiped his mouth on the back of his hand and exhaled deeply.

"Didn't realise quite how thirsty I had become," he stated, "Does that ever happen to you?"

"Oh all the time," replied Nellie, warming to her new chum.

"What do you have planned for the rest of the day, my dear?"

"I'm doing my laundry even as we speak and later I have absolutely nothing lined up," was her rejoinder.

"Well, in that case, may I be so bold as to proffer an invitation for you to accompany me on a promenade by the river and if you so wish I may show you my humble abode," he leaned forward and peered at her with a sparkle of fun in his eyes.

Nellie hesitated.

"I promise you young lady you will be in safe hands. William Short, man of honour, at your service," he announced, jumping to his feet to take a bow.

Nellie believed him. It had been a long hard week and she considered his offer a welcome diversion.

"Thanking you kindly young sir, may I gratefully accept," she said, standing to return his bow with a curtsey.

Nellie bought two sturdy washing bags from a machine on the wall. She embarked on throwing her clothes in as quickly as possible until William stopped her saying,

"Now what's the point in going to all this trouble," he gesticulated at the machines, "If you end up wearing garments that look worse than before you arrived?" he asked, raising one eyebrow at her.

"None, absolutely none," said Nellie. And the two of them folded her belongings neatly into the new shiny bags.

"That's better," said William, with an air of genuine satisfaction.

William escorted Nellie to the flat where she flung the neatly packed laundry onto the settee and they set off gaily towards the river. Nellie did not know her way around London very well and enjoyed the guided tour that her friend was eager to share with her. Eventually, she caught sight of the infamous Thames with its brownish green water lapping against the colourful vessels bobbing along in the light breeze. Nellie loved boats and felt a sudden desire to wave to one of the ferries transporting fresh faced camera bearing tourists. She raised her arm and to her surprise, William followed suit and they stood on the windy bank hoping that the recipients of their greeting would respond. A few of the craft's passengers signalled back at them and they sank on to a bench laughing at their small success.

"I love it here," said Nellie, momentarily freed from her woeful afflictions.

"So do I," responded William, "That's why I decided to set up home here. It's a very desirable neighbourhood you know." He gave a wheezy chuckle which gave way to a rasping coughing fit.

Finally recovering from the unwelcome spasm he said, "I must go and visit my doctor in Harley Street. He's an expert on chest complaints, don't you know?"

"That's a good idea. Are you feeling better now?"

"Oh yes much, let me show you where I live," he replied.

He held up a crooked, right elbow and Nellie accepted by putting her hand gently on his arm.

They walked amiably through the vibrant Sunday morning hordes on the Embankment, stopping for some time at the second hand bookstalls. William was very knowledgeable about a broad spectrum of literature and was only too happy to discuss his opinions with Nellie. Each would become absorbed in a book of particular interest and then put it down to seek out the other and confer on their discovery. Sated with intellectual nourishment, they moved away from the final stand and found that they were positioned directly facing the coffee shop of the National Film Theatre.

Nellie glanced at William and asked, "Shall we have a cup of coffee?"

"I'm afraid I'm a bit strapped for cash," he said, "Just for the next couple of weeks, you understand? I'm just waiting for some news of a project that I've had on the go for a while now; then watch out London here I come!"

"Let me buy them then. We could sit outside with the pigeons and watch the world go by," she offered.

"Well, just this once, I wouldn't normally take out a young lady and expect her to pay," he muttered, slightly abashed.

Seeing his embarrassment, Nellie said, "Don't worry William you can return the favour when you come into your money,"

"OK then, lead the way MacDuff!"

As they sat at their table sipping at the hot strong coffee, William cleared his throat as if he was about to make an announcement,

"You seem a well-educated young woman, Nellie," he began.

"Not really, I've just read a lot," she interrupted.

"A technicality my dear, a technicality...what I was going to say was that there is something that I would like to tell you. It's something that I wouldn't normally divulge to any old Tom, Dick or Harry for fear they may not understand," he continued.

"Oh dear," thought Nellie, "Let's hope he hasn't murdered anyone."

But she said, "I feel distinctly honoured," and waited with some apprehension for the pending disclosure.

He leaned across the table towards his companion and lowering his voice, uttered the words, "I'm something of an author myself, you know?"

"Are you really?" she asked, "What's sort of books do you write?"

"I use quite a wide range of subject matter and I'm just waiting for my last oeuvre to be published."

"That's very impressive," said Nellie, intrigued, "What's it called?"

"Ah!" he replied, touching his nose with the tip of his forefinger, "I don't like to tempt fate, but you will be the first to know when I have been given the go ahead. And the name my dear, I prefer a nom de plume myself. I find it's the only way. What do you think?"

"Well, having never written anything myself I can't say that I've really given it much thought. However, since you mention it, there's a lot to be said for the nom de plume approach, anonymity and all that."

"I knew that you would understand. I could tell when we first met. I said to myself that's a classy lady," and he lifted his coffee cup with the dregs in the bottom and raised it to hers to toast their mutual understanding.

They sat together happily, sometimes in silence and occasionally commenting on a passerby. Nellie felt comfortable with this eccentric man with his crumpled but affable countenance. He had a mass of thick, grey hair framing his weathered, brown face. When he smiled his face erupted with the joy of the moment defying any companion not to smile with him. He pulled his worn, tweed jacket around his person and tucked his stained, silk cravat inside it.

Clapping his hands together, he said, "Well my dear girl, that was splendid. Would you care for a stroll?"

"Yes, I would like that. I need warming up now," replied Nellie.

The two of them ambled up the slopes leading to the Hayward Gallery and considered the posters in its windows.

"All a bit modern and hectic for me," offered William.

"And me, perhaps we'll wait for a more suitable exhibition," replied Nellie, grinning widely at William.

Going back down the steps, William turned to Nellie and said,

"I was going to show you where I lived wasn't I?"

"You were, but don't worry if you don't want to I don't mind," said Nellie, "I'll tell you what, why don't I buy us a little something to drink and we can take it with us."

William took her to the nearest off licence where she bought some more cans of beer, some vodka and a packet of cigarettes.

"This should last us until sunset," she said, laughing and they set off with William leading the way back to the river and just past the Charing Cross Bridge.

"Here it is," he said, pointing to a bench in front of them.

"What do you mean?" asked Nellie.

"This is where I live," he replied, sounding crestfallen, "Its only temporary you know. When I have my novel published things will be very different, you mark my words. I'll be mixing with the hoi poloi and everyone will want to know me then. But for now I make do with this bijou but airy des res."

Nellie was surprised at how shocked she felt. She had known that he would not have been living in the lap of luxury, but for some reason she had not guessed that he was homeless.

In an attempt to conceal her emotion, she said, "You have a very nice view of the river from here, don't you?"

"Yes, and all mod cons too," he replied, pulling out a large misshapen rucksack from behind the bench. "Now let me see, I have two cups in here, we could drink a toast to the great outdoors. What do you think, my dear?"

"Excellent plan, sir," returned Nellie, as William continued to fumble around in the bag.

At one point his arm had disappeared almost up to his shoulder and inexplicably, Nellie felt laughter welling up inside her. She let out a small suppressed chortle and catching her friend's eye, she exploded into an uncontrollable fit of the giggles. William, though not quite understanding the reason for her mirth nevertheless joined in the hilarity of the moment.

Extricating his arm from his baggage, he pulled out two white enamel camping cups and passed one of them to Nellie who immediately filled them with beer from her ready opened can. Nellie opened the packet of cigarettes and passed one to her friend. As William lit his he started to cough again, at times having to hold on to the seat as he tried to breathe.

When he had regained his composure he quipped, "I must give the darn things up. Maybe I will, tomorrow."

Nellie peered round at his flushed face and satisfied that he was recovering, patted him on the forearm and said, "Yes, tomorrow, that will be soon enough."

They sat on their bench chatting and drinking until the light began to evaporate from the sky.

"I shall have to go soon," said Nellie, concerned that she would not be able to find her way back in the dark.

"Would you like me to escort you, young lady?" asked William.

"Would you mind?" she asked, relieved that he had offered.

William tipped the dregs from the bottom of the cups and replaced them in his rucksack. He then stuffed it unceremoniously down the back of the bench, held out his arm for the second time that day and said,

"Let's go this way I need to use the facilities, to put not too fine a point on the matter."

"That's good so do I," responded Nellie, gladly taking his arm.

The pair of them weaved erratically down the road laughing childishly at their obvious unsteadiness. They stopped at some toilets a small walk from where they had been sitting.

"These are open twenty four hours a day so very convenient conveniences for the likes of me," he informed her.

They went their separate ways and met outside a few minutes later.

"So can you have a wash and all that in there?" enquired Nellie, suddenly interested in how a person could keep clean with nowhere to live.

"Well, yes you can, but I prefer to go very early in the morning so that I can have a bit of privacy," he replied pragmatically, "There are other places that I can go though, for a shower and something to eat," he continued.

"Oh that's good," she replied, feeling reassured.

Night had fallen and they were walking alongside the river. Nellie was enchanted by the lights reflecting on the water's surface and the flurry of people making their way to theatres and restaurants. She had a strange feeling of derealisation as she wandered through the crowds. She felt invisible in the midst of their vivacity and their relentless determination. Yet she sensed a comfort in her apparent imperceptibility. Perhaps now she could abdicate from her role in the world.

They reached the cafe all too soon and as they prepared to part, Nellie felt sad at leaving her new pal out in the cold. She knew that it would be inappropriate to ask him to stay. He took her hand and kissed it ceremoniously.

"Now, now my dear, don't you worry about me. It's a nice dry night. Let me just stand here and wait until I see the light go on upstairs. I'll know you are safe and sound then. Goodnight and thank you for a perfectly charming day."

"Thank you William, you will come by for a cup of tea tomorrow won't you?"

"I will indeed, my dear," he responded.

"Goodnight then," said Nellie reluctantly.

She climbed shakily up the steep steps to her cheerless abode and on entering, remembered that William was waiting outside for the light to go on. She turned on the dim bulb and ran to the window to wave at him. He looked up smiling broadly and held up both his thumbs in approval. Nellie pulled the threadbare curtains over in an attempt to cover the darkness and sat on the sofa in the gloom. Reaching over to the stained coffee table she set the clock and sighed. She picked up the photograph of the children and kissing their images she lay down and fell asleep.

* * *

Nellie's work in the cafe followed much the same pattern each day. She found solace in the routine and became familiar with a number of the customers, some of whom were friendly. Stav now came in around eleven or eleven thirty and stayed until the lunchtime rush was over. He had become more relaxed with her and chatted in his strong accent about the trials and tribulations he was having with his teenage daughters.

Every evening, Nellie turned the shop sign around to 'Closed' and set about tidying, cleaning and preparing for the next day's onslaught. She smiled ruefully as she went about these tasks. In an overzealous desire to make her mark she had resolved to scrub the walls and floor and had even toyed with the idea of painting the place. Now, only in her second week of employment she had lost all inclination to do so. Firstly, she was far too tired at the end of the normal day to contemplate any extra work and secondly, she was paid a pittance about which she was already feeling resentful.

During a surge of self-confidence on Friday afternoon after Stav had handed her the meagre wage in a white envelope, she light heartedly asked her employer if there was any likelihood that she might be paid a little more for her efforts explaining that she was finding it difficult to manage on the present sum.

"Oh Nellie, if only it was possible. You are such a good employee. But I don't make enough to pay myself. What with the rent for this place, overheads and the family, I have empty pockets at the end of each day."

He shook his head sadly and continued to count the morning's takings. Nellie would have been more astonished if he had conceded to her request but she was pleased at having had the courage to ask him.

As he departed that afternoon he rested his hand on her shoulder and said, "At least you have a nice flat to go in the evening."

His hand was still on her shoulder and she moved away muttering, "Mmm, I suppose so."

But thinking, "I wouldn't go so far as to say it was nice."

She let the matter go and waving him goodbye, she went behind the counter to serve her next customer. She admitted reluctantly that her lack of funds had ensured that she had been able to get up for work each day in a reasonable condition.

After her final tasks she had dragged her weary limbs up the stairs and sat alone in her living room. Despite the noise from the traffic, she was acutely aware of the silence of the room throbbing in her ears inviting the clamour of her dismal thoughts to invade the space. She recalled Clara Cloud, and realised that she had returned to wreak disquiet upon her far more vengefully than ever before. Nellie knew that there was no class, nor job, nor hobby that would anaesthetise the pain of the festering wound which filled the void her children had left behind. In her darkest hour, she would always be granted a chink of hope from her belief that one day the three of them would be reunited.

In desperation, she reverted back to her old escape route through books. She was now reading Kafka's 'Metamorphosis' and though dismal in the extreme, she felt a ghoulish compulsion to pursue Gregor's plight to its end. It had given her nightmares, but she could not stop reading it. She was intrigued by the intensity of the hero's isolation but imagined a comfort to be had in his bleak remoteness.

Later that evening, she planned a small excursion to the shop to buy some essential items and some beer as a reward for her week's endeavours. Walking out onto the early evening street, Nellie's spirits lifted. Maybe she would tidy the flat when she returned. She scanned the crowds vaguely hoping to catch a glimpse of her new found friend, William. He had popped into the cafe as promised, several times that week and they had managed to exchange a few words with each other in between Nellie's various duties. She provided him with an adequate supply of tea and when possible, supplemented this with a sandwich or a cake. She was careful to ensure that no-one noticed their collusion, knowing that the clientele who frequented the cafe at that time of day would be guaranteed to want the same treatment. However, she continued to give them generous helpings of tea and coffee at Stav's expense. William had alluded to a rendezvous on Sunday and had suggested that they could meet again at the launderette. Nellie was unable to spot him in the milling hordes.

"Never mind," she thought, "Perhaps he will turn up tomorrow and we can confirm our arrangement."

Nellie entered the twenty-four hour shop trying to remember the household items she had intended to buy as the dazzle of the bottles behind the shopkeeper first lured, then mesmerised her. No longer accountable to anyone, Nellie discovered that she preferred to have a selection of drinks with varying impacts. All week she had suffered a nagging discomfort in her belly leaving her with a permanent, unidentifiable anxiety. Leaving the shop with six cans of beer, a bottle of vodka and a bottle of wine in two blue plastic bags, she became aware that the unease had left her. Heartened at the release from her nervousness she rushed up the fire escape stairs and let herself into the dismal quarters and sat down to drink.

She picked up her book, finding herself back in Gregor's flat and imagining the horror of becoming an immobile beetle. Nellie had an aversion to insects, her least favourite being the cockroach. This fear merely served to increase the disgust and despair that the novel had already evoked in her. She became oblivious to her surroundings, hoping against hope that the story would culminate in something more positive than dying the death of a large, upside down, unwanted insect. As she read the last few pages her absorption was complete.

Suddenly, she heard footsteps on the stairs leading up from the cafe to her rooms. She sat transfixed, as the sounds approached the locked front door. Looking around for a possible weapon, she saw the half full bottle on the table before her and picked it up by its neck. Walking silently to the door of the living room, she stood behind it barely daring to breath. Then to her horror she heard a key turn in the lock.

"Oh my God! Oh my God! She mouthed silently.

"Hello! Where are you?" called a familiar male voice.

"Who is it?" whispered Nellie, trembling behind her screen.

"It's me Stav, I come to see if you alright," he said, looming into the dimly lit area.

Nellie nearly vomited with relief at seeing a familiar form. The respite was short lived as she wondered why on earth he was there. He had never shown any concern for her welfare before and there was something strange in his tone and his movements. The combination of her terror and her quite marked intoxication had slowed her reactions. She backed away from him towards the sofa and table.

"I see you have nice celebration. May I join you?" he said, making an uncoordinated sweeping gesture in the direction of her collection of bottles and cans. Finally recognising Stav's own drunken state, she decided that diplomacy was crucial.

"Would you like a drink?" she asked hesitantly.

"Yes, I think I have one of these beers," he replied, picking up a can.

He opened it and gazed inquisitively around the room. As he narrowed his eyes to adjust to the lack of light he settled his gaze on his quivering tenant.

"No need be scared me, Nellie. I come see you, help you," he said.

"That's very kind of you, but I don't need any help. I'm shaking because I thought someone was breaking in," she replied.

"I think you do need help. A little bit anyway," he said slyly, "You said you need more money."

"Yes, I did," said Nellie, with alcohol fuelled courage, "I don't think that you pay me very much. After all, I work very hard and long hours too."

"Exactly!" he bellowed, his face contorting with the emphasis, "So I thought we could come to little arrangement."

"A pay rise sort of arrangement?" said Nellie, light headed from the instant result from her plucky bluntness.

"Maybe you do little favour and you not have to pay rent," he said leering openly at her.

"A little favour?" asked Nellie, puzzled.

In explanation, Stav hurled the weight of his considerable size at Nellie and held her in a vice like bear hug. Squashed beneath the power in his arms, Nellie realised the full implication of all that he had said thus far. Trapped by the flesh of his limbs and his torso Nellie's inebriation evaporated. She could feel her heart pumping with dread at the possible outcome of her vulnerable position. The cloying rancid smell of his sweat combined with his stale beery breath clung to her nostrils. She knew she had to think quickly if she were to extricate herself from his clutches. Instinctively, she relaxed her body against his and his reciprocated in the anticipation of her concession to his desires. Nellie used this animal response to push him away with all her might. He toppled backwards, losing his balance and fell against the corner of the table. As he crashed down to the floor, Nellie stared aghast at the grisly distorted body lying in front of her.

She could see a red patch emerging from the back of his head onto the dirty brown carpet and nausea rose in her throat. Deftly and swiftly she rushed passed him grabbing at her belongings as she went. Picking up her two new laundry bags, she stuffed them full with everything she owned and as she hurried, for the last time, past the coffee table she swept in the bottles and cans and with them, the precious photograph of her two dear children. Nellie gasped with fright as her attacker emitted a long, loud groan. Running towards the open front door, she turned to see him stirring and plunged down the stairs and out onto the street.

Once outside, her head cleared with the coolness of the air. She strode intuitively in the direction of the tube station. The bright lights of the cavernous hall dazzled her and she came to a standstill in front of the ever changing timetables. Staring up at them she saw the central clock which was telling her that it was ten twenty five. Momentarily, she was frozen by her disorientation. The time was meaningless. Was it night or was it day? Why was she here?

"It's dark, it's night time," she reassured herself softly. Then she remembered the bleeding body she had left lying on the floor.

Was he dead? Was she a murderer?

"No he moved. He made a noise," she told her rapidly beating heart.

Then she remembered her new friend William and tried to recall which route they had taken on Sunday to the Embankment. She had no idea where to begin and as she stood alone gripping her bulky laundry bags, despair engulfed her. Huge unwelcome tears started to fall from her eyes and she turned away from the board. She sat on a nearby seat and tried to find a tissue in her chaotic bags. Spasmodically, she let out choking sounds as she attempted to control the relentless sobs that continued to well up inside. A hand appeared in front of her and Nellie screamed.

"I'm so sorry, I didn't mean to frighten you," said a quietly spoken woman, "I was holding out a tissue. You appeared to be having trouble finding one," she continued calmly.

"Oh dear," said Nellie, "I just don't know what's the matter with me. I don't seem to be able to stop crying. You see I'm lost and I can't work out which way to go."

"OK, so where is it that you need to get to?" said the woman kindly.

"I've got this friend, you see. His name is William. He is a gentleman and he lives on the Embankment. He'll help me I know he will but I can't seem to remember how to get there."

"Well that's not so difficult," said the lady patiently, "If I show you how to get to the Embankment by tube, will you be alright once you get there? It's quite late now, you know."

Her voice was soothing and the more she spoke, the more composed Nellie became until her involuntary sobs had all but ceased.

Nellie considered the question carefully, "Yes, that's a good idea. Once I get to the station I will know where to go. My friend lives very near to the station. We walked there on Sunday but now I've forgotten how we got there."

As they made their way to the underground, Nellie's rescuer introduced herself as Mary.

"My name is..." she hesitated, "Nellie, my name is Nellie."

Mary guided Nellie gently by the elbow to the ticket office and bought a single ticket to Embankment station.

She passed it to Nellie waving her hand in dismissal when Nellie rustled in her bags to find the money to reimburse her.

"No, hold on to your money, Nellie. It didn't cost much anyway. Now you need to go down that escalator there," she pointed ahead, "Promise me you will be OK when you get there."

"Yes, Mary I will, I promise," she responded far more confidently than she felt, "And thank you so much for your kindness, goodbye."

"Goodbye, Nellie. Take care." and she waved as she watched Nellie make her way uncertainly down the moving stairs.

Nellie tried to be as inconspicuous as possible on the tube, attempting to squash the plastic bags under her legs as she sat terrified of meeting anyone's gaze. The carriage was packed with late night revellers and theatre goers. The mixture of smells from unwashed bodies, strong perfume combined with garlic and alcohol as it was breathed into the finite atmosphere gave Nellie a light headed sensation. She was glad to leave them all behind as she cautiously stepped through the automatic doors on to the platform. The heavy odours were blown from her by the warm dusty air that replaced the train as it disappeared down the tunnel. She moved along with the thinning crowds until she was outside in the cold air of the night. In her confused state she had been worried that once she arrived she still would not be able to find the bench that William called home.

She scrutinised her surroundings carefully and on recognising the bridge, she breathed a sigh of relief and started to climb its steps. She pulled her coat nearer to her shivering frame as the cruel wind swirled around her at the top of the stairs. Walking across the river, she felt a sense of freedom she had not experienced before. She was glad to be away from the greasy cafe and its lascivious owner. She hoped that he was not too badly hurt, but felt no remorse. Angry to have found herself in yet another vulnerable situation, she resolved to be more cautious in the future. Descending from the bridge at the other end, Nellie bounced down the last few steps at the prospect of seeing her friend.

She strode the short way to the bench they had shared the previous Sunday and her heart soared as she saw William's lumpy, sleeping silhouette. She could just about make out the familiar features of his face as he lay softly snoring into his rucksack pillow. He had lined the slats of the bench with cardboard for warmth and comfort. Nellie suppressed the desire to wake him for her own consolation. Instead, she sat at the feet of her resting companion and gazed out across the river.

Nellie stared into the ink black water with its bright light reflections. At that moment she experienced a sense of peace, gained from the knowledge that whatever happened in the future, she would find the strength and courage to survive. The certainty that she would one day see her children again overwhelmed her and she became convinced that her present plight was merely a punishment for her recent recklessness. There she sat until sunrise, secure in this simple summation of her life.

The city's activity increased with the dawning of the day and William stirred accordingly. Nellie tapped him gently on the leg as he slowly roused. He peered down at her from the other end of his bed. His hair was tousled and he squinted inquisitively at the source of the unexpected human touch.

"Ah!" he said, scratching his head, "Of all the benches in all the world you had to sit on mine!"

Nellie threw back her head, giving way to peals of mirth at his jocular greeting. She had not laughed since their excursion last weekend and the sensation was strangely unfamiliar but very pleasant. She enjoyed the unexpected release she was experiencing so much that she had trouble controlling her increasingly loud guffaws. With tears of joy rolling down her cheeks, her laughter finally subsided and she said,

"Sorry William, I must have needed that."

"Well I must admit I didn't think it was that funny," he said, smiling, "So then young lady, what's the story? Actually, before you begin, I confess I need to use the local convenient conveniences, so would you mind talking while we are walking?"

"Not at all my dear man," replied Nellie, "In fact that it is a very good plan."

They gathered up all their belongings and trundled along to the public toilets, whilst Nellie told her tale. William was a wonderful listener, gifted with the ability to nod, frown or make appropriate noises throughout her description of the horrors that had befallen her.

When she had finally completed her account of events, he turned to her solemnly and said, "So that's it then young lady. You're out on the streets with me."

"It looks that way William and after that horrible place with that awful man, I believe I don't really mind at this present moment."

"What concerns me in all this is whether...how shall I put this? Whether you are tough enough for this life?"

"There's only one way for me to find out, I suppose," she said, feeling a little disappointed that William had already cast a shadow over her situation to which she felt there was no alternative.

"Do not be downcast, Nellie. There's only one thing for it. I shall have to take you under my wing and show you the ropes. What do you think of that?" he enquired, his blue eyes twinkling with mischief.

Nellie sighed with relief, "I think that's just fine." and they went their separate ways into the twenty four hour toilets.

Nellie stopped in front of the mirror to tidy her hair and realised that she did not have a brush. She smoothed it down tucked it into her coat and went to meet her friend. William was waiting for her holding out his crooked arm.

"William Short, man of honour at your service!" he said and Nellie took his arm lightly as they trailed together through the early morning streets of London.

They chatted companionably until they turned a corner and were amidst the noise and bustle of the fruit and vegetable market. Lorries screeched and then performed hair-raising manoeuvres until they were in an appropriate position for loading and unloading their goods. Loud London male voices monopolised the early morning air, shouting greetings and instructions to each other. Periodically there was an eruption of hilarity which echoed off the surrounding buildings. A little bewildered by all the colourful industry around her, Nellie glanced over at William for reassurance.

"Now for a healthy breakfast, my dear," said William, rubbing his palms with gleeful expectation.

William walked up to one of the stands and waved cheerily at the stall holder.

"Morning William, and who's your new friend?" said a man in his forties with a large paunch and a ruddy face.

"May I introduce you to Nellie? Nellie this is Paul, who often provides me with breakfast, and Paul, this is Nellie, she's new to the area, you know," with that William stood back to allow his two friends to shake hands.

"It's nice to meet you Nellie. There are some apples and oranges in the carton over there, William," he indicated towards a wooden tray containing a mixture of his discarded wares.

"Thank you, so much," replied William. He took Nellie with him to rummage around for the best offerings.

They left the market eating their spoils and William led them both to Hyde Park where they watched the early joggers and finished their breakfast.

"Well that was delicious," said Nellie, who could not remember the last time she had eaten anything healthy.

"Yes, now what we could do with is a good strong cup of coffee to set us up for the morning," said William

"Let me treat you," said Nellie, "I still have some money left and I really fancy a hot drink as well."

They bought two large strong coffees in polystyrene cups and resumed their sojourn in the park. The day was warming up and Nellie began to think that William's way of life might just suit her. When they had finished their coffee and smoked a couple of cigarettes from Nellie's dwindling supply, she decided that if she were to manage on the streets she would need to know where all her possessions were and with this in mind she set about sorting out her bags.

The park was still quiet, so she felt uninhibited as she lay out the various things she had collected over the last couple of weeks. Amongst them, was the Freddie's snowstorm paperweight which made her heart leap but she showed it to William and then wrapped it in a sock and replaced it tenderly inside her rucksack. He admired her well kept garden tools and admitted that he had been a bit of a horticulturist in his time. As she went along she folded her clothes and replaced them in an orderly fashion. By chance, the seaside photograph slipped out onto the ground as she pulled out the remaining contents. Nellie jumped up and grasped at it in a frenzied attempt to prevent it from blowing away.

William watched her closely and then asked to see the picture which she readily showed him saying, "These are my two children, Freddie and Daisy. We were on holiday as you can see," she said.

"Well they are handsome, no mistake," he offered.

There was a loud pause. Nellie could not bring herself to give any explanation and waited with dread to be asked about them. She did not have the strength to tell him her story but had he enquired she knew that she would have to be truthful.

William however, merely said, "I think that a picture as important as that requires some protection, don't you young lady?"

"What do you mean?" asked Nellie, glad of the diversion.

"An envelope, dear girl, an envelope," he replied, picking up his rucksack from under the bench, "I think I have just the thing, now wait a minute, yes here it is. I knew it would come in handy one day," and he handed her an unused white envelope.

"Now put it away in a place, remember where it is and I will test you later," he continued.

Nellie gratefully followed his instructions and just as she was about to put the remaining vodka and beer back, she stopped and said, "Let's toast my new circumstances."

The two of them sat and raised William's enamel mugs in the air several times until the drink was all gone but they were left with its warm, golden glow. They sat there until nature called and they moved off in the direction of William's next port of call in his itinerary designed for Nellie's instruction on the how to survive the rigours of outdoor life. Thus William and Nellie embarked on their adventures together, arm in arm undeterred by the weight of their goods and chattels.

* * *

During her first year on the streets of London, Nellie kept close to William. She felt safe with him and he reliably imparted all the information that he had learnt on how to cope with the severity of homelessness. Initially, he had introduced her to the charitable homeless centres and Nellie knew that he secretly believed she was too fragile to weather the brutality of her situation. She was glad that he had because she was able to visit these places when she felt worn down by the discomfort of the pavements, doorways and benches.

She had asked William early on, why it was that he did not accept more of what was on offer in these places. He had replied that he liked to be his own man and that he no longer believed that he was rehabilitation material. Thinking this a bit extreme she tried to encourage him to come along with her when she visited for a meal and a shower, and sometimes for a bed for the night. Occasionally, he would join the seemingly endless but remarkably orderly queue for an overnight stay, but more often than not, he would take himself down to the Embankment after dropping her there. Like clockwork, he would be there in the morning as Nellie fresher for her sound sleep and a shower bounded energetically down the steps with her large carrier bags, to his crooked elbow.

She always asked if he had managed to sleep the night before and he would answer, "Like a baby, my dear, like a baby," and off they would go eager to see what the day might bring.

As time went by, Nellie understood more clearly, William's view on the matter. By then she had experienced various attempts from the delightful staff and volunteers to interest her in her own self improvement. Nellie was curious to hear what was on offer and still far too polite to prevent them from trying. One of Nellie's greatest hindrances was her absolute refusal to tell anyone her tale. On the advice of one of the hostel workers, she spoke to a woman from social services who enabled her to apply for and to receive benefits. For this, Nellie had to be very careful not to tell the whole story of her downward spiral resulting in her life on the streets. She was unhappy about being economical with the truth, but she could not overcome the seemingly impossible hurdle created by her shame.

Nellie was immensely grateful to all the people who helped her, but she became uncomfortable if there were any restrictions made on her. In order to secure a bed for the night it was necessary to start in the afternoon for any chance of being allocated one for the same night. There was also a ten o'clock curfew, which was a very early hour for someone who more often than not had to wait until around one or two o'clock for the evening crowds to die down before positioning the cardboard and covers which were to be her bed. So it was that she joined William in what he laughingly called his specialised status as an 'entrenched' homeless person.

There was an aspect of this nomadic way of life that Nellie had not envisaged. It was the hours of the day during which she was not absorbed in the business of survival and she found herself usually with William at her side, wondering what on earth they were to do. Their meagre income, obtained from their benefits, usually ran out in the first few days however hard they tried to budget. Therefore, their amusement needed to cost nothing.

The advantage of running out of money was that they were relatively clear headed after the first forty eight hours without alcohol and initially, at Nellie's request, they visited all the art galleries and museums that were free to the public. She was careful to plan these excursions on days after she had spent a night in a bed and more importantly, had been able to take a shower. Sometimes, she was able to leave her bags for a few hours.

* * *

One day, as they were visiting the National Gallery together, she was feeling particularly thankful to be clean and unencumbered and she said to her companion,

"See I can pass as a normal human being!"

William stopped, and twisted round to face her. He held her lightly but firmly by the shoulders and said, "You are a normal human being. Please don't say such things. You will do irreparable damage to your soul and far worse than that, my dear, you will make me cry," and as he let go of her and turned away she could see the tears welling up in his eyes.

They sat in front of Van Gogh's Sunflowers whilst Nellie anticipated the elevation of spirit that the painting always promised. The flowers shone from the canvas and filled the vast room and her heart with joy. She held on to the moment for as long as possible and then they moved on to the other chambers.

Nellie was reintroduced to the game of chess which was a preoccupation of a number of homeless people that she met both in the refuges and on the streets. William had a magnetic board enabling them to set up a game at any time and in any place. She had played as a child and remembered teaching her own children the rudimentary moves of the pieces and the general aim but their interest waned if they were not winning. When she was a child, she had spent many an hour playing against her brothers who were all very adept at the game and she hailed her occasional success as victory indeed. Now, with waves of ennui stretching before them, absorption in the game was welcome.

Early on, Nellie became reacquainted with the competitive streak of her youth and took the game to the point of obsession in her attempts to be vanquisher. She suffered an extraordinary plummeting of mood if she sensed that William had the upper hand early on and occasionally would knock over her king when realistically, she still had a chance of winning. Overall, the two of them enjoyed their competitions and they happily whiled away the hours in their pursuit of checkmate.

Their relationship became established and they were known as friends by their street compatriots who occasionally made gentle fun of their fondness for one another. One hot June afternoon, they were engaged in their second chess game of the day, primarily, because Nellie had lost the first one and wanted a chance to depose William from his throne of glory. They were sitting on 'William's' bench on the Embankment and the early evening sun was casting sparkling stars on the water's uneven surface. It was not going well for her. Her defences were all but down and she could see that William was not about to relinquish the chess crown. In a fit of irritation and spite she picked up the small board and flung it like a Frisbee in front of her. They both watched aghast as it flew with the pieces attached, much further than Nellie had anticipated, into the river.

Nellie put her hand up to her mouth in dismay as William turned to her, bewildered and asked angrily, "What on earth did you do that for?"

Nellie sat shamefacedly gazing into the Thames, as if by doing so, she could rectify the situation. She still felt cross because of her earlier imminent defeat and could not bring herself to apologise. William sat staring at her for a few more moments and then stood up shaking his head and shuffled away with his rucksack.

Nellie, still gripped by pique did not watch him walk away. Instead, she fixed her eyes on the buildings on the north bank of the river, feeling justified in her action. She remained seated until the shadows grew longer and the warmth of the day was replaced by a chill breeze. William and Nellie rarely quarrelled and on the odd occasions when they disagreed on something one or other would concede and they would promptly resume their customary affable rapport. This was different. Nellie now knew that what she had done was foolish and could no longer recapture her previous self-righteousness. She was sorry and wanted to express her contrition to her dear friend but he had not returned and she did not know where to start looking for him. She heard Big Ben strike nine o'clock and decided that she would go to St Martin's in the Field to see if they had a bed for the night. It was late but in summertime there was less demand for them and it would give her a purpose while she mulled over the problem of finding William.

She stood up, gathering her bulging bags and plodded reluctantly in the direction of the hostel. She was desolate without her friend and rehearsed several variations of an apology in her head as she walked the darkening city streets. She began to torture herself with the possibility of having destroyed their relationship with her childish tantrum. By the time she reached the church she was in a highly anxious state and wished that she had enough money to buy some alcohol. As she walked through the doors she had resolved to ask one of the kind volunteers if perhaps they would lend her five pounds until benefit day. She was pleased to see Anna who had been working there for three years and who seemed to have a fondness for Nellie. Nellie took a deep breath and plucking up just enough courage, made her request.

"Oh," said Anna, "You know we are not supposed to do that. Anyway, if I did lend you some money could you honestly say that you wouldn't spend it on drink?"

"No I don't suppose I could," said Nellie, feeling cross again and slightly humiliated by the experience.

"I'll tell you what, Nellie. Why don't you stay the night? Go and have a shower. I will find you a change of clothes and then maybe we could have a cup of tea and a fag together. You can tell me your latest news. How's William, by the way?" she asked, having already noted his absence.

"Ah," replied Nellie, looking crestfallen, "I think I may have upset him. In fact, I know I have upset him and now I'm really worried that he might not want to be my friend anymore."

"I see," said Anna thoughtfully, "Well, let's stick to the plan and when I make you a cuppa you can tell me all about it. I'll see if there is any bread left in the kitchen. Would you like a sandwich with your tea?"

The mention of food reminded Nellie that she was indeed hungry and she nodded enthusiastically as she went off for her shower.

Later that evening, she sat with Anna and explained her bad behaviour to her. As she did so she realised how deeply upset she was about the incident and how she would never intentionally want to hurt William. He was such a dear, gentle man who had done nothing but try to look after her ever since they had first met. The prospect of losing him made her feel afraid and big tears started to roll down her cheeks as she sat sipping her tea.

"Now, now Nellie, I'm sure everything will be OK, you mark my words. It's getting late now. How about you go and have a sleep and then in the morning it will all seem different."

Nellie trudged reluctantly to the bed she had been allocated. She tied her boots to the leg of the bed and bundled her possessions under the head end of the bed so that she would hear if anyone tried to steal them in the night. She recalled wistfully that it was William who had taught her these necessary tricks of survival and lay gazing sadly at the peeling paintwork on the ceiling. She listened to the discordant orchestra of sleeping noises and thought that she would never be able to sleep. As she listened, her mind drifted back to her children and their sweet fresh smell when she tucked them in at night and she slept more peacefully than she had for weeks.

She awoke early feeling rested and optimistic about finding her chum. She planned to go back down to the Embankment to see if he had returned there for the night, and failing that, she would try Berwick Street Market where he may have gone for a healthy breakfast. She leapt down the steps and onto the pavement nearly crashing into William who was standing in front of her with a wide grin on his face and an apple in each hand.

"Oh William!" she exclaimed, "I thought I had lost you."

She kissed him loudly on the cheek.

"You would have to try a lot harder than that, my dear," he retorted, chuckling throatily.

"I'm very sorry," said Nellie, turning pink and glancing down at her feet.

"So am I, my dear, so am I."

With that, he handed her an apple, crooking his arm for her to hold and they set off down the warm summer morning streets of London.

151

Nellie never again lost her temper with William. On the occasions where he could see that she was beginning to show signs of irritability he would put his head on one side and raise one eyebrow and say, "Just remember the terrible incident of the chessboard in the river!" This was always enough for both of them to burst out laughing, by which time Nellie had lost any desire to show her anger.

* * *

One day in August the following year, William met Nellie outside the hostel where she had spent the night. They made their way to the Victoria Gardens on the Embankment to enjoy their fruit breakfast which William had collected earlier from his friend at the market. While they were mulling over the possibilities of the day ahead, William seemed restless and eventually her turned to Nellie and said,

"I was talking to Paul this morning," he cleared his throat before he continued.

"Oh yes," said Nellie, "How is he?"

"He's very well. I was chatting to him about what we do during the day and how what we do can seem well, a bit repetitive. He laughed when I said that and asked me if I thought it was any different for him! Anyway, I digress, what I wanted to tell you was that he made a suggestion about something we could do. I would only think about it if you were interested because I wouldn't want to leave you in London on your own," he paused, looking at Nellie who was starting to feel apprehensive about some, as yet, unnamed threat to her security.

"What do you mean? Are you thinking of moving on?" she asked.

She had known a number of her fellow homeless acquaintances who had moved to different areas for a variety of reasons. Some of them took time away from the city to sell the 'Big Issue' in provincial towns, believing that it was easier to do so outside London because the competition was less. These people would return to their original bed places and woe betide anyone who had dared to gazump their doorway in their absence. Others moved on to follow a partially formulated plan based on the hazy notion that happiness may be found in a new environment. These adventures usually met with little success. Those who had conceded to the offers of rehabilitation were often not seen again on the streets, but as Nellie reminded herself, she had only been around for about eighteen months, not years as had William. She did not know if she had the courage to move away but she was quite sure that her itinerant life would prove to be unbearable without her friend by her side.

"No, no, not moving on as such, just taking a little holiday," he reassured her.

"Now William, you are normally such a practical man. Have you lost your marbles and completely forgotten the small matter of money. We don't have any!" she replied, comforted that his plans may just be a fantasy.

"Ah well, that's the clever thing about my plan, though I have to admit it was Paul's idea. He said, "Why don't you and Nellie go fruit picking in September? It would be a change of scenery for a month or so and you could earn some money. It's not much but it's better than nothing." What do you think, my dear? After all it was a gruelling winter last year and I thought it might be a nice thing to do to do before it gets cold again," he finished, stopping to glance at Nellie in order to gauge her response.

Nellie had listened carefully to his words and was considering the unpleasant winter weather they had suffered. There had been a great deal of competition for the better doorways in town but the drawback was that they were not really 'available' until the clientele of the theatres and restaurants had begun their journeys home.

Nellie had found it more frightening and often, following William's advice, had succumbed to the relative comfort of a bed in a hostel. She had also been amazed at the importance that was given to cardboard which had such great insulating qualities. Nellie had actually seen it used as a form of currency on the more bitter nights. A can of Tenants Extra for a large piece of a box seemed a strange but logical transaction. Nellie often asked herself which could give the greater comfort but never found a satisfactory answer.

The prospect of a jaunt away to pick fruit for a few weeks was sounding promising and she asked,

"How would we get there? Fares are much too expensive for the likes of us."

"Paul has kindly offered to take us in his van but he stipulates that we must reduce our baggage to one smallish bag each," William replied, playfully raising one eyebrow at Nellie.

Nellie's mouth curled into a broad smile and she said,

"I think it's a wonderful idea. It'll be like a holiday, just to get away from all this," she said, making a sweeping movement with her hand.

She stopped, looked up at her friend and said, "Well actually, this bit isn't too bad but you know what I mean. When shall we go then?"

"The next lot of picking starts at the beginning of next week, so we can go then if you want to," responded William.

"Monday?"

"Monday it is then," and they fell into a happy silence both thinking about the possibilities of their holiday.

Nellie had considered the problem of the contents of her bags and finally went to the hostel to seek out Anna. Anna had become very fond of Nellie and was delighted that she had an opportunity to go away with William.

"You know we are not really supposed to do that," she said when Nellie asked if it would be possible to store her belongings at the hostel while she was away.

Nellie smiled up at her beseechingly in the knowledge that Anna would do her very best to help her with her baggage dilemma. Anna prefaced most of her responses to Nellie's requests in this way but had always found a way to assist her in the past. She knew that Nellie was not a demanding character and that her desires were not unreasonable. She also benefited from their late night chats over a cup of tea when the other hostellers were raising the roof tops with their snores. So it was that Anna secreted the remains of Nellie's possessions into the back of a cupboard that was kept under lock and key. Nellie had considered cancelling their journey were it not possible to find this storage and in her delighted gratitude, she promised Anna the pick of the crop on their homecoming.

"Just get back in one piece," said Anna, laughing as she waved her off.

CHAPTER SIX

Jack's Farm

On the day, Nellie and William stood, waiting eagerly at the exit of the fruit market for Paul to pack up his van and pick them up to start the drive down to Kent. He bundled them both in and was relieved as he did that they smelt fresh for the journey. It had been Nellie who had insisted that William also stayed in the hostel the previous night so that they could make full use of the washing facilities and start the day with a good breakfast.

Nellie was bubbling with excitement and insisted that they sing.

"It's a long way to Tipperary, it's a long way to go!" she bellowed out tunelessly while the two men chortled at her enthusiasm.

When she had settled down and realised that they were less keen to join in than she had previously thought, she gazed out of the window waiting for the greyness of London to turn to green in the sunlight.

Meanwhile, William had struck up conversation with Paul who lived quite near to the picking farm to which he was to deliver his charges.

"It's only a few miles away from us and my missus suggested that it might be a bit of a break for the two of you," he explained.

"So she knows about us then?" asked William.

"Oh yes, she often asks after you," he replied, and caught William smiling smugly at the thought of his notoriety.

"Which reminds me," he continued, "She has lent you both a tent and two sleeping bags."

"Well," declared William, overcome by the thoughtfulness of a woman he had never met, "Such benevolence, my dear chap, such benevolence. Please convey my deep felt gratitude to your good wife."

Smiling at William's grandiosity, Paul said, "Well you can keep the sleeping bags, but we'll have the tent back when you have finished. The kids play with it in the garden,"

"Of course, my dear man, and we will treat it with the utmost respect," said William.

Nellie had been listening to the men talking. She was overwhelmed by the humanity shown by the couple and had to suppress an unexpected waft of emotion which threatened to bring tears to her eyes. They travelled in silence for a while and, as promised, the cityscape transformed into countryside. The fields of waving golden corn and the meadows of grazing sheep and cows brought with them memories of Nellie's children. She recalled the occasional long car journeys where they had played 'I spy' until the farm animals had appeared on the horizon and for a while their emergence was stimulation enough and peace would subsequently prevail.

"Not far to go now," said Paul merrily interrupting the stillness of his passengers.

Trepidation suddenly gripped Nellie and she asked nervously, "What if they don't think we are suitable?"

"Don't worry Nellie, I know the bloke that runs the place. He's expecting you both. I spoke to him only the other day," reassured Paul.

This allayed her fears somewhat but when they finally arrived at the farm, Paul deposited them at the gate with their bags and turned to wave as he drove off.

Seeing their forlorn faces he stopped the van abruptly and alighted saying, "OK, I'll take you in and introduce you to Jack. Will that help?"

They nodded as he marched them into the wooden shack which was adorned with various colourful signs about 'Pick you own" fruit and was situated just inside the gate.

"Hi," said Paul, to a woman sitting on a chair surrounded by large empty baskets.

"Hello, can I help you?" she replied, continuing to move the vessels around.

"Is Jack about?" he asked.

"He's up at the house. Who's asking?" she answered, eyeing his bedraggled companions with suspicion.

Noticing her disparaging glances, Paul retorted defensively,

"He's expecting us. I think I'll drive up to the house."

The woman shrugged her shoulders and said,

"If you want," and went back to her work

William and Nellie glanced at each other secretly feeling terribly pleased that Paul was taking all this trouble to get them settled. Up at the farm house a large, confident red-faced man answered the door which when it was opened emitted a glorious smell of baking bread.

"Jack, these are my friends William and Nellie. Do you remember I phoned you about them a few days ago?"

"Oh yes, the fruit pickers. Do you want to take them to the camp site so they can get settled in?" and he shook hands with the two of them.

Paul glanced down at his watch and said,

"OK, but I had better hurry. I came up here because Nellie was worried that you might not want her as a fruit picker on your farm."

"Oh I see, pre-picking nerves is it?" he asked her boisterously.

"Yes something like that," she replied self consciously, regretting her earlier foolish fears, "Just point us in the right direction and we'll be alright from here."

Jack told them the start and finish time for their work the next day and informed them that there was a nice little pub adjacent to the camp site.

"See you in the morning!" they called out to their new employer as Paul guided them both by the shoulders onto the necessary path.

"Thank you," said Nellie, looking up at the big kind man.

"Here you are," he said, thrusting a twenty pound note in her hand as he walked away.

"B-but..." she stammered.

"No buts, enjoy! I'll see you in a month. Same time, same place!" With that he made his way back to his van to drive home and pick up his children from school.

Nellie and William meandered down the track that led to the free camp site provided for the seasonal fruit pickers. The first job they had was to construct their tent. There were no convenient doorways in which to shelter when the rain fell from the skies and they were both aware of the necessity for cover if they were to start work at eight o' clock. Unfortunately, neither of them was adept at the task and amidst a muddle of canvas and tent pins, Nellie started to become frustrated.

William glanced over at her with his raised eyebrow and she said rattily, "I know, I know, the chessboard and all that," and she started to smile impishly as she went on to say, "However, old chap, if the Thames were in front of me now I would not hesitate to hurl the whole lot into its murky depths!"

"Good job it isn't then, is all I can say," he muttered, fiddling unconstructively with the unyielding equipment which lay before him.

"I know," said Nellie, "Why don't we go and try the pub that Jack told us about? We might meet some fellow pickers who know a little more than us about this tent business."

"Not a bad idea, my dear," and he held out his arm for her, "Do you think they'll sell a spot of cider seeing as this is apple country?"

"I think they might," replied Nellie and they strolled together towards the pub, their pace quickening as it came into view. Neither Nellie nor William had visited a pub for a long time but they felt that they could mingle with the best of them now that they were away from the London where no-one knew them. They were both relieved that they had taken the trouble to smarten themselves up before embarking on their adventure. They entered the doors of the quaint country inn with confidence and were instantly drawn to the gleam of the bottles behind the bar with its polished brass fittings.

"Good evening," said the dark haired, bespectacled man standing behind the bar polishing the handle of one of his pumps.

"Good evening," replied William, "And what delights have you to tempt us with?"

"Local cider, very tasty," he said without hesitation.

"Two pints," returned William with equal certainty.

"Are you down here for the picking season?" asked the barman, conversationally.

"We are indeed," replied William, warming to the man. "This is our first time."

"Well there are some fellow pickers over there. Would you like me to introduce you to them?"

"Yes that would be good of you."

With that, he carried the two full pint glasses round the bar and to a long table in the corner of the pub which was surrounded by a lively group of people of varying ages, shapes and sizes.

He turned to William and Nellie and asked, "And your names are?"

"William."

"Nellie."

"Hello pickers, please welcome William and Nellie to your merry band," he placed the glasses carefully on beer mats and turned to them saying,

"My name is George."

"Thank you George," they chorused and sat down at the table in front of the glasses of cider.

"This is all very friendly, don't you think, my dear?"

"I do, old chap, cheers!" said Nellie, and as they raised their glasses to each other the rest of the table joined them in a resounding, "Cheers!"

As the evening wore on and Nellie's fears fell away from her with the city dust, she began to feel the possibilities of life once again. The disparate group of fruit pickers included healthy brown youngsters who allured the rest of the party with their ebullience, enticing them to share the hopeful promise to which only they held the key. Nellie found herself joining in with the increasingly hilarious banter, noticing that the younger members seemed to have acquired a natural leader.

This tall, dark haired individual had large, facial features rendering him almost ugly. This he countered with a wit and magnetism so powerful that the young girls appeared to be listening to his every word and watching each considered movement he made. Nellie had made them laugh earlier by recounting her and William's attempts to erect their wilful tent and as the bell for last orders rang out he came over to Nellie and held out his hand.

"Hi, my name's Connor. I heard your story about the tent and wondered if you would like some help putting it up? I think it may rain tonight and you wouldn't want to be catching a cold before your first day in the fields, now."

Nellie looked up into his dark eyes as his lilting Irish brogue drew her in. She instantly understood the fascination he held for the girls.

Shyly, she replied, "Yes, we really need some help. I didn't think that it could be so complicated."

"OK, let's go then," said Connor, gently guiding Nellie with a hand on her shoulder.

William stood up unsteadily and followed them out onto the unlit path which led to the site. As they walked along side by side, Connor asked her where she came from and why she had decided to come to this particular farm. Nellie responded as best she could. She did not have a coherent explanation and was fearful, as always, of probing questions about her past. Fortunately, he appeared to lose interest as she fumbled for words to answer his enquiries and they were both distracted by the crash and groaning of William falling into an unseen bramble bush. Connor immediately took out a torch from his pocket and shone it at the flailing body.

"Keep still, old man," said Connor, "You'll make it worse. Here give me your hand and I'll pull you out."

As he grabbed William's hand and successfully disentangled him from his snare, William muttered,

"I'll have less of the old man if you don't mind!"

"William! Don't be so ungrateful," reproved Nellie sharply.

"Well, I tripped," he said, and added grudgingly, "Thank you, I suppose I was a bit stuck."

He brushed the undergrowth from his clothing and staggered along between Nellie and Connor as they held his arms. Connor set about the construction of the unassembled tent and presented them both with adequate sleeping quarters within minutes. He rubbed the palms of his hands together to remove the dirt and said,

"There you go, can you manage from here?"

"Thank you so much," said Nellie, "Yes, we've got our sleeping bags and stuff. Could you give us a shout in the morning? I'm a bit worried we might oversleep."

"Yep! I'll do that. Sweet dreams," and he strode away waving his hand as he went.

"I don't trust that young man," said William, shaking his head, "I don't know what it is about him but I don't like it whatever it is."

This damning verdict was unlike William and took Nellie by surprise.

"What on earth are you talking about? He just helped you out of a bush! What more do you want?"

Later that night, Nellie lay looking up at the moon shining through the canvas roof. William was snoring earnestly beside her and she thought about Connor. He seemed so gentle and concerned about her welfare. Could it be that he actually liked her? She felt grateful that she had been able to leave her baggage in the hostel and in her unencumbered state thought that perhaps she would be able to blend in to this new world. As she had when she first went to London, she again felt the security of her anonymity which seemed to invite her to act extemporaneously. She slept peacefully and awoke to the sound of Connor's distinctive lilt informing them of the time and the weather from the door flap of their tent.

During their first week on the farm, William and Nellie formed a routine whereby they were able to perform the strenuous work expected of them, eat, sleep and spend a couple of hours in the local pub. The exertion took its toll on William and Nellie. They ensured that they did not stay too late, enabling them both to have adequate sleep in preparation for the day ahead.

By Friday, they were both exhausted and looking forward to the weekend. They had the option of working on Saturday, but Nellie, concerned about her friend's wellbeing, insisted that the two of them took a break. They were paid daily at piecework rates which suited them both. Nellie enjoyed having enough money to eat and drink without worrying about it running out and William had secreted some of his earnings at the foot of his rucksack, "For a rainy day."

The weather had been fine all week and they were both sporting healthy suntans. Nellie loved the rhythm of the work in the fields, unperturbed by the strength it required. It seemed like such a long time since she had worked on the earth and she wondered if this unforeseen heaven would have to end. She was constantly aware of the whereabouts of Connor, but she told herself that she was foolish to think that he would have any amorous interest in her, not least because of his ever present entourage of young, beautiful girls.

Unlike the rest of the pickers, Connor had an old Volkswagen camper van which was parked on the edge of the camp site. Every evening, she would see the girls knocking on the sliding door which he would open leaning out with his curly dark hair blowing in the breeze and greeting them with his charming, white smile. Despite herself, Nellie felt a pang of jealousy each time she witnessed this and would turn away and pretend to be otherwise occupied.

On the Friday night, Nellie washed and tried to find a less utilitarian outfit to wear in celebration of the ensuing two days of freedom. She had packed the gypsy outfit she had bought the day before she started work in the cafe nearly eighteen months previously. It was torn in places but she trusted that the overall effect could still work. William greeted her as she returned from the women's showers,

"What a sight for sore eyes, my dear,"

"Do I look OK? There are no mirrors here, so I need to trust your judgement," said Nellie.

"You look fabulous, my dear, absolutely fabulous," and he gave a chesty chuckle.

William had also made an effort with his appearance. He wore his tweed jacket with a yellow silk cravat which had seen better days and the pork pie hat that he had been wearing the day he had met Nellie outside the launderette.

"You don't look so bad yourself!" laughed Nellie.

William held up his arm for Nellie to hold and they sauntered down to the village, soaking up the fading sunlight.

Nellie sensed a tension in the air of the smoke filled bar. They were not alone in dressing for the occasion and a strong acrid smell assaulted her nostrils as she traversed the room with her companion. She recognised it as a combination of perfumes and aftershaves some of which on their own were pleasant but blended in this eclectic fashion were quite noxious. As she prepared to sit on a bar stool and order their drinks, she heard a familiar voice.

"Hello there, you scrub up well," Connor remarked, immediately luring Nellie into the depths of his eyes.

"Thanks," said Nellie, blushing, "Do you want a drink?"

"No you're alright, I've got one here," he looked down at a full glass of cider in front of him.

"So what have you and the old boy got planned for the weekend then?" he asked.

"We're going to explore the countryside," she replied, feeling ashamed that she had not reprimanded him for the derogatory way in which he spoke about William.

"Very nice too," he said, "If you are around tomorrow night, would you like to come over to the van? Maybe we can get to know each other a bit better," he continued, his eyes sparkling with mischief.

"What just me?" said Nellie nervously.

"Well yes, maybe pop over when the old codger is asleep." And with that, he grasped his drink and swung round to join the girls, most of whom had been watching him whilst he was talking to Nellie.

"What did he want?" said William tersely, taking the pint of cider that Nellie held out to him as he arrived. He had been engrossed in conversation with an elderly lady sitting in the corner enjoying her bottle of stout.

"He was only asking how we were getting on with the fruit picking," she said, alarmed at how the lie tripped so easily off her tongue.

"I don't trust him," said William.

"So you said," replied Nellie crossly, "Anyway, let's not ruin the evening before it has begun. Who was that lady you were talking to?"

"Oh, let me introduce you to her. She knows the area quite well. She might have some good suggestions for our day out tomorrow."

William regained his normal sunny demeanour as he introduced her to Rita, who was proud to proclaim that at eighty years old she was the oldest fruit picker on the farm. She was from Antrobus in Cheshire and had spent the last thirty years travelling up and down the country sometimes for months on end, but always returning to her cottage in the village.

"My husband died when I were fifty and my son died in a farm accident when he were a teenager," she explained in her broad northern accent.

Ignoring their mutterings of "Oh dear," and I'm so sorry, she continued, "So I thought, 'Rita, you can spend the rest of your life feeling sorry for yerself or you can do something interesting.' Well the house were paid for so I only needed enough money to feed misself and a bit extra so I started to do seasonal work wherever I could get it. I stayed fairly local at first, but then I got braver and I found myself in all sorts of places. Some of them nicer than others mind.

I always go home to my little cottage for a few months in a year. I have a neighbour who keeps an eye on it for me; not that there's anything to steal mind; just to make sure that there aren't any leaks or the like." She paused and took a sip from her glass.

William stood up and asked her, "Would you like another drink, Rita?"

"No, that's me lot, one bottle of stout after work and two on Friday. Anymore and I'll forget me name," she cackled.

As William made his way to the bar, Rita glanced over at Nellie and enquired, "And what about you, young lady? Where are your children?" Nellie, who had begun to smile at being described as a young lady, let her face fall abruptly as a stabbing pain rose from her belly at the mention of Daisy and Freddie. For a moment she could not speak and then she uttered slowly,

"How do you know that I have children?"

"It's written in your eyes, girl, an absence of light where they once were. Only a shadow, but it's there alright."

She held her gaze while she waited for the answer to her question. Nellie did not know what to do. She had told no-one of the circumstances leading up to the loss of her children and she had no desire to do so now.

As a diversion, she rustled in her shoulder bag and pulled out the envelope containing the happy seaside photograph of the three of them together. She glanced at it briefly as she passed it across the table to the waiting Rita. As she caught sight of the happy faces smiling for the camera, she felt the pang of loss, which though always present in the form of a dull ache, had not caused her such severity of pain for some time. She was shocked by the sense of time slipping away from her. They would be older and bigger by now and maybe there would come a time when she would no longer be able to recognise them. She was called back to the present by Rita's words,

"What a handsome pair they are," and she handed the picture back to Nellie, saying, "Put it away somewhere safe, dear. You wouldn't want to lose it now, would you?"

William arrived back with the drinks just as Nellie was replacing the envelope in her bag.

As he put down the drinks on the table, he commented to Rita, "Yes, they're a credit to her, don't you think?"

"Aye," agreed Rita and said no more on the subject.

Nellie could feel tears welling up in her eyes and after taking a large gulp of cider she rushed off to the toilets to try to staunch their flow. When she returned, William and Rita were having a lively discussion about the various options open for the exploration of the of the surrounding country side.

"Nellie, listen, Rita has been on some walks around these parts and she was saying that one of her favourites was up Ferny Hill, she has even kept the map with the route and everything. What do think, my dear? Shall we blow the cobwebs away? Apparently, the forecast is good, during the day, at least. I was thinking, maybe we could buy some provisions from the village shop and make a day of it." William's face was glowing at the prospect of an adventure and Nellie's spirits rose with his.

"I think it is a fantastic idea. How on earth do you find the time and energy to do all these things, Rita?" she asked.

"Why? Just because I'm an old woman doesn't mean I'm ready to be put out t'grass!" she said, grinning at Nellie's worried expression.

Seeing her smiling eyes, both Nellie and William laughed with her.

"I'll pop over and pick up the map. As a special treat I'll lend you my plastic map holder and you'll look a proper pair of hikers."

"We'll walk back with you, Rita. We'll make an early start tomorrow," said William. As he stepped over the threshold, he paused and waited with both his arms crooked in readiness for the ladies. Nellie twisted round as she went through the doorway and looked in the direction of Connor, who winked at her as she waved. Nellie and Rita took William by the arm and the three of them meandered amiably back to the camping field.

That night, as William lay snoring, Nellie thought about Connor. What could he want from her? She did not dare to think further than walking up to the camper van and knocking on the door. She knew that however much William disapproved, she would not be able to stop herself. She fell asleep and slept soundly, waking early following a dream about Daisy and Freddie. It was a happy dream, set in a time not yet forgotten and instead of the hollowness of loss which usually roused her from such a reverie, she greeted the day with a renewed hope, remembering their day's rambling ahead.

The morning was warm, heating the surrounding vegetation and causing it to emit the thick, sweet smell reminiscent of childhood. They both breathed in its magic recalling their own juvenile memories as they trudged silently through the redolent undergrowth. The route was taking them up a steep incline and the exertion was causing them both to pant.

"Shall we stop soon?" asked Nellie, noticing that William was having trouble catching his breath.

"Yes, my dear, if you feel like you need a bit of a rest. Perhaps we could have a drop of tea from the flask that Rita so kindly lent us," replied William.

"What about here?" said Nellie, pointing to a sheltered alcove in the hillside.

"Ideal!" And they threw themselves down onto the mossy ground and gazed down at the farm below.

"I've always loved being outdoors," said Nellie, "Mind you, it's a good job I do, I suppose."

William laughed and said, "I used to play in the grounds all day long when I was a boy."

"The grounds!" exclaimed Nellie, "Are you secretly a rich person then?"

Nellie realised that despite the time they had spent in each other's company, she knew very little about William. She knew that he had been married and that he had spent many years on the streets of London, but she had no idea how he came to be there. Before she let her curiosity take hold she remembered that she too, had spoken rarely of her past and never of the events leading up to her arrival in King's Cross.

William rubbed his chin and then said cautiously, "I come from a wealthy family, with all the advantages that money and good breeding can offer, but, let's just say, I was a disappointment; to my father, to my mother and later to Kathleen my darling, beautiful wife. I let them all down, one by one and over a long period of time until none could stand my presence any longer. If I was to be considered consistent at anything, it would be at being a disappointment."

"You've never disappointed me, or let me down, come to that," encouraged Nellie.

"That may just be because you have never had any expectations of me," replied William, "Which is not such a bad thing," he added regretfully.

"Well I believe that you are a kind and dear man. Look at this wonderful place you have brought me to. It's perfect. If I could bottle the way I feel now, at this precise moment, so that I was able to open the bottle and breathe in these sensations whenever I felt downcast, I don't think it would be possible to be unhappy again. I would no longer be afraid. I would have enough courage to find my children and then I could share it with them."

"Where are they, Nellie?" he asked softly.

"William, I just don't know. Careless, I know, but I have no idea where I would start looking. I love them so much," she said wistfully and for once she did not feel crippled by the pain of talking about them.

"I know that, my dear," uttered William with kindness in his gravelly voice.

"The moment has gone," said Nellie, "Let's move on."

They gathered their rucksacks and climbed contentedly up the hill, resting occasionally, until they reached the top.

"Wow!" gasped Nellie, "What a view! I didn't think we would really make it. Doesn't it feel like an achievement?"

"Yes, my dear, it does. And I have just the thing to celebrate our not inconsiderable triumph."

"Ooh! What's that then?" said Nellie, waiting with child-like glee to see what William had brought with him. After much fumbling and muttering he said,

"Ah ha! Here we are. Just what the doctor ordered," and he presented Nellie with a flagon of cider and his two enamel cups.

As they sat drinking and congratulating each other on their intrepid feat, the noon day sun beat down on them.

"When I was a child summer days seemed to last forever. I know that it is an illusion, but I like to believe that the days were actually longer than they are now, do you?" asked Nellie whimsically.

"I suppose so," replied William dreamily, "It's a funny thing, though, Nellie, my dear, but somehow I feel more comfortable in London. I've been living there, in the way I do, for such a long time that these open spaces make me nervous. I don't mean that I have an actual phobia or anything; it's just that the buildings, the river, the constant movement of people makes me feel safe. I have a sense of belonging and an understanding of who I am. Does that make any sense to you?"

"Yes it does, but I like the quiet and the space. I feel free out here," she replied, "But I know that we will have to go back in a few weeks, so don't think I am getting ideas beyond my station."

William chortled softly and said,

"I know that, my dear, but I am so glad that you like it here. I thought you would and it's a bit like having a holiday, don't you think?"

"It's a lot like having a holiday," she responded and raised her enamel mug to his and drank its contents, smacking her lips with pleasure as she finished it.

"Oh look," she said, as she picked up the container that William had so considerately carried up the hill on his back,

"We've nearly finished it."

"Oh good," said William, taking the cider and pouring the remainder in to their cups, "That'll be a weight off my shoulders!"

They drunk the dregs as grey clouds moved across the sun.

"Where did they come from?" asked Nellie, "Do you think they're rain clouds?"

"I think they might be, perhaps we had better make tracks," he replied.

They repacked their rucksacks and as they stood up Nellie tittered,

"I had better watch my step. I don't feel altogether sober, do you?"

"Not entirely, my dear, not entirely," he responded and wobbled into a standing position.

They retraced their footsteps, carefully at first and then with increasing confidence as the gradient eased with the descent. Light rain had begun to fall by the time they were half way down becoming increasingly heavy with each step. Eventually, they reached the tent, rainwater dripping from their hair and noses.

"Let's get in the tent and try and get dry," said Nellie seeing William shiver in his soaked shirt. William hesitated and Nellie realised that he wanted some privacy in which to change out of his wringing clothes.

"You go first. I'll wander down to the village and find somewhere to keep dry," she said.

"Wait a moment," he said and bent down to enter the tent through its flap. He came out with some money and pressed it in to her hand saying,

"Buy yourself something to eat and drink, Nellie. I'm all in. I think I'll have an early night." With that he crouched down and disappeared into their canvas home, leaving Nellie clasping the note.

She sloshed slowly towards the houses through the hedge at the end of the now familiar pathway. Pausing at the road, she considered her options for the evening. She remembered Connor's invitation and settled on going to the pub for a couple of drinks so that she might find enough courage to knock on the van door. She could eat there too if she felt hungry. So she rounded the corner and entered the convivial atmosphere of the village local.

It was crammed full of wet, underdressed fruit pickers like herself who by their raucousness must have been there since the rainfall had started. Weaving in and out of the revellers, she made her way discreetly to the bar and ordered a pint of cider and a large whiskey, paying with the note that William had kindly given her. She sat at a table in the corner where she was able to survey the scene without obstruction.

There was no sign of Connor, which was unusual but his attractive entourage were all in a group causing quite a stir with their loud incessant chatter interspersed by piercing screams of laughter. Behind them sat Rita with her single bottle of stout. Nellie waved but she did not see her and so she contented herself with her drinks and her surroundings.

When Nellie had spent all the money, she left the pub and returned to the camp site observing on arrival that the engine of Connor's camper van was running and the lights were on behind the floral curtains covering the windows. Courageous in her cups, she knocked loudly on the door and waited. She heard the bellowing shout of a very angry man from within and instinctively retreated. But the door slid noisily open and Connor stood, leaning on the handle with a broad grin,

"So you decided to come, after all," he stated, inviting her in with a sweep of his arm.

Nellie's heart was pounding with excitement as she climbed into the cramped accommodation. She automatically looked around for the owner of the gruff voice.

"There's no-one here but me," said Connor looking puzzled. With an understanding look, he picked up a dark rectangular object and showed it to his guest.

"I was on the phone," he explained, "People just don't do what you want them to do they?" Nellie remained silent and he showed her to the wooden seat positioned under the windows.

"Cup of tea?" he asked.

"Yes please," answered Nellie.

"So you've earned a bit of money this week then?" he asked.

"Yes, some but I think I've spent most of it already. I'm not very good with money." She gave what she hoped was a coquettish laugh but started choking on the tea that she had inadvertently inhaled in the process. Connor passed her some tissue which he tore off from a toilet roll and passed it to her to wipe the tea she had dribbled from her chin.

"Anyway," he continued, more brusquely than before, "If that's the case I can offer you credit with special terms if you prefer."

"What would I want credit for?" she asked, baffled.

Connor peered at her and said, "Why are you here? I thought you came over to buy something. I have quite a selection at the moment all pure stuff. Coke, skunk, blues to name but a few."

"Drugs?" Nellie's eyes widened, "I don't take drugs."

"So let me ask you again, why are you here?"

"I thought..." and she trailed off.

"You thought what?" asked Connor impatiently. Then the light of comprehension flooded his fleshy features and they contorted in revulsion.

"What? You thought that you and me? But you're a bag lady aren't you? Correct me if I'm wrong, but you are a bag lady?"

Nellie sat with her hands clasped on her knee as he continued to fire angry words at her.

"Have you looked in the mirror lately?" he raised his voice as his wrath mounted, "Perhaps you should," and he thrust a blue, plastic rimmed mirror at her and she took it meekly, overcome with embarrassment.

She dutifully peered into its smeared surface and saw the image of a bloated woman, with blood shot eyes encircled by dark shadows. Her mouth hung open in horror and she could see the unsightly gaps where her teeth had fallen out. She so rarely studied her face that she had forgotten she had lost them. Her hair fell down in untamed clumps around the blotched surface of her loose, lined flesh. She silently handed the treacherous glass back to its owner as she moved falteringly to the door.

Outside, the rain continued to fall and she narrowed her eyes to clear her vision. She spotted the tent, which Connor had helped them put up only a week ago. How on earth could she have been so stupid? She thought of all the pretty young things that listened admiringly to his every word and recalled with a jolt the reflection in the mirror. She pulled open the wet canvas door flap and went in.

William was sleeping fitfully. His limbs were twitching and he shouted in terror at some unseen horror. Then he settled back into his rhythmic, reassuring snoring. It was clammy inside the tent. Nellie wished there was somewhere else for her to go, but she dare not leave the tent for fear of seeing Connor. She shuddered, pulling out various items of clothing from her bag and putting them on. She wriggled into the damp sleeping bag and eventually dozed despite her discomfort. She dreamt a dream where she was still young and was out walking with her old school friend, Jane. They were sniggering as the young men ogled them and whistled. She felt the warm confidence of youth envelope her.

Suddenly, from nowhere, came gruesome grunts and groans. Her heart pounded heavily against her ribs. She awoke to find William flailing his arms in the air and shouting. She shook him,

"William! Wake up! You're having a nightmare."

He opened his eyes but continued yelling,

"Kathleen! Don't go! Please come back!"

"William! It's me, Nellie. What's the matter?" asked Nellie, becoming increasingly concerned for him.

"Ah! There you are! I knew you'd come back. Please don't leave me again Kathleen. You won't leave me will you?"

He clasped Nellie's wrists and she could feel the heat of his body through them. She touched his burning forehead with the back of her hand just as he started to cough uncontrollably. She helped him to sit forward to ease the spasm and when it finally passed she lay him back down gently.

"William, you're poorly, I need to get some help, so please just stay here and I will be back soon."

She left him and ran off to the farmhouse. She beat furiously on the front door, thinking that they would still be asleep, but Jack answered almost immediately, looking freshly washed and dressed.

"Oh, thank goodness you're up!" exclaimed Nellie.

"I am a farmer," said Jack, "This is quite late for me. Now what on earth is the matter?"

Nellie told him and cried with relief, as he took command of the situation and called an ambulance. She ran back down to the tent to sit with William while they waited. The ambulance men did not take long to assess William and decide to take him to the local Accident and Emergency Department.

As they were putting him into the ambulance, Jack, who had remained to oversee the proceedings, handed Nellie a piece of paper and said, "Call me when you know what is going on. Use my address for his details. I have written it on here with my telephone number."

Nellie thanked him and climbed the steps into the ambulance. She sat watching her friend fight for breath while the paramedic gave him oxygen and tried to maintain his consciousness. As they drove along the winding country roads, pitching from side to side, her fear mounted.

"Please, please let him be alright," she said over and over again inside her head, as if by repeating the mantra it would not fail him.

His condition had deteriorated during the journey and he was rushed straight through to the resuscitation area, whilst Nellie sat outside waiting for news. She watched the nurses and doctors bustling purposefully in and out, wondering how she ever managed to work as a nurse. She had found picking apples quite taxing and admired the determination and efficiency of the team around her. Many hours had passed by the time a doctor came out and spoke to Nellie.

"Are you a relative?" he asked.

"No, I'm his friend. He hasn't had any contact with his family for some years," she replied, waiting for the news.

"Would you like to be his next of kin, for now, for our records?"

"Yes I would," said Nellie, thinking that it was a promising request and asked, "How is he? Is he going to be alright?"

"It's a bit early to tell. He has pneumonia and will need big doses of intravenous antibiotics and lots of fluids. I'd say he was stable at the moment. Would you like to go in and sit with him?"

"Yes please!" said Nellie.

She shuffled quickly along the corridor beside the doctor and let him show her to his bed. She thought she had been taken to the wrong bedside at first. She could see nothing in the body or face of the man before her that resembled her dear friend, William. She was about to call the doctor back and tell him so when she caught sight of his wedding ring as she twisted round. It was distinctive because it had their initials engraved on the outside of the band with the indentations of a heart between them.

She picked up his hand and held it for a moment before kissing it and saying, "Come on my friend, you can do it."

She sat holding his hand for hours. The curtains concealing the bed opposite were green with orange whorls. Nellie sat and counted the garish coils, trying to convince herself that if there were a certain amount and she was able to tally this number, everything would be alright again. But the orange began to blur with the green into some ghastly psychedelic effect until she fell asleep with her head resting on the side of the bed.

The nurses came in and out throughout the day and as evening came again, Nellie was jolted awake by the sound of William coughing and trying to push a tube out of his mouth.

"William!" she called and the nurse who had just left his bedside turned around.

She stood over him while his consciousness returned and held the tube as he spat it out. He coughed, spluttered and gasped for breath.

"Where am I?" he asked, in a deeper more gravelly voice than usual.

Nellie explained to him what had happened. He looked as though he was struggling to understand, but he recognised her and squeezed her hand in gratitude.

"Don't you worry about anything right now, dear friend. You just rest and get better, please," instructed Nellie."You gave me a terrible fright, you know."

Overcome with relief and utterly exhausted from the anxiety, Nellie could barely keep her eyes open.

The nurse tapped her on the shoulder and said, "Perhaps you should go home for some rest."

Nellie did not know quite what to do or say. She was not inclined to tell this stranger that she had no home to go to but she was aware that perhaps she should leave William to recover.

Then she remembered Jack's words, "Call me when you know what's going on."

She felt in her pocket and pulled out the piece of paper with his address and telephone number and asked, "Could I use your telephone please?"

"Yes, I'll take you to the ward phone; this one is for emergencies only."

She led her into the ward office, gave her an outside line and left, shutting the door behind her.

"Jack, this is Nellie. He's a bit better now. I thought he was going to die," and with that she broke down into tears.

"OK Nellie, I'll come down and see him. You just wait there."

Jack arrived shortly after the call and following a muffled conversation with the nurse in charge, he approached William's bed.

"Well, you gave us a nasty shock, I'll have you know," he said in a jovial tone.

"Sorry," said William, "It didn't do much for me either." He mustered up a half hearted laugh and then shut his eyes.

"Nellie," said Jack, indicating with his head that he wanted to speak to Nellie out of earshot of her friend. They moved away and Jack continued,

"I've been thinking and since I promised Paul that I would keep an eye on the two of you, I wondered if you would like to stay in our holiday cottage until William is well enough to go back to London? It's vacant at the moment and I don't think living in a tent will do much to aid his recovery."

Nellie's spirits rose at the prospect of having a roof over her head, but she frowned and said, "But Jack, I don't have any money to pay rent or anything," and she gazed down at her dilapidated shoes.

"I thought about that and I have a proposition for you. If you tend our cottage garden and our vegetable patch for the time you are there I will count that as payment enough. Sarah, my wife, has had to help me on the farm with the harvesting and she hasn't had time to do it. Have you ever had any experience in gardening?"

"I have actually. I did a course once and I always really enjoyed working in my own garden. Everything seemed to grow alright, anyway."

"OK, I'll take you back with me tonight and you can get settled in. It will only be temporary, though," he said, "And there is one other thing..."

"What's that?" asked Nellie, looking up at him expectantly.

"Please, no drinking or drunkenness while you are there. Sarah can't abide alcohol and she won't have you there if you are drinking. I had to persuade her as it is," he finished.

"No alcohol it is then," said Nellie smiling.

After Jack had given her a brief tour of the house, Nellie went down to the tent to see if she could salvage any of their belongings. It had not rained since the night before and the tent had almost dried out. She took it down, trying to keep track of the pegs, so that she could give it back to Paul in a reasonable condition.

While she was happily condensing the various items, she looked towards the end of the field and noticed that Connor's camper van was no longer there. She looked around the field to see if he had moved it and to her relief, saw that it had gone. As she was searching for it, she caught sight of Rita waving from the gate. Nellie returned the greeting and beckoned to her to come over. As she approached, Nellie embarked on the tale of William's sudden illness and explained that she was going to stay in the farmer's holiday home.

"The poor old thing," she said, "Please wish him better from me. I'll come up and see him when he gets back. By the way, you missed a right carry on here this morning."

"Why? What happened?" enquired Nellie, looking up from her packing.

"Well, there were sirens and police cars all down t'lane. They took him away," she said, pointing to the space where Connor's van had been parked.

"Really? I wonder how the police knew about him," she said, thoughtfully.

"Well, I'll deny it if anyone asks me, but I told them. I were sick to death of him peddling to all those young'uns. Can't abide drugs and that's a fact," she said, folding her arms for emphasis.

Nellie felt a waft of admiration.

"Well done you!" she said to the old lady who stood grinning mischievously at her.

"I'll see you soon. Mind you look after him well. Lots of rest and good food," and she turned back towards her own tent with a wave of the hand.

Back at the cottage, Nellie sorted through the wet, dirty clothes she had collected and attempted to use the washing machine in the kitchen. When she saw that the laundry was being rotated in soapy water she relaxed and explored the other rooms.

There were two bedrooms with twin beds made up with floral counterpanes and a light pink bathroom with complementary soap and fragrant white towels hanging neatly on a heated rail. Nellie was excited at the thought of staying in such a pretty, clean place and her thoughts naturally turned to a celebration in the form of cider. She remembered the stipulation that she had agreed to only a couple of hours ago and knew that she must not break her word.

She went downstairs into the living room and put on the television. The theme tune to Coronation Street was playing and she sang along to it as she used to with the children.

"Laa la la la la laa!" she laughed and then tears filled her eyes, blurring the screen.

She took a deep breath and tried to concentrate on the plot. She watched the characters and felt as if she was in the warm company of old friends. She watched it to the end and was pleased to have seen it but after visiting the Rovers Return, she found herself thinking about drinking again.

It was not yet dark, so she decided to go for a short walk around the garden. She realised, to her dismay, that she had better not venture near the village for fear of being drawn into the pub. She walked around the simple country garden, pondering when her drinking had become such a problem that only two or three hours after promising not to drink, and with good reason, she was finding it almost impossible to stop herself from running down the road to buy alcohol.

"Well I will just have to find something to occupy me until William is better and then we can have a little tipple to celebrate," she thought, earnest in her intent.

She no longer possessed any books to satisfy her old passion, but she recalled seeing her trowel and hand fork in the bottom of the rucksack. At the time she had questioned why they were there, but now she was glad and went indoors to fetch them. She rummaged in the bag and her hand touched the envelope containing the picture of the children. She could not resist the temptation to take a peek at it, although she expected it to disturb her. She sat on the soft floral covered sofa and held it in front of her. She peered as long and as hard as she could, as if to take away her eyes from their images might make them disappear forever.

The light began to fail and she reluctantly returned the photo to its envelope, placing it carefully in the internal pocket of the grubby bag. She took out her gardening tools and resolved to use them in the morning, but now she was exhausted and she went upstairs to bed.

She lay under the fresh linen, breathing in its fragrance and acquainting herself with the night noises of the building. Nellie was not afraid, which surprised her. In the past, a first night alone in an unfamiliar place would have found her checking under beds and in wardrobes for concealed murderers, rapists or burglars. She was too worn out to bother and hoped that sleep would come and take her soon. It did, but not without a price. A world of untold horror unfolded before her. Monstrous creatures laughing at her as they swiped her with their colossal talons, tossing her carelessly into a pit of cockroaches, which lying in wait for her, ran all over her body as she tried to escape them. Shouting and shouting in this mad realm, she finally forced her fevered mind back to consciousness. She lay still. Sweat poured off her body and her heart beat rapidly and loudly in her chest and ears.

"Oh my God!" she said to the empty room, "What is happening to me?"

Cautiously, she switched on the bedside lamp and soaked up the scene, unhindered by monsters or creepy crawlies.

Nellie knew now that what she had just experienced was not real, however, what she also realised, was that what she had just suffered was her first attack of the delirium tremens. She recognised the symptoms from long ago when she had trained to be a nurse. She had heard some of the drinkers who slept on the street talking of them. She recalled the distaste she had felt when listening to their descriptions of the 'terrors', but she had never thought it would happen to her.

She got up and went downstairs to the kitchen and ran the water cold before filling one of the tumblers she had found in the wall cupboard. She drank it down as quickly as she could with the uncontrollable shaking of her hand. Now, she was afraid of going to sleep, but exhaustion was encasing her again. Slowly, she made her way back up to the bedroom and lay down on the bed. "Please God, don't let me go back to that nightmare," she said, as she stared at the ceiling.

The night passed in short fitful sleeps filled with vivid dreams but without the abject horror of her first attempt. When she awoke she gazed upon the sunlit flowery curtains of the bedroom. Although she felt weary, she was heartened by the reprieve from the hideousness of the previous night. She went to the bathroom pondering over the reassurance that daylight brought. How was it that in the same place, in the same situation and surrounded by the same things it was possible for emotions to range from fear of death to being quite pleased to be alive simply because morning had broken? Unable to satisfy herself with an adequate answer to her question, she washed and dressed in readiness for the work planned in the kitchen garden. She was looking forward to it. She ate a good breakfast in preparation for the hard work ahead; then she filled a plastic bottle with tap water and set off for the farmhouse.

The garden was in dire need of attention. Nellie started weeding the vegetables first, knowing that if she could rescue them from the clutches of the perennial weeds, they would have a better chance of life and bear greater rewards, despite the lateness of the season. She became absorbed in her work, formulating a sequence of necessary tasks in order of priority. Nellie had always loved working close to the earth. She was at ease under the sun with the smell of the warm, moist soil rising up from between the plants.

She focussed purely on the ground directly in front of her and only when she was happy with that patch, would she move on to the next. Her reward for her application was a mind devoid of negative thoughts. The welfare of the vegetables took precedence. She remembered to drink plenty of water, and though she was still shaky, she was beginning to recover from her alcohol withdrawals. At midday, Sarah came out of the house with a large doorstep sized cheese sandwich and a mug of tea.

"Well, you're making good progress Nellie, thank you," and she handed her the lunch.

Nellie sat back and admired the vegetable patch, while she ate.

"Oh this is the best!" she said out loud and resumed her toil.

When Sarah came back from harvesting on the farm she called out to Nellie.

"Hi there! I think that's enough for the day, don't you?"

"I suppose so," said Nellie reluctantly, "I am quite tired now."

"Why don't you go and get washed up? If you like you can come over here for supper, save you having to cook."

"That would be fantastic," realising that she was ravenous. "I could eat a horse!"

"I'll see what I can do," returned Sarah, smiling at Nellie's enthusiasm.

As Nellie walked down the passage at the side of the building, Sarah opened a door and called to her.

"Nellie, don't be offended, but I was turning out some drawers and I thought you might like these," and she handed her a plastic bag full of clothes, "I just thought that your stuff must have got very wet and you may need something to tide you over while you wash them."

Nellie was delighted and told her so. She skipped up to the cottage thrilled at the thought of wearing something different.

The three of them ate heartily that evening and Nellie felt like royalty in one of Sarah's cast off dresses. Jack phoned the hospital and was pleased to report that William was making steady progress. The nurse in charge informed him that he may be well enough to be discharged by the end of the week.

"I'll pick him up if that is the case and the two of you can stay for another week while he recuperates. The cottage is booked for the week after that, so if he is not well enough to go back to London, we'll have another think about it."

"Thank you so much for helping us, Jack. It really is very kind of both of you. I really enjoyed working in your garden today," said Nellie.

"Yes, we had noticed," said Sarah.

"Better than picking apples then, Nellie?" asked Jack.

"Much!" she replied emphatically.

That night Nellie slept a long and peaceful sleep, waking early to the sound of birdsong from the eves of the roof.

The week passed quickly and Nellie's physical state improved with the regular food, fresh air and exercise. The cottage garden was responding well to her touch and she had managed to harvest the bulk of the vegetables. In the evenings, she practised making soup for William's pending convalescence and read books that Sarah had lent her.

Occasionally, at the end of a hard day's work she contemplated the possibility of going down to the pub, for what she considered a well earned pint of cider. She dismissed the thoughts when they came, remembering Jack's cautionary words and the excruciating agony of her withdrawals. She comforted herself with the promise of a rewarding drink when she and William returned to the streets of London deciding to take care, in future, not to overdo it.

On Saturday morning, Jack drove to the hospital to pick up William. While he was gone, Nellie ran around the cottage tidying the house and airing his bed. She made a pot of soup with the vegetables she had tended, then sat and waited for his arrival. She heard the car pull up at the farmhouse and ran to greet him, just as Jack was helping him out of his seat.

Nellie's heart was pounding with excitement at the prospect of seeing her friend. She stopped in her tracks when she caught sight of him. She was stricken by his haggard appearance but tried not to show her dismay. Jack passed William the walking stick that he had brought back with him from the hospital. He thanked him, leant on it, then straightening his back he looked over at Nellie.

"Look at you! You look like you've been on holiday in the Bahamas," he chuckled at his joke and held out his free arm, as she ran up to him so he could put it round her shoulder. They wobbled up the winding path to the cottage, William leaning on Nellie for support. Jack shook his head and smiled fondly at the two of them as they chatted about their activities in their week apart. He carried the plastic hospital discharge bag containing William's belongings up to the house and left it in the hallway as he waved goodbye to them.

The walk from the car had left William breathless and exhausted. Nellie guided him gently to the chintz chair under the window and supported him as he lowered himself carefully into its welcoming arms.

"I've made some soup from the vegetables in the garden. I thought you might need building up when you got back. Shall

I go and heat it up? It tastes lovely and it'll be really good for you," she stopped her excited chatter when William raised his arm shakily,

"Thank you so much Nellie, but what I'd really like now is a cup of tea," he said. "Perhaps I could have a drop of soup with you later."

"Yes, of course, William. I'm getting carried away doing my impersonation of a housewife. It's just that I'm so pleased to see you, I've missed you so much," she could feel tears rising and she left the room hurriedly to boil the kettle.

She stood in the kitchen staring out onto the garden she had so lovingly nurtured and for the first time since William's collapse, she was afraid. How would he manage the severity of street-life, especially now that winter would soon be here? Would he have to stay in a hostel? She could not imagine him anywhere that might choke or crush his spirit. She sighed, then concentrated on brewing the tea and carried it in to the lounge.

"There you..." she looked over at her friend.

He was snoring softly with his mouth slightly open, turned up at the corners giving him the appearance of smiling. Perhaps he is, she thought, continuing to study his ravaged features. She drank her tea watching his peaceful countenance, happy that they were together again. She stayed with him as he slept for several hours until darkness filled the room.

Eventually, she switched on the lamp next to the chair where he slept and he woke up squinting at the light.

"I'm sorry William, I didn't mean to wake you. It was getting dark," she said.

"That's OK my dear, I feel quite refreshed. I must have been sleeping for a long time," he replied. "Now did I hear mention of some delicious soup or was I merely dreaming?"

Nellie went happily back to the kitchen and returned with a tray of soup and farmhouse bread for the two of them. They ate in easy silence, as the crescent moon rose in the darkness that settled behind the drawn curtains. Nellie glanced up as she finished her meal and gazed at the familiar profile of her friend. Something had altered in his demeanour other than the pallour and the prominence of his cheek bones. She could not define it; but it caused her disquiet.

"William, what was it like in hospital? Were you very scared?" she asked softly.

"No Nellie, my dear, I don't believe I was scared. But I did think that I was going to die. I really thought that my time had come," he said thoughtfully.

"What was that like? Thinking that you were about to die?" questioned Nellie.

"It was alright really," he replied, "You know how people say that your life flashes before you? Well it didn't happen in the way I had imagined that it would, but it did happen. There wasn't a succession of images, of people I had known or events that were important to me.

What I had were emotions. Big, powerful waves of sadness, anger, loss and then happy ones too; joy, peace and laughter. I remember laughing out loud and not being able to stop but now that I look back I'm not sure whether it really happened or not.

So I would feel, say, a whoosh of joy and once I had identified it, then I could see Kathleen and I walking down the aisle of the church where we were married smiling at the congregation. I could see the glimmer of pity in my eyes as I watched and I recalled the sensation that I had had on that day."

Nellie had been listening intently to William's account and her face had suddenly changed into a perplexed frown.

"I know Nellie, sounds bizarre doesn't it? It's quite simple really. I had forgotten right up until that moment in hospital that despite the wonder of that day, my main emotion as we made our way back to the church door as man and wife was that I felt desperately sorry for the members of the wedding party and indeed the rest of the world because I knew that they could never feel as blissfully happy as I did then.

As this process continued, I began to feel numbness creeping up my body from my toes and my fingertips. Then I saw hers, her fingers I mean. Just her fingers and her wedding ring: I tried to reach out and touch them with mine, but by that time they wouldn't move and I had lost all sensation in them. Her hands disappeared before I could reach them.

Then I heard lots of clattering and voices while I was shoved about all over the place. I suppose the doctors and nurses were busy saving my life. Anyway, they did. And here I am to tell the tale."

Nellie was struck by the flatness of tone, in which he had related the latter part of his story and asked, "Are you sorry? That you didn't go, I mean."

"I don't know Nellie. I think there must be a reason for me coming back to this mortal coil. Maybe to look after you," he pondered.

"Maybe," but she was thinking that the way things were it would be her caring for him.

"William?" said Nellie, "Is Kathleen dead?"

"Yes," said William.

"You didn't tell me," she went on.

"No, I was ashamed. I wasn't with her when she died. I thought we would always stay together and then she left me. She became ill soon after that and then I heard that she had died. I wasn't even told about her funeral."

He stopped and looked out of the window.

Then he continued, "But I know we will meet up again. I'm more convinced now than ever but I expect there are a few things in store for me before I do and I have you as my companion."

Nellie smiled at him. Now she could see what was missing. The light of hope had gone from his usually twinkling eyes and in its place was acceptance of his situation.

"What I want, more than anything, is to make amends for the pain that I caused her. I don't know if that will be possible but I would like the opportunity to find out."

William sighed and turned to his friend, "I'm all done in, my dear. Could you help me up the stairs and show me where I am to sleep?"

Nellie waited until William was in bed and she could hear the regular sound of his breathing before she went back upstairs. Lying on the bed, gazing up at the white ceiling she thought about William and Kathleen. Then her mind turned to her children. Would she see them again? She had always believed that she would but she still had no idea where they were. In a moment of panic she leapt out of bed to check that she still had their picture in the envelope. After the usual scrabbling that preceded the occasion, she lay on the bed staring at the faces of her two dear children.

She suddenly felt unnerved, as she realised how much they must have changed by now. She remembered how amazed she had always felt when she looked back at pictures of them which had been taken only a year before. The change then was remarkable. What did they look like now? She resolved to set about finding them when they returned to London and William had recovered some of his old zeal for life. She fell into a dreamless asleep with the battered photograph on her chest.

Aware that their time in the holiday home was limited, Nellie focussed her efforts on helping William to regain some physical strength. She was still working on the garden but most of the autumn harvesting had been done and Jack seemed content to leave them to their own devices. As William became stronger, they both tried to enjoy the luxury of their surroundings. They slept well, ate regular meals which were sometimes prepared for them by Sarah and in the evenings they watched television or went for a short stroll. Nellie had told William about the prohibition of alcohol and he agreed that walking near to the pub might be unwise.

So it was with great delight, that they received a visit from Rita towards the end of their stay.

"Hello you two, I've missed you at the pub. How are you now William?"

"Much better thanks to Nellie's kind attention. It's knocked the stuffing out of me though, I can tell you. It's lovely to see you. How are you?"

"Fair to middling, I'd say," she replied. She handed him a large, mixed array of wild flowers wrapped in a piece of newspaper.

"Oh how kind!" exclaimed Nellie, "Shall I put them in water for you?"

"Aye you'd better else they'll die," said Rita on William's behalf and she sat down on the sofa.

Nellie went into the kitchen and made them all a cup of tea. When she came back into the lounge the pair of them were laughing and William was having trouble catching his breath. She felt a pang of jealousy at the old woman's ability to amuse her friend, who she had not seen so happy since he was taken ill. She composed herself and said nothing as she handed out the cups of tea.

"I'm going back up north tomorrow," said Rita, "And I wanted to catch you before I went. I've really enjoyed your company and you know how it is, we may not meet again. I have to say Nellie, you look years younger."

Nellie did not know how to respond to her observation but she assumed that it was a compliment and replied, "Thank you."

"Must be off, goodbye William," she bent over and kissed him on the cheek, "Could you see me to the door, Nellie?"

Nellie obeyed, reflecting that this was a strange request for one as independent as Rita, but she was a little afraid of her bluntness and obliged with bemusement. William raised his arm in a wave as they left the room and at the front door Rita turned around and faced Nellie.

"You take care of him now lass," she ordered and then prodding her on the shoulder with her index finger she went on,

"And lay off the drink. It'll be the death of you, mark my words."

Then she was gone, leaving Nellie stunned by Rita's manner and her words.

"What a cheek!" she thought, "How dare she come in here and give me orders! Of course I'm bloody well going to look after William and as for the drink, well I'll have a skinful as soon as I get back and I'll think of her when I do! That'll show her!"

Nellie felt her heart racing with anger and had to take a minute or two to restore her composure before re-entering the room where William still sat.

"What did she want then?" he asked, as Nellie sat down.

"To impart some pearls of wisdom," Nellie said scathingly.

"Oh," said William, noting her irritation.

He pursued the matter no further.

Jack informed them that Paul had telephoned and planned to pick them up at 5am on Saturday morning. With this knowledge, Nellie organised their clothes so that they were washed and packed. By four thirty that morning, they were both ready and waiting in the lounge. They wore a cloak of silent gloom as they awaited the sound of his van on the gravel of the drive.

Paul greeted them with loud morning bluster and helped them load their baggage into the cab of the van. Sarah ran out of the house as he restarted the engine and handed Nellie a large parcel of sandwiches and a flask in a plastic carrier bag. She waved them off with Jack by her side. They turned and went back indoors.

CHAPTER SEVEN

Wilderness

Paul dropped them off near the Embankment and they walked slowly down to the river, only to find a stranger sleeping soundly on 'William's' bench. They looked at each other. William sighed and they climbed back up the steps to the stirring streets of London. They had forgotten the unwritten laws of vagrancy. One of them being, that if a pitch were left vacant or unguarded for any length of time, it would be usurped. They still had a little money from their fruit picking. They decided to put it to good use by celebrating their return. By midday they were drunk and Nellie's impassioned ambitions to find her children were instantly drowned in the sea of alcohol which she had so ardently imbibed and thus they were, by default, relegated once again to dreams.

Despite the renewed fervour with which she returned to drinking, Nellie sustained a sense of responsibility towards William who was now far frailer than he had been before their departure to the countryside. Her main concern was to find him shelter at night, so that his greatly weakened lungs did not become infected again. Her plans for this were hindered by William's ability to obstruct her at every turn when she attempted to secure him a place in a hostel for the night.

"I can't stand being told what to do. There are too many rules and regulations in those places. Anyway, they're full of smelly, windy old tramps. Why would I want to be there when I can roam to my heart's content in the great outdoors?" he would say.

Finally, in desperation, Nellie succeeded in persuading her friend to spend as much of the night as they could get away with, in the mainline railway stations, during the winter months. They both enjoyed the light and general commotion of the environment. One of the hazards of being there was the regular patrolling of the transport police and some of the station staff.

Nellie became quite adept at spotting them from a distance and moving on accordingly. It was not long before their faces were known to the officials but fortunately, for them, they were not considered a priority in the course of their day's work. As a result, William and Nellie managed to spend protracted periods of time under cover with the added benefit of human activity to watch.

As well as serving as a diversion to them during the long hard days of winter, Nellie gained an indefinable sense of security from being amongst people. She was aware, by now, that she and William were almost invisible to the regular passersby and this, she found, enhanced the pleasure of being an observer.

* * *

One winter's evening, whist comfortably ensconced on one of their favourite seats in Euston station, Nellie noticed a young girl of about thirteen walking slowly across the departure hall. Her heart leapt at the sight of her. From a distance, the teenager was the image of Daisy and Nellie did some haphazard mental arithmetic and realised that she could easily be her. Without further thought she launched her aching body in her direction.

As she approached the child, she realised that her face was shockingly unfamiliar. Nellie paused, but the girl had already noticed her and she seemed to be frozen to the spot.

Recovering from her disappointment she tried to reassure her,

"I'm sorry if I frightened you, it's just that you looked so much like my daughter," she felt the strangeness of the word on her lips and stopped.

The youngster remained still in front of her and Nellie saw that she was afraid. It was around midnight and she wondered where she was heading at such a late hour.

"Do you need some help? Are you lost?"

The girl shook her head. Nellie could see her limbs shaking. She was poorly dressed for the harsh weather and was only carrying a small bag with her.

"I'll tell you what, we'll go and find somewhere where you can get a cup of tea."

Nellie went over to William, who was watching them from the bench and told him what she had proposed. She bent down and took out a cardigan from one of her bags, shook it off and handed to the terrified creature.

"William, will you stay here and keep an eye on my bags for me?" she asked.

"Of course, my dear," he said, "You take care of the little one."

Wriggling his frail frame into a more comfortable position, he waved her off.

Nellie took the girl to the nearest burger bar and bought her a strong cup of tea, putting the sugar in for her. She still had not uttered a single word.

Gently, Nellie cajoled her into speaking her name, "Lily," she whispered.

"That's a very pretty name," encouraged Nellie.

By now, Nellie was sure that Lily had run away from home. She had seen a lot of young boys and girls who had fled from angry, violent families seeking a better life and finding solace on the shared streets of London. It caused Nellie great pain to watch these children lose their youth and hope to predators and drugs but she knew that she did not have the power to protect them. She sat with Lily as she sipped her tea and she relaxed a little as it took effect.

"I can't go back," she said eventually.

"I know," said Nellie, "Let's go back to the station where we can keep warm and then maybe in the morning, I can help you find a place to stay."

They strolled back in silence to the bench where William now slept. The three of them stayed for as long as they could and then reluctantly walked out on to the streets for the last cold hours of the night. At William's suggestion they made their way to the Embankment where, as he had hoped, there was a group of homeless people who had made a fire and were in varying stages of drunkenness and sleep. Amongst the regular faces were three young people who Nellie and William had not met before. After brief introductions, Lily moved towards them and stayed in their company for the rest of the night.

When the sun rose to herald the dawning of another cold winter's day, Nellie remembered her charge and went over to the young group who were still remarkably lively after the harsh night outdoors and said to Lily,

"Would you like to come with me to a hostel and we can see if they can help find you a place to stay?"

Lily looked up at the bedraggled woman gazing down at her with concern.

She appeared baffled and then recalling Nellie's kindness the previous evening said, "Thanks Nellie, but Joe, Ben and Nathan are going to find a squat today so I thought I'd go with them. They said they'd show me the ropes," she paused, "You don't mind do you?"

Nellie shook her head, touched by Lily's consideration of her feelings.

"No, but you take care Lily. I'm usually somewhere in this area if you want someone to talk to," and she left it at that.

A short while later, the four of them stood up unsteadily, laughing at their inebriated state and set off on their day's adventure. Nellie never spoke to Lily again. Three weeks later she found her in a shop doorway; cold, dead and with a needle hanging from her torniqueted arm.

* * *

Nellie drank away the pain of Lily's untimely death as she drank away everything else. A sunny day, an unhappy day, a cold bitter night or an amiable time spent with people she knew. The promise she had made to herself on the farm not to 'overdo it' was long forgotten, as she eagerly threw her whole being into the clutches of King Alcohol. Now she had no desire to curtail the wreckage to her mind or her body. Each day was spent in the pursuit of enough money or guile with which to acquire her poison. The benefit she received only lasted a few days and merely touched the surface of the amounts she now required to blot out the world.

She met up with a group of buskers for a short period of time and despite William's admonishments she threw herself wholeheartedly into the role of street singer motivated by the prospect of a capful of coins. She was mocked and jeered at but she continued undeterred until the group asked her to leave. They said that she was an embarrassment to them and anyway, she could not really sing in tune.

It was soon after this foray into the world of street arts that Nellie decided to do something that she had never previously countenanced. She started to beg. She tried several approaches that she had seen others engage in. One was to ask for the price of a cup of tea. Another was to invent an emergency for which it was imperative that she had a coin for the telephone. Lastly and most reluctantly, she sat with a hat on the steps of the Embankment Bridge gazing sorrowfully into the faces of scurrying passersby. The latter provided the most reliable income and she soon became able to defy her innermost disgust in order to provide the money for her next drink.

Her time on the streets had taught her the use of different forms of currency. Cardboard was at a premium during the autumn and winter months due to its ability to transform a cold, windy doorway into a habitable abode for the night. Nellie would always forgo comfort for the sake of a drink and as time went by she found various places where cardboard had been discarded by shopkeepers and market stall holders on to the street. She would then drag her findings back to the most popular venues for her compatriots, in the hope that someone would have enough drink to make a worthwhile transaction.

There were a few factors that influenced the regulation of what would have been her twenty four hour consumption of alcohol. One of these was passing out. This could happen at any time and in the most unlikely of places. She would come to often in a place that she swore she had never set foot in before, only to discover that she had absolutely no recollection of the events preceding her arrival. Though alarmed at this ever more frequent occurrence, she never contemplated the possibility of reducing her alcohol intake; in fact, it only served to increase her pursuit of further oblivion.

Another sobering responsibility was her inconsistent desire to care for her street companion, William. He could no longer drink with the enthusiasm of his younger days and Nellie was guiltily pleased at the amounts that naturally came her way. However, his fragility became more apparent particularly when the days were inclement. At these times she tried to coax him to the greater comforts of a hostel. On the rare occasions this was possible she would take a bed for the night as well. Due to the infrequency of their visits, she no longer knew any of the volunteers. Anna had left soon after they had returned from the farm and she was no longer able to build up a rapport with any of the others.

The prerequisite of sobriety was now abhorrent to Nellie and the best she could muster was to turn up without slurring or swaying about. The fear of the inevitable delirium tremens coupled with her entrenched obsession and physical addiction to alcohol rendered all attempts to resist impossible. The result was that one by one the hostels barred her attendance. She had no sense of loss. On those rare occasions that she had been admitted, she had not used the washing facilities or any of the other opportunities open to her such was her need to escape and resume the endless cycle of intoxication which had her in its grips.

Nellie knew that she did not care for William in the way that he had for her. She did not know that she was now incapable and thus carried around heavy feelings of guilt for her apparent neglect. Often she awoke in a strange place only to find that he was not there. Sometimes it would take all day to find him and she would hang her head as he recounted tales of her drunken conduct.

Being away from William frightened her because her behaviour became even more erratic. She often found herself in dangerous places with the most unpleasant of characters. She had learnt early on simple rules such as not making eye contact with angry drug abusers. This seemed to allay the possibility of having their irrational fury aimed at her. Regrettably, without her friend by her side, she often forgot this and there had been several incidents whereby Nellie had become embroiled in a meaningless altercation which often ended in violence. The police were sometimes called and once Nellie's injuries were so bad that she was taken, by ambulance, to the local accident and emergency department.

She came to on a trolley, woken by the agony from the wounds to her face where she had been repeatedly punched during a brawl over a sleeping space. Without the pain, Nellie was unlikely to have remembered the scene. As it came back to her in incoherent images she realised how vulnerable she had become. How could she have been so stupid? She lay back on the pillow behind, grateful for the safety and warmth of the hospital. She listened to the clatter and footsteps. Then she heard the suppressed giggles of two young girls immediately outside her curtains.

"OK," said one of them, "Your choice is A: smelly, drunk women with blood all over her face or B: clean but creepy man with something nasty wrong with his private parts. Which is it to be?"

"Not much of a choice, but I think I'll opt for smelly, drunk woman on this occasion. Good luck with yours!"

Nellie was starting to smile at the light hearted repartee until the latter speaker swung in behind her curtain and said,

"Hello, my name is Charlotte, I'm just going to examine you."

Nellie was mortified by her earlier description and remained speechless as the young girl took her blood pressure and peered at her injuries.

"I'll get the doctor to come and see you as soon as possible," she said and added, "You'll probably need some stitches in that." And she left as breezily as she had come.

Recovering from her humiliation, the only demonstration of her outrage that she could contemplate was to leave. She heaved her aching limbs off the trolley and crept stealthily to the gap in her screens. Everyone was far too busy to notice her movements and she walked, trying to hold her head high, out on to the streets fading into their consoling cloak of obscurity.

The next day, when she finally found William they sat together at the water's edge on their bench by the Embankment. Nellie was too unwell to beg which meant that they had no money. She had started to shake and sweat despite the punishing wind. William glanced over at her and shook his head in despair. Nellie had said very little and was now terrified of the consequences of not drinking.

"William, I don't know what to do. I feel terrible," she uttered in a whisper.

As if in answer to an unsaid prayer an acquaintance of theirs, Dennis, strode towards them rubbing his hands together to warm them.

"Hello Nellie, hello William old chap, how are you both?" he said loudly. He peered at Nellie's battered visage and continued, "Not so good then?"

The dejected pair shook their heads in silence. Then William said,

"I'm sorry Dennis I'm forgetting my manners, would you care to sit with us a while? Maybe you could share some of your sunny disposition with two despairing, cloudy souls."

"Well it's funny you should say that but I was just on my way to a meeting," he said with a glint in his eyes.

"What meeting would that be, my man?" asked William, noticing that this normally dishevelled man was clean shaven and presentable.

"It's a meeting of Alcoholics Anonymous. I've been going for two months now and I feel fantastic," he replied.

"What do you do there?" asked William, curious to know why this man was suddenly so animated.

"They teach you how to stop drinking and then they teach you how to live without drinking," he answered simply.

"Sounds like a barrel of laughs!" mumbled Nellie, wrapping her arms tightly around her body in an attempt to stop the feeling that her brain was rattling about in her head.

"I don't know my dear," said William thoughtfully, "Does it cost a lot of money this Alcoholic business?" he asked.

Dennis laughed, "No, it doesn't cost anything to go to your first meeting. Why not give it a try?"

He looked over at Nellie and said kindly, "You'll get a free cup of tea."

"Oh alright, if William wants to go I'll come along and keep him company."

"We might even learn something, my dear," and for the first time in a long time, he held out his arm for her to take and they followed Dennis to a church hall a few minutes' walk away.

Nellie felt very shaky as they approached the door displaying the AA sign and thought,

"What on earth have I let myself in for now?"

She also considered running away when William was not watching but the opportunity did not arise and before she knew it they were in the middle of a crowded room amidst greetings and chirpy chatter.

Then she heard something which was both familiar yet strange. She realised after a few moments that it was the sound of carefree laughter. It was a completely different noise to that of the mocking, forced cackles of the street. Then there was a lot of muttering and shuffling and she was somehow seated on a rickety wooden chair with a half-filled cup of tea in her hand.

The room was filled with peaceful silence and the meeting had begun. For its duration Nellie felt a serenity she had not experienced for years, if ever, and when it ended a lady came up to her and asked her if this was her first meeting.

"How did you know that?" asked Nellie.

The woman took Nellie's shaking hand and said, "I haven't seen you here before."

They spoke for a while and then everyone seemed to be moving off, so Nellie made her way to the door. As she did, the lady who had spoken to her handed her a piece of paper with her telephone number and a small paper package.

"Call me when you feel like drinking and just keep coming back."

She hugged Nellie tightly and kissed her on the cheek. Nellie felt tears well up in her eyes and forgot that she had been the unsavoury, smelly, drunk woman on the hospital trolley only hours earlier.

"Well they were a friendly bunch," said William, sounding perkier than he had for some time, "And generous," he added, holding up a ten pound note.

"Where did you get that?" asked Nellie.

"One of the chaps came up to me after the meeting and put it in the palm of my hand. I tried to give it back but he wasn't having any of it. He said that he'd been coming to those meetings for three weeks now and he hadn't felt so good in years. He told me to buy a meal for you and me. He said that it would make us feel better. So what's it to be my dear?"

"I know what will make me feel better!" said Nellie, clasping her hands together in childish glee as she threw William a beseeching glance.

"Oh OK then," said William.

They walked into the nearest off licence and carefully divided their windfall between cans of Special Brew and cigarettes. As they left the shop, William turned to Nellie and said,

"Not a bad day after all, my dear. Shall we stroll down to the river to enjoy our booty?"

"Excellent idea, old chap!" responded Nellie, pulling the ring-pull from one of the cans.

They never went back to another AA meeting but they often talked about the people they had met that day. Occasionally Dennis would seek them out and ask whether they would like to come along with him but they shied away, thinking that, overall, their own drinking life was preferable.

* * *

Time passed and months grew into years. Nellie's days were differentiated primarily by the weather and thus by the changing seasons. William's health improved in the summer months and reliably deteriorated during the winter. Although he was able to maintain a degree of well being for the latter months of the year, by late January and February his resilience to the elements was compromised to the extent that he would usually have at least one hospital admission for treatment of a severe chest infection. At these times, Nellie tried hard to maintain a routine of daily visits to his bedside but sometimes she failed to get there due to unexpected events caused as a direct result of her drunkenness or simply because of intoxication itself. When this happened she suffered terrible pangs of guilt and remorse.

On resuming her duty to her friend she would try and make an extra special effort with her appearance and when possible, would bring him a treat of some description to salve her burning conscience. On the occasions that she permitted herself to dwell on his poor health, Nellie became immersed in the darkness of lonely dread. She genuinely did not want her trusted companion to endure pain or discomfort, but she was unable to avoid contemplating the implications to her when left alone on the streets of London.

Each day spent without William, Nellie would try to remember to be careful where she went and to whom she spoke. But with her ever increasing consumption of alcohol, it became inevitable that she would find herself in unpleasant and often dangerous situations. She continued to become unnecessarily involved in street brawls and at times sustained blows from her adversaries leaving her with resultant scars and loss of teeth. On his discharge from hospital, Nellie would welcome William back 'home' with a celebratory drink acquired in anyway necessary and they would sit on their favourite bench by the river congratulating themselves on their good fortune.

* * *

One fine summer's evening, William and Nellie sat on their Embankment bench gazing at the murky, familiar current of the river. A cool breeze relieved them of the sticky heat of the day and they sipped on cider enjoying the satisfaction gained from the security of still having a bottle and a half waiting in reserve. Nellie savoured a rare carefree moment and wanting to share her contentment with her companion, turned to William and said,

"Not such a bad life, old chap," and poured another drink for them both.

She looked back at the river; she then turned back towards him raising her cup in a toast. As she caught sight of his heavily tanned, leathery face she noticed him wince and then attempt to recover his composure.

"What's the matter William? Is it your indigestion playing you up again?"

"Mmm maybe," he replied, but now he was unable to hide his pain. He clutched his abdomen and tried to breathe slowly and deeply until he felt some respite. He had been experiencing considerable abdominal discomfort for the last few weeks but up until now had managed to disguise or conceal it completely from Nellie. He believed that the pain was indicative of something much more severe than indigestion and was far too afraid to find out its cause. More than the actual knowledge of his condition, he feared the indomitable control of the medical profession once succumbing to its care. It was not death that he dreaded most but the treatment, however thoughtfully that might be bestowed on him to cure his ailing body. Seeing the look of alarm on Nellie's face, he knew that he could hide the truth from her no longer.

"Have you had a pain like this before?" she asked suspiciously.

"Once or twice," he responded, sighing as he felt release from its grips.

"You must see a doctor, William, they'll be able to find out what is wrong and they can treat you."

"That's what I'm afraid of," he said sorrowfully.

He took a large gulp from his cup and refilled it.

"Maybe this will help it to go away," he continued, trying to sound optimistic. The next agonising wave was upon him within half an hour and Nellie decided that she must take the matter into her own hands.

"William, you need to go to hospital. Can you walk there?"

She had to wait until the pain subsided before he was able to answer her.

"I think so," he faltered and for the first time, Nellie noticed that the whites of his eyes were yellow.

She realised, with a sinking heart, that his unusually healthy, bronzed appearance had actually been jaundice. She assisted him as he hobbled haltingly up the steps and on to the street. The effort exhausted him and he had to sit down on the pavement to rest. Nellie sat with him flummoxed by her impotence. He started to writhe in torment and Nellie stood up and started to search the faces of the men and women who were so conscientiously ignoring him.

Anger rose inside her until finally, she let out a bloodcurdling howl. Several people stopped, searching for the source of the unearthly sound which assaulted their ears.

"Now will you help him?" bellowed Nellie.

A man wearing a vicar's collar came forward from the gathering and knelt down beside William. He took his hand and pulled out a mobile phone from the top pocket of his jacket. When he had called for the ambulance, he looked down at William and said,

"They won't be long William. Just take a few deep breaths."

"Hello Reverend, I wasn't expecting to see you, especially as I am somewhat indisposed at the moment," the discomfort had eased temporarily and William was relieved to see the vicar's face. They had met several times when William had sought comfort in the church attached to one of the hostels in which he and Nellie sometimes stayed.

"This is Nellie," he offered and then clutched his belly once more, unable to speak.

"You don't have to say anything William," reassured Nellie, "The paramedics will be here soon and then they will take you to hospital and get you well again. You know how good they are there and they like you too. I know because the nurses always speak to me when I come and see you. You see, it'll be alright," but her faltering voice belied her words and she fell silent. The crew knew both Nellie and William and were kind to them, allowing Nellie to ride with them in the ambulance regardless of the amount of baggage that came with her.

Nellie remained with her sick friend in the Accident and Emergency Department until the following morning, when he was finally admitted to a ward. He had been given various investigations and when the doctors where satisfied that they had made an accurate diagnosis they had waited for a bed to become vacant. Nellie helped him to settle into his newly made bed and then he said to her,

"Nellie, you go now and get some rest. Why don't you go to the hostel? You could pop into the church and thank Reverend Timothy, on my behalf, for his great kindness."

"Is there anything that you want me to fetch for you, William?"

"Yes, a razor please and perhaps a spot of shaving foam if you can lay your hands on any," he lay looking up at Nellie. "Don't you worry now everything will be OK, just wait and see."

Nellie was loath to leave him but she took his request as a sign that he wanted to rest. He had been given several analgesic injections and though the agony had subsided he was now exhausted. She bent and kissed him on the forehead. He seemed very frail and yellow, as he took out his arm from under the cover to make a small waving motion as they parted.

She took the stairs down to the ground floor and out onto the street. She walked creating a steady rhythm to soothe her disquieted soul. She had ascertained the severity of William's condition over the duration of the last twenty four hours by paying close attention to the frequent hushed discussions between the doctors and nurses following each test that had been performed. They merely confirmed what she had already known when she had looked at him on the bench before his collapse. William was dying.

Without having consciously directed her feet, she had arrived on the steps of the church. She entered its ancient oak doors and let the musty coolness of its interior surround her. She sat at the back of the church gazing upwards at the sun shining through the elaborate stained glass image of Mary nursing the baby Jesus behind the altar and wept. Hearing the sound of a man's footsteps she lifted her head and saw Timothy walking towards her with a book in his hand. He sat beside her and asked how William was.

"He's not very well. I don't think he will live much longer." and she felt the resurgence of sobs choking her words.

He laid a hand on her forearm and waited for her grief to subside. Then he said,

210

"William's a good man. Is he in much pain now?"

"Not so much, they've given him quite a lot of pain relief so he is more comfortable. Do you think he'd want you to come and see him, you know... if he's dying?" she asked in a melancholy voice.

"Well I can visit him anyway. I have always enjoyed our chats and then if he wants anything he can let me know himself; how about that, Nellie?"

"Oh thank you so much, I just didn't really know what to do," she looked down at the floor, took a deep breath and went on, "There's something else that I wanted to ask you..."

"What's that, Nellie?"

"Well, I don't know what to do if he dies. What happens to a person like William? He hasn't got any family, well he hasn't seen any in all the time I've known him and that's quite a few years now. Is he still allowed to have a funeral?"

The thought of losing her dear friend began to overwhelm her again and she paused.

"Nellie please don't worry about that. I will take care of the arrangements myself if you are sure that there is nobody else that can do it. Now what about you? Perhaps you should have a meal. Shall I come over to the hostel with you and see if there is some food going?"

"Yes please, do you think they might let me use the showers and keep my stuff for me while I go back to the hospital? I don't want to be gone for too long, you know."

"Yes I understand, let's go and see who is on duty today. If you like I can meet you and we can walk back there together."

"Thank you, I would like that."

Nellie had a much needed shower and a change of clothes from the selection stored at the hostel. She had always liked to try and look presentable when visiting William in hospital. She had a vague notion that her own fresh appearance might lessen the terror of illness. She met Timothy as arranged and they set off to comply with the afternoon visiting hours. Feeling brighter after a cooked meal and lighter without her baggage, Nellie's optimism returned and she wondered whether she had not been a little melodramatic earlier.

One glimpse of her friend's yellow, gaunt face in the sea of white bed linen removed this fleeting hope. His eyes were closed and his breathing was laboured. She took his bony hand and held it until he awoke.

"Hello my dear," he said with just a hint of a twinkle in his eyes, "How lovely to see you."

She smiled and turned to Timothy.

"Ah Timothy, so good of you to come," and William held out a shaking arm.

Timothy gently shook the man's hand.

"Nellie, could you give me a minute or two alone with the Reverend?"

Nellie nodded and left his bedside. She sensed the world changing without her consent. She childishly wondered if there was any one thing that she could do now that would alter the inevitable outcome of William's disease. She walked out onto the street and looked for a newsagent. She bought ten cigarettes with the pennies she had found in the clothes she had thrown away after her shower. She walked into the park across the road and found a bench on which to sit and smoke. She watched the smoke swirling above her and hoped no-one would come to share her seat. How long had he known about his illness?

She felt a rush of anger towards him for not having told her but she knew that he would have refused any lengthy treatment that was offered. He had lived on the streets far too long to tolerate a long stay in any institution, let alone a hospital. Despite this knowledge, the rage continued to mount. She wanted to break something or hit someone and found that it took all the restraint she could muster to remain seated.

Finally, in a deafening, furious howl she stood up and yelled,

"DON'T LEAVE ME ON MY OWN! PLEASE DON'T LEAVE ME!"

Nurses, builders and office workers taking an afternoon break in the pleasant gardens looked over in alarm. Nellie remained standing with her arms rigidly at her sides supporting her clenched fists.

Moments later, unable yet to see beyond the red mist of anger before her eyes, she felt the firm grasp of hands on her wrists as they were gently lifted up and as she released her fingernails from her palms she heard a familiar voice.

"It's OK Nellie," and she began to make out the features of Timothy's benevolent face.

He gestured to the seat behind her and they both sat down. The onlookers returned to their safe worlds relieved that, on this occasion, no action was required by them.

"Nellie, I think it is nearly his time," she nodded slowly, "Nellie, he's waiting for you."

Silently, she arose and trod carefully, with Timothy supporting her arm, back to the hospital entrance. Timothy escorted her to William's bedside and then departed.

Her friend appeared to have shrunk even more since she had left him such a short time ago. His breathing was erratic and taken in gasps. It seemed as if he was now so near to death that he was forgetting to inhale the vital oxygen that he had spent all his days remembering.

He opened his eyes and as he focussed on Nellie's expectant face he smiled and said, "Nellie, my dear, you came back."

"Of course I did, old chap, of course."

"Nellie I must say goodbye to you now. Thank you so much for being a most wonderful and dear companion..."

His voice was husky and fading, as he paused to take a breath.

"I'm not frightened now Nellie. Remember I am going to see my dear, sweet Kathleen. Let's hope I make a better husband there than I did here," and he choked on his feeble chuckle.

Nellie moved closer and held his cold hand in hers.

"William, what shall I do now?" she said plaintively.

"Look for your children, Nellie. I think you're ready to do that now, don't you?"

His words were barely audible under the crackle of his failing breath.

"But I don't know where to start, William," panic rising in her chest.

With one final exertion he uttered,

"At the beginning my dear, at the beginning."

His eyes closed. As the already icy hand fell limp, Nellie lay it down carefully by his side and with large, mournful tears rolling down her cheeks; she rose and leaned across the bed to kiss him on the forehead. Leaving the ward, she turned back and waved to her dearest of friends, then walked out onto the hazy, summer street, bewildered and alone.

* * *

Timothy had dealt with William's effects and the arrangements necessary for his funeral in the knowledge that there was no-one else able to perform these duties. Thus it was that Timothy held a funeral service for William the following Thursday at the parish church where he and William had first met and beside the hostel in which Nellie had stayed in preparation for this day. Her grief had left her in a bemused and detached state of mind which had aided her enforced abstinence from alcohol. Her body and mind had suffered the indignity of withdrawals but her disturbing sense of derealisation masked the abject horror of the process, bringing her to a state of reasonableness by the day of the interment.

She stood at the church door and peered in. Timothy was standing at the altar and on seeing her, beckoned her inside. She walked up the aisle and sat at a pew in the echoing, empty building. There had been intermittent rain showers that morning and she was damp in her borrowed black mackintosh.

Timothy approached her and asked, "Would you like to say anything, Nellie?"

She shook her head and replied, "I think he would like it if we sang this song. He used to sing it a lot when... he used to sing it a lot on happy days," and she handed him a crumpled piece of paper on which were scrawled the words of a song.

Timothy took the damaged document and as he read the first few words his face relaxed into a smile of recognition,

"I know this, my mother used to sing it when I was little; we could sing it together if you like," he suggested.

"My singing isn't very melodious," she replied hesitantly.

"I don't think that really matters do you?"

"I suppose not."

They were disturbed by the sound of men's feet at the door and they turned to watch the pall bearers carry William's simple coffin to the altar. Nellie was then lulled by the sound of Timothy's voice as he spoke of William's life. As the service came to an end Timothy said,

"And now we will sing, "I'll take you home Kathleen," for William."

The combination of Timothy's unaccompanied, powerful tenor and Nellie's cracked but enthusiastic tones were joined, unexpectedly, by a third voice from a homeless man who Nellie recognised from the hostel. He had slipped in unnoticed during the service with the intention of sheltering from the rain.

215

I'll take you home again Kathleen
Across the ocean wild and wide
To where your heart has ever been
Since you were first my bonnie bride.
The roses all have left your cheek
I've watched them fade away and die
Your voice is sad when e'er you speak
And tears bedim your loving eyes.

Oh! I will take you home Kathleen
To where your heart will feel no pain
And when the fields are fresh and green
I'll take you to your home again.

I know you love me, Kathleen, dear
Your heart was ever fond and true.
I always feel when you are near
That life holds nothing, dear, but you
The smiles that once you gave to me
I scarcely ever see them now
Though many, many times I see
A dark'ning shadow on your brow

Oh! I will take you home Kathleen
To where your heart will feel no pain
And when the fields are fresh and green
I'll take you to your home again

To that dear home beyond the sea
My Kathleen shall again return.
And when thy old friends welcome thee
Thy loving heart will cease to yearn.
Where laughs the little silver stream

Beside your mother's humble cot
And brightest rays of sunshine gleam
There all your grief will be forgot.

As the three of them rounded into the final chorus, Nellie's gaze lifted to the stained glass window and she watched the sun break through the clouds to shine into the church above Mother Mary's head. She smiled up at what she perceived to be a sign from William indicating that all was now well with him.

After the service Nellie thanked Timothy and left the church. She went back to the hostel, returned the borrowed coat, collected her bags and walked with her head held high to the Victoria Embankment Gardens. She searched around for a good spot and when she had decided upon one, sat cross legged with her bags on either side of her and began picking the daisies. She was particularly looking for those with longer stems and once she had collected enough to start, she embarked on weaving a daisy chain. William and Nellie had sometimes amused themselves with this pastime on a balmy summer's evening. Now, completely immersed in her child-like pursuit, Nellie smiled at the fun they used to have on that very patch of grass. Nellie continued her craft with absolute focus until she had achieved her aim. She had woven several rings of daisies into one. As she held it up to inspect her handicraft, she nodded slowly, satisfied with the result.

She stood up carefully as she felt her joints click and waited until she was able to move without pain. With great care she managed to manoeuvre her bags with the flowers around her neck down to the bench on which she had shared her time with her departed companion. She hooked the home-made wreath around the end of the seat where William had always preferred to sit. For a moment, she considered trying to will him back there, but thought better of it.

Instead, she blew the empty space one last kiss and said, "Goodbye William and thank you for being my friend."

With that, she set off, for the first time in years, in the direction of 'home'.

* * *

As she began her journey through the streets and alleys that were now so familiar to her, she was aware that she was bidding them farewell. Although she knew a number of people in the vicinity, there was no-one to whom she felt the need to say goodbye. In her heart, she believed that she would be forgotten soon enough, if indeed, she was remembered at all. Instead of sadness at this realisation, she experienced a sense of freedom, almost hope that now she could go anywhere and achieve anything.

She felt immense gratitude towards William for the patience he had shown her when trying to improve her sense of direction and educate her on the geography of the great city. Its skyline had changed immeasurably during their time together on the streets but it was his insistence on the importance of knowing how to navigate them that enabled her now to find her way through its maze of roads and alleys with ease.

"Thanks William, I never did know what was good for me!" she uttered to the ether.

She decided as she trudged, to avoid the busy roads where possible and as a result found herself at the cafe in Russell Square gardens. She had some money saved from her benefits that would normally have been spent by now and she bought a cup of coffee with a sandwich. As she started to eat, she became aware of how hungry she had become. Sitting at a metallic table with a good view over the park, she pondered, as she had so many times before at the steadfast movement of the majority of the capital's inhabitants. Where were they all rushing to at the same time? Surely they must stop or at least slow down sometimes.

The food and drink began to give Nellie a clearer head and she considered where she might sleep that night. She tried to quash the sense of foreboding that was welling up inside. Would she be safe on her own? Then she remembered the money that she still had in her purse. It was a considerable amount for her and she ruminated upon the possibility of buying some alcohol. She knew herself well enough by now to know that it would be foolhardy to purchase any now since her expedition had barely begun. Her pattern of 'stocking up' for later in the day always ended in her becoming much drunker, much sooner than planned, usually with the direst of consequences. She prevaricated on her dilemma whilst throwing crumbs to her entourage of pigeons and thought of William. What would he suggest? Then she came up with the idea of having her own private wake for him. Unable to consult him, she felt sure that, if he were there, he would approve wholeheartedly of this plan.

As the sun lowered in the sky, she rounded into Park Crescent and after taking a few moments to admire the beauty of the Regency buildings that swept its curves she made her way, with trepidation, to the gates of Regent's Park. Originally, she had planned to survey the situation and assess whether it would be possible to find a suitable spot to sleep in; then hang around dodging the park attendants while they locked the gates for the night. Once there however, she was not so sure that she would be able to carry this out. Certainly, there were far more people than she had expected and with a sinking heart she realised that she did not have the nerve to follow through with her plan. Despondently, she left the green space and walked back out on to the noisy traffic infested roads.

By chance, she saw an off licence as her gaze moved temporarily upwards from her feet and the pavement in front of them. She stood at its window and read the tempting offers scrawled in white over the glass. In preparation, she took out her shabby purse from its position in one of her larger plastic carrier bags and entered the shop. Overwhelmed by the vast selection of bottles and cans, she paused before selecting two large bottles of cider. She had already begun to feel calmer whilst standing there and added some crisps to her purchases, mindful that she intended to celebrate the life of her dear friend William just as soon as she found a place where she could relax and do so in comfort. She asked the vendor for some cigarettes, then exchanging the correct amount of cash for her items, packed them away carefully and left the premises.

She still had a few pounds remaining and reflected on the inevitable transferring of her benefits that would need to be dealt with on her arrival in a new area. Just as she was considering how long she could survive with the money she had left, she saw a bus coming towards her, she looked at the front and saw that she recognised the number and on closer inspection realised that it terminated at her destination. In a flurry of excitement, she rushed to the bus stop, thankful that she had not replaced her purse in her bag.

She heaved her belongings up to the waiting driver and asked how much she had to pay. It was darker in the bus and she could not see the coins clearly. As she held the purse up to her face for closer inspection, she was jostled from behind by an impatient passenger and it flew from her hand spraying the change above her head and onto the floor. As Nellie watched it fly and then tinkle down onto the filthy, grooved floor, her complete lack of control began to tickle her and she started to laugh. It began as a suppressed titter and was followed by a shoulder heaving bellow. Taking a deep breath, she attempted to regain some decorum and bent her head to the ground to search for her fare. But the tears of merriment blinded her and she conceded to the mirth emitting a louder, more raucous guffaw than ever.

Eventually, as the passengers became tired of the inconvenience, a smartly dressed middle aged woman took Nellie by the hand and sat her down at the long seat at the back of the bus with her bags. She then picked up as much of the dropped change as she could find, bought her ticket and gave it all back to her. Although embarrassed and bemused by the scene she had caused, Nellie enjoyed the euphoria that ensued. Suddenly, the bus was a brighter place and she settled with only the occasional urge to snigger.

Though she had acquired her seat by default, she was pleased to be sat in a position whereby she had full view of its passengers. She was also higher up on the back seat and was able to watch the activity out on the street as the bus wheezed its way along the busy roads. Stopping and starting in lurches, sounding at times too tired to go on, the bus finally left behind the congested traffic of the city and ran more easily into the leafier suburbs. Carried away by the freedom of movement, the bus shook with excitement as it rattled up to the last leg of the journey.

Nellie's heart leapt with joy as she watched familiar sights come into view. Now, she had a memory for each part of the ride and when she dwelled upon them she could not believe that she had been away for so long. So much of her surroundings had remained unchanged. The sun was setting in the sky but she no longer felt afraid of the night ahead. She was astonished at the difference that knowing the area made to her. She was aware that she would have to find somewhere to sleep but she also recalled the places where she had seen the homeless sleep when she had lived there. The bus pulled into its final resting place and discharged its occupants onto the street with the sound of a pressure cooker releasing its steam.

Nellie stood still and took in the sights of her home town. The large church tower divided the road into a natural fork. The glow of the burger bar to its right reflected on the puddingstone wall as it always had at this time in the evening. As if being drawn by its promise of warmth and comfort Nellie found herself walking towards the cafe. She entered through the door wedged open by a piece of folded cardboard. She sat in the corner seat by the window which she and the children had always favoured. She was exhausted from her travels and slipped into a trance in which her children were sitting in front of her eagerly putting in their requests for food. They had all loved to come here as it was considered a treat of the highest order. She pictured Daisy and Freddie so clearly that when they started to laugh she could hear the tinkling of their childish voices.

"Hello, what would you like, madam?" Nellie was startled from her reverie by the recognisable sound of George's voice with its hint of a Greek accent that he no longer wished to lose. She looked up knowing what she would see; George, standing smartly with his small pad and pencil, donning a broad smile which accentuated the lazy squint in his right eye.

As their eyes met, she watched as George controlled his horrified recognition of his customer.

Recovering his composure with practiced skill he asked, "How are you? How are the children? They must be big now."

Nellie had not anticipated being immediately identified as a former customer and was momentarily at a loss for words. She looked down, took a deep breath and replied,

"I'm terribly sorry but I've never been to this town before." She continued," This is my first visit here," as if to compound the lie would dispense with any further misunderstanding.

She went on, "It must be a case of mistaken identity; it happens to me all the time," she smiled beatifically, exposing her brown stained, decaying teeth as she did.

"Of course," said George, "Can I get you a cup of coffee?"

"That would be just the ticket!" she said with excessive enthusiasm in an attempt to hide her discomfiture.

She eyed the laminated menu in its holder on the table and by holding her head slightly to one side she could read the price of the beverages. When she had ascertained the amount required, she counted out the correct change and pushed it in front of her just as George returned with a piping hot mug of coffee with exactly the amount of sugar she had always taken placed neatly in the saucer.

Seeing the small pile of money on the table, George slid it back to Nellie saying, "This one is on the house, enjoy!"

Nellie sat sipping her coffee and gazing out of the window. She could see the graffiti scratch marks on the glass that had upset George so much, many years ago. He had just had a new window put in at great expense due to its size. But all these years later the marks were still there and George no longer seemed to see them.

There was one other customer in the cafe sitting at one of the inner tables. She had seen him look over to her table earlier and she had looked away to avoid any interaction with him. He was a large man in his early forties with a slightly vacant look in his eyes. She could feel the impending possibility of conversation and delved needlessly into one of her bags to postpone the moment. As she stared unseeing into the pile of possessions that lay within she heard another man enter and greet her neighbour.

"Hello Jim," he called cheerily, "How are you today?"

He was a slightly built man with an air of bewildered sincerity.

"Not so good," replied Jim in melancholy tones, "It's my head, I'm waiting for an operation you know?"

"So how is your head?"

"Why are you asking me about my head? I was beaten up when I was at school and really I needed an operation then, you know," answered Jim, who was now sounding quite angry.

"Yes, I know that, I have a bad head as well remember!" retorted the other man.

George walked up to Nellie's table watching the two men as they countered each other's ailments with increasing vigour.

He placed a plate of chips in front of Nellie saying, "They would have gone to waste anyway," as she attempted to say that she was not really hungry.

Abandoning this, she whispered to him, "Are those two alright? They seem to be getting very cross."

"Ah! They always do this; they've known each other for years. Don't worry I'll keep an eye on them." He smiled at Nellie and winked as he walked away from the table.

"My head! My head! Why does every one ask me about my head?" shouted Jim, banging on the table, "You just don't know what it is like!"

"But I do, you know I do, I've told you before about my terrible accident twenty three years ago. I banged my head so badly that I can't remember things. I forget people's names. I forget how to get dressed. I get up in the morning and I forget what I am supposed to be doing. My head is so bad that I have to take thirty three tablets every morning before I get up but the trouble is that I forget to take them.

So I do know what it's like and I ask you how your head is because I know you have a bad head and I'm trying to show that I'm interested and I understand!"

The last sentence was uttered with loud exasperation followed by a moment's silence in which Nellie considered the sadness of these two men with bad heads, one trying to help the other.

"Do you want a fight?" challenged Jim, rising to his feet and clenching a fist.

224

George appeared behind the smaller man who had not yet sat down. He took him firmly by the shoulders and sat him at a table away from Jim and Nellie.

"Burger and chips and a cup of tea, please George," he requested politely, shrugging his shoulders in the direction of Nellie as if to apologise.

Nellie smiled back and nodded. From behind the counter, a young man came out with a tea towel in his hand. He seemed familiar and then with a shock, Nellie realised that he was George's son, the little boy who had been in the same year at school as Freddie.

"Oh my God!" thought Nellie, "He's so tall and grown up."

It was then that the enormity of the years lost from her children's lives made a full and painful impact in the pit of her stomach. The agony temporarily immobilised her as she watched the youngster walk past Jim's table.

"Hello Jim, how are you?" he enquired.

"I don't know what to do. I have a very bad head. I was diagnosed with a brain tumour last week and I'm waiting for an operation. My head hurts," he replied earnestly.

"Go to the doctor, he will make it better," he offered, as he wiped the table next to his. He then returned to the rear of the restaurant.

The ease and confidence with which he spoke to the suffering man overwhelmed her. Was Freddie able to deal with people in a similar manner? It was this, more than the boy's size and maturity, that had overwhelmed her and brought home to her how much she had missed and how little she would know about her son now when they next met. The thought made her feel nervous and excited all at once. Was there a chance that she might see him again? What about Daisy? Would she actually see her one day? Sighing, Nellie stood up and slowly gathered her bags together, careful not to leave anything behind. She remembered that she had a good supply of cider with her and all she needed now was somewhere quiet to sit and drink. She glanced up at George as she was leaving,

"Thank you, George," and then blushed when she realised that, by using his name she had made obvious her earlier duplicity.

Nellie had known since alighting from the bus where she would sleep that night. She made her way towards the park where she used to take her children. She managed to find the gap in the hedge which seemed to have always been there and found the bench which Old Joe had always chosen to sleep on. There was no-one else in the park that night as Nellie pulled out the folded cardboard she had saved from London and some clothes to lay down as her pillow. After drinking some cider from the bottle, she took out the picture which was still in the now tatty envelope. Although she could not see her children's faces in the darkness, she held it to her breast as she fell into a peaceful sleep.

CHAPTER EIGHT

Home

Nellie awoke refreshed and warm. She could feel the softness of the mattress beneath her body and after a few moments she remembered where she was and the lovely evening she had spent with Tom. She looked around the room and could see no sign of him so she pulled herself up from the floor where her bed had been and went into the kitchen. There was a note on the side by the kettle.

Good morning Nellie,

Didn't we have a great time last night? I have to go out and see to a bit of business. I'm hoping to have a surprise for you this evening. I'll be back about six or seven to tell you all about it. Make yourself at home. There should be plenty of hot water and there's some food in the fridge.

See you later

Tom.

Her bones ached less and she opened the back door and looked out onto the overgrown garden.

"What a shame, I bet there are some nice things still in the ground under all that. I think I'll have a little go at it when I've had a cup of coffee," she said out loud.

Nellie enjoyed making coffee in a kitchen on her own. She tried to remember the last time she had been in such a privileged position and realised that it was all those years ago when she had cared for William at the farm. She daydreamed about the little cottage and its bountiful garden. She rarely dared to hope that one day she might live in such a place but this morning she allowed herself a few moments of cheerful optimism as the kettle boiled. As she pushed open the back door, the sun poured down through the cold skies and she climbed down the crumbling patio steps. She pulled her various garments tightly around her as she perched on the low wall, sipping her coffee.

She lit one of the cigarettes left over from the night before and coughing heartily, she thought, "One day I'll give these up, maybe when I move into my little house with its little garden at the back. I'll dig in proper beds and plant herbaceous and mixed borders."

She imagined all the different plants that she would include, with the tallest at the back and tapering down to the front in swathes of similar or contrasting colour.

Her daydream was broken by the song of a robin who had decided to keep her company.

"Hello, are you hungry?" she asked, "Let's see if I can find you a small snack."

She went back into the kitchen to look for some bread. When she came back out with some bread, a saucer full of water he had gone.

"I know what will bring him back!" she said, recalling the robin that used to keep her company in the garden of the family home she had shared with Philip and the children.

She returned with the hand fork and trowel that she had showed off to Tom the previous evening and started to clear a small patch of ground near the house. As she pulled away the debris she uncovered the shoots that she knew were there waiting to be found. She dug gently around them, regaining the rhythm of happier days and in a short while the robin was back on the low patio wall watching her. She worked for about an hour and feeling her knees aching from the cold earth underneath them, she stopped, sat up on her heels to admire her work.

"That'll do for now," she thought, "I'd better not overdo it like I usually do."

Her efforts had made her hungry so she went into the small kitchen to make some toast and more coffee. While she was eating her breakfast, she re-read the note that Tom had left her and was reminded of his invitation to 'make herself at home'. Would she dare to have a bath? Tom would not be home all day so there was no reason not to but she felt strangely nervous at the prospect.

Warily, she walked into the bathroom and inspected the toiletries on offer. She picked up the soap with its familiar clean smell and with glee spotted some bubble bath on the window sill next to a bottle of shampoo. That was it. It simply had to be done. All those wonderful smells and the luxury of a tub full of hot water, how could she resist?

Trying to curb her excitement long enough to think the matter through, she realised that she would not be able to put on the same clothes again and went in search of the charity shop bag from which her new boots had been conjured. On finding it, she selected various items that were likely to fit and to cover her adequately, even discovering a well-tailored linen jacket with a matching silk headscarf. After laying out her new outfit on the sofa in the living room, she put the plug in the bath and ran the water on to a generous helping of bubble bath. With a thrill, she noticed that the large mixer tap sported a shower attachment with which she would be able to wash her hair.

She began to undress. As she removed each of the many layers of clothing, she placed them into a bin bag which she had brought with her into the bathroom. She was hoping to tie the bag and dispose of it before Tom returned. As she neared the final layers, she realised that she was much smaller than the impression given by her normally bulky appearance. Noticing the cuts, scars and bruises displayed on her pallid legs, she was grateful that there was no wall mirror in the room. She tested the water and carefully climbed into the frothy white bubbles. She knelt down in the warm water and then lay back with her head resting on the edge of the bath. She let the heat embrace her battered body and she closed her eyes.

Lying still in the fragrant water, she realised that the warmth had alleviated all the discomfort from her limbs. At that moment, she was able to let her mind drift back to a happier time. The familiar smell of the bath bubbles evoked an acute memory of her nightly baths taken when both the children had been tucked safely in to their clean beds. Since the day she had lost both of them she had been unable to combine, in her mind, the life she had had with them with her present world alone. But behind her closed eyelids in the warm, soothing water she could imagine that when she reopened them she would be back in her bathroom at home.

Many years had passed since those halcyon days. The time elapsed had struck her cruelly when she first saw George's son the day she arrived back in her home town. She had made the journey primarily in the hope that she would one day find her children but once there, she had not known where to start. Many a time she had wished that William were still alive so that she could ask him what she should do. Her attempts to discover the whereabouts of Daisy and Freddie were always overpowered by her immense guilt for the manner in which she had so carelessly lost them both and by the shame at what she had become. The intensity of these emotions was always too much for her to bear and she resorted, every time, to the bottle rendering her incapable of any clarity of thought.

She could feel the water cooling, so taking a deep breath, she opened her eyes and gazed, without surprise, but nevertheless with a modicum of disappointment at the browning grout between the cracked tiles of Tom's bathroom. The analgesic effects of the water gave Nellie a sense of physical well-being and thus hope of a comfortable day ahead. It was with renewed gusto that she thoroughly shampooed her hair ensuring that it was rinsed to the squeaky clean degree that she had always enjoyed. The strenuous massaging of her scalp, followed by the sensation of clean running water on her head resulted in an unexpected rush of optimism.

As she fastidiously dried and dressed herself she began to hum the tune to Louis Armstrong's 'Wonderful World' bringing the song with its words to a crescendo as she tied her hair into a pony tail with her newly acquired silk scarf.

Rejuvenated by her ablutions, she held up the small shaving mirror that Tom kept on the window sill and thought,

"Not bad, I could do with a bit of lippy though," and she went to her bags in the living room and started to search through them.

As she rummaged, she came across a brightly patterned shoulder bag that she had picked up along the way with the intention of using it for 'special occasions'. Considering the day exceptional enough, she began to transfer necessary items from her larger bags and in doing so, she found an old red lipstick that she had not used since her days in the cafe in King's Cross. She carefully applied a little to her lips and smoothed it in with the tip of her finger. She admired the results in the mirror and checking the shoulder bag for money, cigarettes and envelope containing her precious photograph, she left Tom's house by the back door, delighted by the freedom from the weight of her cumbersome belongings.

The sun shone as she strode confidently on to the street and she was undeterred by the sharp north-easterly breeze which found its way easily through the linen of her tidy jacket. She was wearing the boots that Tom had given to her the night before and as she increased her pace to keep warm she noted, with satisfaction, that they were every bit as comfortable as she had hoped.

Reaching the town centre she decided to make the most of being unencumbered for the day by visiting the library. She walked through the automatic glass doors and into the foyer. The building was modern and had replaced the fusty, crumbling library of her childhood which she secretly preferred. However, she was met with the reassuring, slightly stale air of an institution that favoured closed windows. Walking through the barriers that greeted her, the smell of books of all ages wafted forth and her spirits rose in anticipation of what she might find within. It was still early and the comfortable chairs by the floor to ceiling windows were mostly vacant. It suddenly became imperative that she find something soothing to read and then occupy one of the luxurious seats before they all became filled.

She kept an eye on the entrance for interlopers as she made her way to the poetry section feeling that a dose of Dylan Thomas or T.S. Eliot would set her up well for the day ahead. She walked past the display of leaflets that were neatly arranged on a mobile display unit at the entrance to the poetry aisle. She gave them a cursory glance and recalled as she looked away how she used to periodically peruse these information booklets with a view to finding an outlet for her unsettled soul. Occasionally, she would follow through and attend a group or a class with the intention of starting up a new hobby. She smiled at the memory that came to her that morning of the hideous time she had spent with the local 'French Society' where, with her inadequate knowledge of the language she had attempted to give a presentation on an aspect of Algerian history. Her toes began to curl as she saw herself again, standing in front of a kindly but self important group of middle class men and women waiting expectantly for her to begin. She had tried to speak and although she had prepared a little for the ordeal she had mistakenly thought that she would be able to rely on her ability to improvise. As she looked at the sea of shiny, well-coiffed heads, all French words that she had ever known left her consciousness and her summation of Algerian history remained unspoken. She fled from the room, tears of abject humiliation falling from her eyes, never to return.

Relieved that she no longer felt obliged to take part in uncomfortable activities, she still experienced a pang of loss in the knowledge that she had no use for informative leaflets of any kind anymore. At this thought, she shrugged and chose her books before nestling into the armchair with the best view of the world outside. She became immersed in the lilting words of Thomas and Eliot's eloquent austerity. She put the books to one side and gazed out of the window. Maisie was already enthusiastically embarking on her second round of unbidden trolley collection and Cyril had bought his meal for one and was sitting with the younger men as they opened their first cans of beer of the day. It was warm in the library and Nellie started to feel sleepy. She knew that she would be asked to leave if she dozed off so she fidgeted in her chair from time to time to prevent the possibility of slumber.

Her head was beginning to feel hot and she was not sure if it was the atmosphere inside the building that was causing it or whether she had a temperature so she returned the two anthologies to their correct shelves and went out into the crisp February air in an attempt to clear the muzziness accumulating around her brain.

She took the quieter roads behind the shopping centre. Her limbs had begun to feel painful and she realised that she must be ill. Undeterred by her self-diagnosis, she continued on her way, deciding as she did to spend her last few coins on something to drink. She would visit the off licence at the bottom of the hill as she had not been there for some time.

Nellie preferred to alternate the places in which she bought her alcohol supplies, convinced that by doing so, none of the vendors would know exactly how much she drank. Unfortunately, her theory was flawed by Nellie's habit of returning to the same place when drunk, having forgotten that she had been there only hours earlier. She walked down the hill to the row of shops by the school that her children had attended. When she had first come back to the area she had found it agonising each time she had revisited an old haunt but the passage of time and the effects of long term drinking had numbed the pain to a dull ache.

Nellie pushed open the door of the off licence and was greeted by the owner.

"Hello Nellie, how are you?"

"Alright," began Nellie, then remembering that she had felt quite unwell on her way there, "Actually, I'm not really feeling very well today, since you ask. I think I might have a touch of flu and my bones are really achey."

"Oh dear," said the lady kindly, "I could make you a hot toddy, do you think that would help?"

Nellie's face lit up.

"Oh yes!" she exclaimed, "That should do the trick."

"OK, well you sit there and I'll boil some water. I might even join you," she said cheerfully.

Nellie was enjoying sitting on the wooden chair admiring the bottles when a cardboard mounted advertisement for a well known brand of cider caught her eye. It was a picture of a pretty young girl laughing while seemingly absorbed in an intimate conversation with a casually dressed, handsome boy. They both held glasses of cider with bubbles accentuated by the glow of the evening sunshine.

Nellie thought she could sense the warmth of their moment and thought, "That looks a good cider, I think I'll buy some before I leave."

The lady returned with two glasses of warm brown liquid with spoons clinking on the sides.

"There you go, Nellie. Give it a bit of a stir to get the honey moving through it."

"Thank you," she replied, focussing completely on the task she had been set.

She licked the sweet spoon and then took a sip of the strong warm fluid. The whiskey caught the back of her throat just the way she liked it and she waited while she felt the warmth flow through her. The kindness of the act, her feverish state and the welcome drink all served to engulf her in emotion. Tears began to well up in her eyes and she waved her free hand in front of them hoping they would dry and save her dignity.

Seeing Nellie's apparent distress, her companion said, "You look nice today. Are you going somewhere special?"

"No not really, I stayed with a friend last night and I've been able to smarten myself up a bit. I thought I'd go for a slightly different look..." she trailed off unconvinced by her empty words.

She took the last gulp of her drink and stood up ready to buy her cider. The lady handed her a bottle of cider and ten cigarettes with the words,

"Have these on me, you can save your money for something to eat later."

"You are kind, thank you," said Nellie, slightly abashed again by her generosity.

Nellie began the steep haul up the hill passing the courts where she had played tennis with her brothers when she was a child. They were well kept now and it was free to play on them. She grinned as she recalled how she and her brothers would try and get a free game by tricking 'Parky' into thinking that they had been there less time than they had. He was a gruff old man and would shout at them if he thought that they had stayed longer than the hour they had paid for. Whilst musing over the fact that they were less well used now that they were free, she found that she needed to stop and catch her breath.

Sweat was trickling from her brow and she wiped it away with her sleeve before it ran into her eyes. She stood still facing down the hill and let the chill wind cool her febrile head. She was beginning to wish that she was back at Tom's curled up on the mattress on the floor but she continued on upwards until she came into the main area of the recreation ground.

The sun had long gone and the sky was full of ominous clouds preparing to break. Nellie regretted the vanity of not wearing a coat so that she could show off the linen jacket that she had so eagerly claimed. Nevertheless, she pulled it tightly around her and walking against the wind, went over to the pond to see if the ducks were also braving the cold. Satisfied that they were all present and correct she ambled over to the bench where she had so often slept.

She sat down and took out the bottle of cider that she had purchased earlier and grimacing ruefully at how she had been so easily seduced by the glamour of the advertisement, she unscrewed the cap and began to drink.

Due to the sudden drop in temperature, the park was almost empty and for this, Nellie was immensely grateful. As she was waiting for the alcohol to take effect, she was disturbed by the scraping sound of a pushchair and footsteps as they neared her seat. Unperturbed but curious she looked up. One of the reasons that she chose to sit on that particular bench, was that she was obscured from the direct view of people entering the park but she however, was able to observe them, unseen.

She heard the sound of a young woman's voice as it broke the silence,

"Let's just go down to see the ducks and then we'll go back and get something to eat."

Nellie saw the toddler's feet clad in blue shiny, wellington boots above the wheels of the push chair. She fleetingly thought that there was something terribly familiar about the sound of the voice she had just heard but she knew that there was no-one of that age group that she knew around there and instantly dismissed it.

The mother and child continued on to the pond. Nellie coughed and the woman turned around to see who was there. Reassured that it was merely a woman sitting there alone, she gave the little boy some bread and they started to feed the hungry ducks. Nellie now quite disorientated by the fever that was engulfing her, sat stricken as she watched the young girl help her son break the bread into small pieces. When the woman had turned towards her, Nellie had seen her own face. Her heart beat loudly in her chest and she thought that perhaps she was delirious and had started to hallucinate, but they were still there and she continued to watch them.

Absorbed in her observations, she realised that not only did the girl look like her, but she moved like her too. The bread had run out and the boy was being secured into his buggy once more. His mother, smiling over at Nellie took the brake off the wheels and started to push. Then she knew.

Leaping up, Nellie walked towards them and called, "Daisy!"

The young woman turned, not knowing whether to run or stay but the decision appeared to have been made for her because she was unable to move. Rooted to the spot, she narrowed her eyes as if to enhance her sight in the dark light of the wintry afternoon: then putting the brakes back on, she moved towards Nellie. As she came closer she saw a time ravaged woman holding her breath and gazing at her. Then she saw the gleam of excitement and hope in the older woman's own eyes and felt their familiar warmth.

"Mummy?"

Nellie stood still as she absorbed the word into her psyche. The years of desolation fell away and she knew that she had come home. Daisy approached tentatively and put her hand up to her mother's puffy cheek.

"Where did you go Mummy? I was so worried about you," she asked, tears welling up in her blue-green eyes.

Nellie placed her index finger on her daughter's brow and traced its line and the curve of her upturned nose. She smiled and said,

"I thought it was me when I first saw you but I'm not feeling too good at the moment so I put it down to a funny moment and then you smiled and I knew that it was you," she paused, "I didn't leave you, Daisy. I didn't leave you and Freddie. I made a mistake and when I came back, you were gone."

Daisy stared at Nellie, overcome by her mother's despoiled features.

"I know Mummy," she said quietly, and then in a whisper, "What happened to your pretty face?"

"Lots of things Daisy, lots of things have happened. Will you sit with me?" she asked, suddenly exhausted.

"Yes," she replied, "Let me bring Luke over here so that I can keep an eye on him. He's quite tired so I'll have to take him back soon."

"Is he...?" began Nellie.

"Yes, you're a Grandma. That's quite something don't you think?"

Nellie reached over to the little boy who was sucking his thumb and dozing. She touched his head gently; then stroked his dark hair as his eyes closed. She sat back up and turned to her daughter. She wanted to hug her and hold her but she did not want to frighten her away so she sat with her hands by her side and waited. Daisy took her mother's hand and began to talk. The words came from a place deep within her and sounded strange to her as they hit the cold air.

"I came back here to look for you. I didn't know where to begin. It's been such a long time. I went to our house yesterday. It's not our house anymore," she stopped and stared into the space in front of her.

Nellie filled the silence, "I went there once a couple of years ago. I came back here to look for you and Freddie. A friend of mine suggested that I start at the beginning and that was as far as I got. It looked like the soul had gone from the bricks and mortar. There was nothing to show that we had been there at all. I stood and stared at the outside for quite a long time and I wanted to see inside but I didn't dare knock on the door. Then a woman came out with a shopping bag in her hand and I could just see into the hallway. It wasn't our house. It's a funny thing because all those years I used to think about it as if it was still our home and I realised then that of course it wasn't. Why should it be?" Nellie could hear her voice breaking with grief.

Daisy squeezed her hand and said, "This is home. You and me here on this bench."

Nellie could feel tears of gratitude falling from her eyes. Hearing her sniff, Daisy rustled in her shoulder bag, which Nellie observed, was remarkably like her own. She held hers up to show her and they laughed.

While Nellie blew her nose and wiped away the tears, Daisy continued, "Dad died five months ago..."

Nellie gasped, "How?"

"He had a heart attack. He was always working: he didn't really have to these last few years but he just did anyway. I'm not sure why; it wasn't as if he really enjoyed it anymore and he used to get so angry all the time. Then he went to work one morning after having a massive row with Patricia, his partner," Daisy glanced at her mother to see how she was taking this and seeing that her expression had not changed, she went on,

"He collapsed at his desk. They couldn't resuscitate him."

"Where were you living?" asked Nellie, unaccountably nervous about the answer.

"Dubai, we moved there when... you know, then," she stumbled, "Anyway, the thing is that I finished sorting through his stuff a few weeks ago and I found the letter: the letter that you wrote to Dad on that day..." she took a deep breath.

"Oh that letter," said Nellie looking down.

"But Mummy, it changed everything. I had always believed that you had left me and Freddie as well as Dad. When I read what you had written, I understood that that had never been the case. Dad told us that you had run off with a man and that you were never coming back. He lied. He told us that you cared more for this man than you did for us. I cried and cried when he told us that we would never see you again. He said that we had to forget about you.

In my heart, Mummy, I couldn't understand how you could have just left us behind, nor could Freddie. But Dad was so angry that he wouldn't even let us talk about you when he was in the room. We used to make up secret plans about how we would save up enough money and get on a plane and come and find you. But we had no idea how to or where you were," Daisy choked back the sobs that had arrived to accompany her freely flowing tears.

"I came back on the Sunday and you were already gone. I could see your Mother's Day card on the table and I couldn't get in," Nellie baulked at the recollection that until that point in the day she had been so absorbed in her own activities, that she hadn't even known it was Mother's Day.

"That was the surprise that Freddie nearly told you about when we came here the day before you went away," Daisy explained simply." Do you remember the last time we came here?"

"Of course I do. I have wished so many times that we could have gone back to that day and then I would have done everything differently and I would never have lost you."

She took out the battered envelope containing the picture of the children and passed it to Daisy.

"This was all I had left. I used to kiss your faces and say night, night to you."

Daisy looked up from the photograph and fixed her gaze on Nellie.

"When I was little I used to cry myself to sleep and on those nights I would often dream that you came into my room and stood at the door. You would say, "Night, night, sleep tight. See you in the morning," just like you always did. In the morning when I woke up I would remember the dream and although I desperately wanted you to be there I would feel better, as if you really had come to see me.

As I got older I had a terrible time with Dad. I think he found it really hard the more I grew to look like you and I was just so angry with everything that I left home when I was sixteen and came back to England. I worked in hotels and restaurants but I had no purpose," she paused, "And I drank a lot. Then I had a baby and I went back to Dubai so that we would have somewhere to live. It didn't really work, but Freddie was always very good with Luke; they are quite alike so he probably feels like he can identify with him even though he is only little."

Daisy took a breath.

"Where is Freddie? Is he alright?" asked Nellie, aware of the absurdity of the question, as the boy's mother.

"Oh Mummy, he's gone to Afghanistan," replied Daisy despondently.

"Why?" asked Nellie naively.

Daisy turned and looked at her mother's face suddenly comprehending the degree of detachment from reality in which she was living.

With a surge of irritation she snapped, "The war, there's a war on, you know!"

"Daisy, I'm sorry, I do know, but I can't imagine Freddie wanting to fight. Why would he want to fight?"

Recovering her composure Daisy said, "Actually, he isn't. He's a reporter and now he seems to be on some sort of one man peace keeping crusade. I wish he'd come home where I could keep an eye on him. We talk on e-mail and I saw him at the funeral. But I miss him and I don't entirely trust him to look after himself properly even though he's a grown man.

"Does Freddie cope with things? Remember how we used to worry so about him?" asked Nellie.

"I think so; it's hard to tell really. Do you remember all that bizarre stuff he used say, trying to work things out and be funny all at the same time? Well he isn't much different now. He just does it in a slightly more grown up fashion. But I know he's just our little Freddie underneath it all. Luke reminds me of Freddie, a lot. Talking of which, I'd better get him back to where I am staying: it's getting cold and he needs his tea. We're at a friend's house so shall I ask her if she will babysit and then I can maybe meet you here in an hour? Would you like to go for something to eat? I'd take you back with me now but it isn't my place and I just think that it might be too difficult for all of us."

Nellie felt that she might burst with happiness.

"Of course, I would love to do that. It'll be better to meet here, just me and you and I don't want the little chap to catch cold."

"You don't have to wait here until then, you know," said Daisy.

"I know but I will, I have no pressing engagements to disentangle myself from," she said, trying to sound jovial.

Daisy stood and Nellie followed suit wobbling as she got to her feet.

"Are you OK?" asked Daisy, looking concerned and noticing her mother's flushed face. She raised her hand and felt her burning forehead with the back of her hand.

242

"You do feel hot, Mummy," she said, "I'll bring you some paracetomol when I come back and take this," she handed Nellie the blanket that had been covering Luke's small body, "We haven't got far to go."

Nellie took the light blue tartan rug and said as cheerfully as she could, "Thanks Daisy I'll be alright now. Off you go and see to the young man. Give him a good night kiss from his Grandma," she said, with pride, "The sooner you go the sooner you'll be back."

The two women faced each other and embraced. Nellie held Daisy so tightly that she had to pull back in order to breathe and as she did she smelt the sweet, stale odour of alcohol and saw the light of her mother's love shine through from her soul, dispelling the lonely dread that resided in her own. She took the brakes off the buggy, waved to Nellie and walked briskly out of sight.

Nellie sat upright clasping the wooden seat as if to prevent her from running after them. She watched as they disappeared from view, immediately willing the hour to be up and for Daisy to be sat once more with her on the bench, holding her hand. She heard the half hour toll from the tall clock tower in the town centre and knew that the next time the single chime sounded, Daisy would be there again.

Amazed at the serendipity of the meeting, Nellie gladly accepted their providence and wondered whether to walk a little to fill the hour ahead. Concluding that fate had already generously smiled upon her, she was not prepared to risk missing her daughter's return and decided instead, to wait patiently. The temperature seemed to have dropped a few more degrees and she pulled the baby's blanket to her putting it automatically to her nose, to breathe in the fragrance of clean washing and toddler that clung to its fibres, before laying it proudly on her knees.

She still clutched the envelope in her hand and as she put it back into her bag for safe keeping, she felt the bottle she had purchased earlier that afternoon and drew it out with the intention of celebrating her good fortune. She tried not to drink the cider too quickly aware that she did not want to appear inebriated when she and Daisy went out to eat. She felt eternally grateful that they had encountered each other on this day, the day that, for the first time in a long time she had had the opportunity to wash and wear clothes that would pass muster on the streets of this town. As she continued to imbibe, she began to glow with pride at the thought of her beautiful daughter and delightful grandson.

She imagined sitting in a smart restaurant with Daisy, as they embarked on the animated conversation that would naturally ensue and she realised that she wanted her daughter to be proud of her.

"I can do that," she said out loud, "I'll have perfect manners and I'll speak quietly but clearly and she can tell me everything she has to tell and then..."

Nellie took another swig from the bottle and disregarded the disquiet this thought had brought with it.

"After all, I had no idea that we would finally see each other again today, so who knows what tomorrow might bring?"

She hummed a tune quietly and became aware that it was the tune to 'Oh, Susanna,' that she had played on the piano when she was a child and sang to her children in later years. She proceeded to sing the words of the strangest, yet saddest verse of all whilst playing the notes with both hands on imaginary keys.

It rained all night
The day I left
The weather it was dry
The sun so hot
I froze to death
Susanna, don't you cry

And then, abandoning the musical accompaniment she belted out the chorus with gusto:

Oh, Susanna,
Oh, don't you cry for me
For I come from Alabama
With my banjo on my knee

She giggled quietly when she had finished and stopped when she heard footsteps. Delighted that Daisy had managed to get back there early she leapt up to greet her only to see the council attendant pulling the padlock chain through the railings and entwining it through the gate. She moved back stealthily behind the shrubs to prevent him from seeing her and as she stood there listening to the metallic click of the padlock being turned. She heard the solitary chime that she had been so eagerly awaiting.

Her heart sank. Childishly, she had interpreted Daisy's hour to be exactly that. She reminded herself that children had unexpected needs and perhaps Luke had been unhappy that his mother was planning an outing without him and she was consoling him. With the tolling of the next hour her hope was extinguished.

She sat with dogged resignation, refusing to leave the one place that her daughter would be able to find her. She stared ahead, no longer expecting to see Daisy and with a tidal wave of clarity understood the devastation she had caused when she had failed to reappear on that fateful day. Had Daisy simply used this situation to teach her the ultimate lesson? If she had then Nellie had finally been quick to learn. As she toyed with this unthinkable concept, she concluded that it was unlikely that Daisy would be so unkind. The years had not taught her first born the common harshness that so many people possessed as an instrument for survival and yet why had she not come back?

Knowing that she could not answer that question, she examined the large bottle from which she had been drinking and congratulated herself on her relative temperance because she now had quite a quantity left with which to numb the searing pain that was burning into her battered soul. She gulped the liquid down as fast as she could until the agony had diminished. She sat for a long time pleased with the solace her drunkenness offered. Her body temperature fluctuated between cold and hot bringing the discomfort of both shivers and rigours until she suddenly felt spent.

Momentarily, she questioned ever having seen Daisy at all until she caught sight of the beautiful blue rug on her lap. Content that she had a souvenir, she took out the picture of the children from its envelope and kissed their faces,

"Night, night, sleep tight, see you in the morning," she whispered even though she could no longer see their images in the moonless dark.

She put her shoulder bag on the bench as a pillow and pulling the blanket up around her neck, she lifted her legs, one at a time and lay down to sleep. The night was quiet now and allowed Nellie to meander back through the day in her mind. Daisy's face as they parted was the last image Nellie saw as slumber overrode her reflections.

The smile remained on her lips as she slept. It stayed as the heavy flakes of snow fell on her face during the coldest February night for years. She dreamt a dream of childhood where her own children were her friends and the three of them ran freely on endless summer evenings. Then they sat on the warm, heavily scented cow parsley meadows and made chains from the profusion of little white and yellow flowers that grew each time they were picked. As Daisy raised the floral crown to place it upon her head, Nellie exhaled for the last time under the snow that covered her bed.

246

EPILOGUE

Daisy awoke before sunrise to find the heavily curtained room strangely lit up. Rubbing her eyes she walked sleepily to the window and gaped out onto the normally harsh landscape and saw that it had been transformed by a thick blanket of fairy tale white snow. Then she remembered the snow falling as she sat in the taxi being driven back from the hospital. She had taken little notice as she was still recovering from the trauma of Luke's head injury, sustained by a fall from the upstairs banister during a frenzy of high spirits. The hours following the doctor's reassurance that there was to be no lasting damage were torturous. Long waits for sutures, dressings and a final discharge clearance delayed their return until midnight with Luke proudly displaying his neatly dressed wound. Daisy relieved, but exhausted, settled the little boy into the bed they were temporarily sharing and lying down next to him promptly fell asleep.

Now fully alert her thoughts leapt to her mother who she had been unable to meet. Dressing rapidly, Daisy ran into the bedroom where her friend lay, still sleeping. She shook her shoulder and said,

"Sally, Sally, wake up!"

Sally stirred and opening one eye reluctantly, asked,

"What is it? Is Luke alright?"

"Yes he's fine. Please could you look after him while I go out? There's something I really must do."

"Yes, OK but bring him in here with me," and she rolled over to continue her slumber.

Daisy trudged intuitively back to the park where she had waved good bye to her mother the previous evening.

"Please be there, please be there," she chanted under her breath as she crunched her way arduously through the freshly laid snow.

Turning into the wide entrance of the park, she saw the secured gate padlock glistening in the lamplight. She automatically turned towards the place in the hedge where there had always been a gap. She recalled her mother showing her when she was little and remembered how proud she had been to be privy to such a special secret. She had to knock down large drifts of snow before she could access it but once found, she went straight through and into the silent grounds. Her movements were muted by the thick layer of undisturbed snow and she felt her spirits plummet as she saw it's unbroken surface, informing her that no-one else had trodden the path since it's falling. She was about to retrace her tracks when she had a sudden desire to see the bench where she had spent those precious minutes with her mother the day before.

Daisy vaguely sensed that her actions were not necessarily those of a sane woman, but she could think of no other way to find her mother and when she had, she determined never to lose sight of her again. She rounded the end of the snow laden hedge and walked toward the now white bench wondering how long she would be able to wait before having to relieve Sally of Luke.

Glad that she had picked up her phone in her rush to leave, she checked it and saw a message from Freddie. Daisy had been e-mailing her brother when Luke's accident occurred and she could not remember whether she had pressed the send button.

Apparently she had, "Wow! Give her a big hug and kiss from me and tell her that I love her. Must see her. Will book a flight to London. Text you the details asap. Love FreddieXXX"

Daisy could not make out the definition of the bench and thinking that her sight was being hindered by the glare of the snow she rubbed her eyes as she approached. She stood over the snow mound on the seat and felt bemused. Then she saw the mere glimpse of a familiar colour contrasting with the purity of its white surroundings. Instinctively, and with unknown dread in her belly she began to gently scrape the snow away, revealing the linen of the jacket her mother had been wearing when last she saw her. Shaking she continued the repetitive movement until the upper portion of the body and face were visible. Though the features were recognisable, her mother was gone. Daisy looked down at the hands that lay clasped together on her chest and prised from them the picture that her mother had for so long cherished.

* * *

Tom woke up early from an uncomfortable night's sleep on the sofa. He surveyed the room as he always did to assess his surroundings and then remembered why he had slept there. He had returned to the house in the early evening and pleased with his achievements of the day called out to Nellie to tell her about them and to announce the outing that he had planned. The sun was low in the sky and the rooms were dark. As he walked from one to another he turned on the lights and was surprised at the level of his disappointment he was experiencing as her absence became apparent. However, he noted happily that most of her belongings were still strewn about the living room and content that she would soon be coming through the door he settled down on the settee to wait for her. His day had been busy and on the way home he had stopped to share some cans of lager with Cyril and the boys leaving him a little worse for wear. It was not long before he had fallen into a deep sleep.

As Tom walked out into the kitchen, he glanced out of the window and gasped at the white carpet of snow that covered the garden. He began to worry about Nellie who had not returned as he had expected. He made a cup of coffee and whilst doing so decided that it might be an idea to take a flask with him in case Nellie had foolishly spent the night outdoors despite his invitation to stay. He knew from his own experience that she would be in instant need of warming fluids. He put on his duffel coat, scarf and mittens over the clothes he had slept in and set off towards Nellie's favourite place, the park. He smiled as he saw the Nellie sized footprints and followed them through the hole in the hedge and up towards her bench. He fumbled in the pocket of his jacket which he wore under the overcoat to search for the two train tickets to Frinton which he had purchased the day before. As he pulled them out with a flourish to present to her, he was stopped in his tracks by the sight of a young woman scraping at a heap of snow on the bench saying over and over again,

"Mummy, Mummy please come back. Mummy, Mummy please come back."

* * *

The three mourners stood momentarily on the steps of the church. Tom declined the offer of a space in the cortège to the crematorium and handed the carrier bags, which he had placed discreetly in the lobby during the service, to Daisy. She thanked him and passing one to Freddie, walked with him in silence to the waiting car.

As she put on her seatbelt, she fixed her gaze on the expensive floral arrangement spelling 'MUMMY' displayed in the hearse. She turned away from it, knowing that it was not enough. Neither were her stumbling words from the pulpit nor Freddie's booming recital of 'Fern Hill', her mother's favourite poem.

The snow had finally begun to melt and the brown slush that bordered the roads and pavements in the watery sunshine, served only to reinforce the misery of the day. The cars drove slowly through the shopping centre. Maisie looked up briefly at the shiny black vehicles that were passing by, before catching sight of a displaced shopping trolley and bustling towards it to add it to her collection.

THE END